Bruno, Chief of Police

Martin Walker

Bruno, Chief of Police

Martin Walker is the senior director of the Global Business Policy Council and editor emeritus and international affairs columnist at United Press International. Formerly Moscow and U.S. bureau chief for Britain's *The Guardian*, he is also a senior scholar at the Woodrow Wilson International Center for Scholars in Washington, D.C. His books include *The Cold War: A History*, a *New York Times* Notable Book and short-listed for the Whitbread Book of the Year Prize; and *The Caves of Périgord*, a novel. He has written for *The New York Times*, *The New Yorker*, and *The Times Literary Supplement*. He lives in Washington, D.C., and the southwest of France.

ALSO BY MARTIN WALKER

NONFICTION

The Iraq War

America Reborn

The President We Deserve

The Cold War: A History

Martin Walker's Russia

An Independent Traveler's Guide to the Soviet Union

The Waking Giant: Gorbachev and Perestroika

The Eastern Question

Powers of the Press

A Mercenary Calling

Daily Sketches

The Infiltrator

The National Front

FICTION

The Caves of Périgord

Bruno, Chief of Police

Bruno, Chief of Police

Martin Walker

Vintage Books

A Division of Random House, Inc.

New York

FIRST VINTAGE BOOKS EDITION, APRIL 2010

Copyright © 2008 by Walker and Watson Ltd.

All rights reserved. Published in the United States by Vintage Books,
a division of Random House, Inc., New York. Originally published in
Great Britain in slightly different form by Quercus, London, in 2008,
and subsequently published in hardcover in the United States by
Alfred A. Knopf, a division of Random House, Inc., New York, in 2009.

Vintage and colophon are registered trademarks of Random House, Inc.

The Library of Congress has cataloged the Knopf edition as follows:
Walker, Martin.
Bruno, chief of police / Martin Walker.—1st U.S. ed.
p. cm.
1. Police chiefs—France, Southwest—Fiction. 2. Country life—France,
Southwest—Fiction. 3. North Africans—Crimes against—Fiction.
4. World War, 1939–1945—Underground movements—Fiction.
5. France, Southwest—Fiction. I. Title
PR6073.A413B78 2009
823'.914—dc22 2008042740

Vintage ISBN: 978-0-307-45469-0

Book design by Virginia Tan

www.vintagebooks.com

Printed in the United States of America
29 28 27 26 25 24 23 22 21 20

For Pierrot

Bruno, Chief
of Police

1

On a bright May morning, so early that the last of the mist was still lingering low over a bend in the Vézère River, a white van drew to a halt on the ridge that overlooked the small French town. A man climbed out, strode to the edge of the road and stretched mightily as he admired the familiar view of St. Denis. The town emerged from the lush green of the trees and meadows like a tumbled heap of treasure; the golden stone of the buildings, the ruby red tiles of the rooftops and the silver curve of the river running through it. The houses clustered down the slope and around the main square of the Hôtel de Ville where the council chamber, its Mairie, and the office of the town's own policeman perched above the thick stone columns that framed the covered market. The grime of three centuries only lately scrubbed away, its honey-colored stone glowed richly in the morning sun.

On the far side of the square stood the venerable church, its thick walls and squat tower a reminder of the ages past when churches, too, were part of the town's defenses, guarding the river crossing and the approach to the great stone bridge. A great "N" carved into the rock above the central of the three arches asserted that the bridge had been rebuilt on the orders of Napoleon himself. This did not greatly impress the town's inhabitants, who knew that the upstart emperor had but restored a bridge their ancestors had first built five centuries earlier. And now it had been established that the first bridge over their river dated from Roman times. Across the river stretched the new part of town, the Crédit Agricole bank and its parking lot, the supermarket and the rugby stadium discreetly shaded by tall oaks and thick belts of walnut trees.

The man enjoying this familiar sight was evidently fit enough to be dapper and brisk in his movements, but as he relaxed he was sufficiently concerned about his love of food to tap his waist, gingerly probing for any sign of plumpness, always a threat in this springtime period between his last game of the rugby season and the start of serious hunting. He wore a uniform of sorts, a neatly ironed blue shirt with epaulettes but no tie, navy blue trousers and black boots. His thick, dark hair was crisply cut, his warm brown eyes had a twinkle, and his generous mouth seemed ready to break into a smile. On a badge on his chest, and on the side of his van, were the words POLICE MUNICIPALE. A peaked cap lay on the passenger seat.

In the back of the van were a crowbar, a tangle of battery cables, one basket containing newly laid eggs from his own hens, and another with his garden's first spring peas. Two tennis rackets, a pair of rugby boots, sneakers, and a large bag with various kinds of sports attire and a spare line from a fishing rod added to the jumble. Tucked neatly to one side were a first-aid kit, a small tool chest, a blanket, and a picnic hamper with plates and glasses, salt and pepper, a head of garlic and a Laguiole pocketknife with a horn handle and a corkscrew. Tucked under the front seat was a bottle of not-quite-legal eau-de-vie from a friendly farmer. He would use this to make his private stock of *vin de noix* when the green walnuts were ready on the feast of St. Catherine. Benoît Courrèges, chief of police for the small commune of St. Denis and its 2,900 souls, and universally known as Bruno, was always very well prepared.

He chose not to wear the heavy belt that weighs down almost every policeman in France with its attachments of holster and pistol, handcuffs and flashlight, keys and note-book. There was a pair of ancient handcuffs somewhere in his van, but Bruno would have to conduct a search to find them. He had a flashlight but it could use a new set of batteries. The van's glove compartment held a notebook and some pens, but the notebook was full of various recipes, the minutes of the last tennis-club meeting and a list of the names and phone numbers of the *minimes,* the young boys who had signed up for his tennis lessons.

Bruno's gun, a rather elderly MAB 9mm semiautomatic, was locked in his office safe in the Mairie, and in recent years he had taken it out only for his annual refresher course at the gendarmerie range in Périgueux. He had worn it on duty on only three occasions in his ten years in the Police Munici-pale. The first was when a rabid dog had been sighted in a neighboring commune, and the police were put on alert. The second was when the president of France had driven through

St. Denis on his way to see the celebrated cave paintings
of Lascaux nearby; he had stopped to visit an old friend,
Gérard Mangin, who was the mayor of St. Denis and Bruno's
employer. The third time was when a boxing kangaroo
escaped from a local circus. On no occasion had Bruno's gun
ever been used on duty, a fact of which he was extremely but
privately proud. Of course, like most of the other men (and
not a few women) of St. Denis, he shot almost daily in the
hunting season and usually bagged his target, unless he was
stalking the notoriously elusive *bécasse,* a bird whose taste he
preferred above all others.

Bruno gazed contentedly down upon his town in the
freshness of the early morning. His eyes lingered on the way
the sunlight bounced and flickered off the eddies where the
Vézère River ran under the arches of the old stone bridge. The
place was alive with light, flashes of gold and red, as the sun
magically concocted prisms in the grass beneath the willows
and danced along the honey-colored façades of the ancient
buildings along the river. There were glints from the weather-
cock on the church spire and from the eagle atop the town's
war memorial, where Bruno would later that day attend one
of the ceremonies that punctuated the nation's year.

All looked peaceful as the business of the day began, with
the first customers heading under the crimson awning into
Fauquet's café, tucked into the alley beside the Mairie. Even
from this high above the town he could hear the grating
sound of the metal grille being raised to open Lespinasse's
tabac, which sold fishing rods, guns, and ammunition alongside the cigarettes. Bruno knew without looking that, while
Madame Lespinasse was opening the shop, her husband

would be heading to the café for the first of many little glasses of white wine that would keep him pleasantly lubricated until lunch.

From the secretaries and social workers to the street sweepers and tax assessors, the staff of the Mairie would also be at Fauquet's, nibbling their croissants and taking their coffee at the long zinc bar, eying the *tartes aux citron* and the mille-feuilles they might take home for lunch along with the essential baguette of fresh bread and scanning the headlines of that morning's *Sud Ouest*. Alongside them would be a knot of old men studying the racing form and enjoying their first *petit blanc* of the day. Bachelot the shoemaker would take his morning glass there, while the neighbor he despised, Jean-Pierre, who ran the bicycle shop, would start his day at the Café de la Libération. Their enmity went back to the days of the Resistance, when one of them had been in a communist group and the other had joined de Gaulle's Armée Secrète, but Bruno could not reliably remember which had been in which. He only knew that they had not spoken to one another since the war, had never allowed their families to speak beyond the frostiest *"Bonjour,"* and each man had devoted many of the years since to subtle but determined efforts to seduce the other man's wife. The mayor had once confided his conviction that each had attained his objective. Bruno, as a careful guardian of his own privacy in such tender matters, was content to allow others similar latitude.

He enjoyed the continuity these morning movements represented. They were rituals to be respected—rituals such as the devotion with which each family bought its daily bread only at a particular one of the town's four bakeries, except on those weeks of holidays when they were forced to patronize another, each time lamenting the change in taste and texture. These little ways of St. Denis were as familiar to Bruno as his own morning routine on rising in his old shepherd's cottage in the hills above the town: his exercises while listening to Radio Périgord, his shower with a special shampoo to protect against the threat of baldness, the soap with the scent of green apples. Then he would feed his chickens while the coffee brewed and share toasted slices of yesterday's baguette with his dog, Gigi.

Across the small stream that flowed into the main river, the caves in the limestone cliffs drew his eye. Dark but strangely inviting, the caves with their ancient engravings and paintings drew scholars and tourists to this valley. The tourist office called it the Cradle of Mankind. It was, they said, the part of Europe that could claim the longest period of continuous human habitation. For forty thousand years, through ice ages and warming periods, floods and wars and famine, people had lived here. Bruno, who reminded himself that there were still many caves and paintings that he really ought to visit, felt deep in his heart that he understood why those people had chosen to remain in this gentle valley.

Down at the riverbank, he saw that the rider known to the town as the mad Englishwoman was watering her horse after her morning ride. In the town of St. Denis, everyone had a nickname, and since she was devoted to her horses and invariably carried treats to give to other people's dogs she evidently conformed to the English stereotype of bizarre affection for animals, even those that did not hunt. Along with her love of privacy and her odd habit of filling in the *Times* crossword as she walked from the Maison de la Presse to collect her morning croissant from Fauquet's café, this justified her title. As always, she was correctly dressed in gleaming black boots, cream jodhpurs and a black jacket, and her auburn hair flared out behind her neat black riding hat like the tail of a fox. Of course, she was anything but mad. Moreover, she appeared to make a good business of running her small guesthouse. She even spoke comprehensible French, which was more than could be said of most of the English who had settled here. Bruno looked further up the road that ran alongside the river and saw several trucks bringing local farmers to the weekly market. It would soon be time for him to go on duty. He took out the one item of equipment that never left his side, his cell phone, and called the familiar number of the Hôtel de la Gare.

"Any sign of them, Marie?" he asked. "They hit the market at St. Alvère yesterday, so they are in the region."

"Not as of last night, Bruno. Just the usual guys from the museum project stayed here and a Spanish truck driver," replied Marie, who ran the small hotel by the station. "But remember, after they were here last time and found nothing, I heard them talking about staying in Périgueux and renting a car there to put you off the scent."

Bruno, whose loyalty was to his local community and its mayor rather than to the nominal laws of France, particularly when they were really laws the European Union made in Brussels, played a constant cat-and-mouse game with the inspectors who were charged with enforcing E.U. hygiene rules on the markets of France. Hygiene was all very well, but the locals of St. Denis had been making their cheeses and their pâté de foie gras and their *rillettes de porc* for centuries before the E.U. even existed, and did not take kindly to foreign bureaucrats telling them what they could and could not sell. Along with other members of the Police Municipale in the region, Bruno had established a rigorous early-warning system to alert the market vendors of their visits.

The inspectors, called "the Gestapo" by some locals in a part of France that had taken very seriously its patriotic duties to resist the German occupation, had made their first visit to the markets of Périgord in an official car with red-and-white Belgian license plates. On their second visit all the tires had been slashed. Next time they came in a car from Paris, with the telltale "75" as the last two digits of the plate. This car, too, had been given the Resistance treatment, and Bruno worried that the local countermeasures were getting out of hand. He had a good idea who was behind the slashings, and had issued some private warnings that he hoped would calm things down. There was no point in violence if the warning system could ensure that the markets were clean before the inspectors arrived.

Then the inspectors had changed their tactics and come by train, staying at local hotels. But they were easily spotted by the hotel keepers, who all had cousins or suppliers who made the *crottins* of goat cheese and the foie gras, the jams, the oils flavored with walnuts and truffles, and the confits that assured that this corner of France was known as the very heart of the nation's gastronomic culture. Bruno, acting with the support of his mayor and all the elected councillors of the commune, including even Montsouris the communist, made it his duty to protect his neighbors and friends from the nuisances of Brussels, where the idea of food was known to stop at *moules* and *pommes frites,* and where perfectly good potatoes were adulterated with an industrial mayonnaise they did not have the patience to make themselves.

So now the inspectors were trying this new tack. They had succeeded in handing out four fines in St. Alvère the day before, but they would not succeed in St. Denis, whose famous market went back more than seven hundred years. Not if Bruno had anything to do with it. After one final gaze into the beautiful little corner of the world that was entrusted to him, Bruno climbed back into his van and headed for the market.

2

Bruno probably kissed a hundred women and shook the hands of at least as many men each market-day morning. First this morning was Fat Jeanne, as the schoolboys called her. The French, who are more attuned to the magnificent mysteries of womanhood than most, may be the only people in the world to treasure the concept of the *jolie laide,* the plain or even ugly woman who is so well at ease in herself and so cheerful in her soul that she becomes lovely. Fat Jeanne was a *jolie laide* of some fifty years, almost perfectly spherical in shape. The old brown leather satchel in which she collected the modest fees that each stallholder paid for the privilege of selling in the market of St. Denis thumped heavily against Bruno's thigh as Jeanne, squealing with pleasure to see him, turned with surprising speed and proffered her cheeks to be kissed in ritual greeting. Then she gave him a fresh strawberry from Madame Verniet's stall, and Bruno broke away to kiss the roguish old farmer's widow on both wizened cheeks in greeting.

"Here are the photos of the inspectors that Jo-Jo took in

St. Alvère yesterday," Bruno said to Jeanne, taking some printouts from his breast pocket. He had met with his fellow municipal policeman the previous evening to collect them. They could have been e-mailed to the Mairie's computer, but Bruno thought it might be risky to leave an electronic trail of his private intelligence operation.

"If you see them, call me. And give copies to Ivan in the café and to Jeannot in the bistro and to Yvette in the *tabac* to show their customers. In the meantime, you warn the stall-holders on the far side of the church. I'll take care of the ones toward the bridge."

Every Tuesday since the year 1346, when the English had captured half the nobility of France at the Battle of Crécy and the grand Brillamont family had to raise money to pay the ransom for their seigneur, the little Périgord town of St. Denis has held a weekly market. The townspeople had raised the princely sum of fifty livres of silver for their feudal lord and, in return, they cannily secured the right from him to hold the market, understanding that this would guarantee a livelihood to the tiny community, happily situated where the stream of Le Mauzens ran into the river Vézère, just beyond the point where the old Roman bridge thrust its remaining stumps from the flowing waters. A mere ten years later, the chastened nobles and knights of France had once again spurred their lumbering horses against the English archers and their long-bows and had been felled in droves. The Seigneur de Brilla-mont had to be ransomed from the victorious Englishmen all over again after the Battle of Poitiers. By then the taxes on the market had raised sufficient funds for the old Roman bridge to be crudely restored. So, for another fifty livres, the townsfolk bought from the Brillamont family the right to charge a toll over the bridge and their town's fortunes were secured forever.

These had been early skirmishes in the age-old war between the French peasant and the tax collectors and enforcers of the power of the state. The depredations of the market inspectors (who were Frenchmen, but took their orders from Brussels) were simply the latest campaign in an endless struggle. Had the laws and regulations been purely French, Bruno might have had some reservations about working so actively, and with such personal glee, to frustrate them. But since that was not the case, he was entirely comfortable. The local farmers and their wives had their living to earn, and would be hard put to pay the inspectors' fines from the modest sums they made in the market. Above all, they were his friends and neighbors.

In truth, Bruno knew there were not many warnings to give. More and more of the market stalls these days were run by strangers from out of town who sold dresses, jeans, draperies, cheap sweaters, T-shirts, and secondhand clothes. Two coal-black Senegalese sold colorful dashikis, leather belts, and purses, and a couple of local potters displayed their wares. There was an organic-bread stall and several local vintners sold their Bergerac and the sweet Monbazillac dessert wine that Providence in its wisdom had kindly provided to accompany foie gras. There was a knife-sharpener and an ironmonger, Diem the Vietnamese selling his spring rolls, and Jules selling his nuts and olives while his wife tended a vast pot of steaming paella. The various stalls selling fruit and vegetables, herbs and tomato plants, were all immune so far from the men from Brussels.

But at each stall where they sold homemade cheese and pâté, or ducks and chickens that had been slaughtered on some battered old stump in the farmyard with the family axe rather than in a tiled abattoir by people in white coats and hairnets, Bruno delivered his warning. He helped the older women to pack up, piling the fresh-plucked chickens into cavernous cloth bags to take to the nearby office of Patrick's driving school for safekeeping. The richer farmers who could afford mobile cold cabinets were always ready to let *Tante* Marie and *Grandmère* Colette put some of their less legal cheeses alongside their own. In the market, everyone was in on the secret.

Bruno's cell phone rang. "The bastards are here," said Jeanne, in what she must have thought was a whisper but wasn't. "They parked in front of the bank and Marie-Hélène recognized them from the photo I gave to Ivan. She saw it when she stopped for her *petit café*. She's sure it's them."

"Did she see their car?" Bruno asked.

"A silver Renault Laguna, quite new." Jeanne read out the number. Interesting, thought Bruno. It was a number for the Department of the Corrèze. They would have taken the train to Brive and picked up the car there, outside the Dordogne. They must have realized that the local spy network was watching for them. Bruno walked out of the pedestrian zone and onto the main square by the old stone bridge, where the inspectors would have to come past him before they reached the market. He phoned his fellow municipal police chiefs in the other villages with markets that week and gave them the car and its number. He had protected his friends from the inspectors; now he had to protect them from themselves.

So he telephoned old Joe, who had for forty years been the town's chief of police before Bruno. Now Joe spent his time visiting cronies in all the local markets, selling an occasional oversized apron and work coat from a small stock that he kept in the back of his van but more often nursing a *petit rouge.* Joe had been a good rugby player two generations ago and was still a pillar of the local club. He wore in his lapel the little red button that labeled him a member of the Légion d'honneur, a reward for his boyhood service as a messenger in the Resistance. Bruno felt sure that Joe would know about the tire slashing, and might well have helped organize it. Joe knew every family in the district, and was related to half of them.

"Look, Joe," Bruno began when the old man answered with his usual gruff bark, "everything is fine with the inspectors. The market is clean and we know who they are. We don't want any trouble this time. It could make matters worse, you understand me?"

"You mean the car that's parked in front of the bank? The silver Laguna?" Joe said, in a deep and rasping voice that came from decades of Gauloises and the rough wine he made himself. "Well, it's being taken care of. Don't you worry yourself, *petit* Bruno. The Gestapo can walk home today. Like last time."

"Joe, this is going to get people into trouble," Bruno said forcefully, although he knew that he might as well argue with a brick wall. Joe must have been in Ivan's café when Jeanne was showing the photos around. And he had probably heard about the car from Marie-Hélène in the bank, since she was married to his nephew.

"This could bring real trouble for us if we're not careful," Bruno went on. "So don't do anything that would force me to take action."

He closed his phone with a snap. Scanning the people coming across the bridge, most of whom he knew, he kept watch for the inspectors. Then, from the corner of his eye, he saw a familiar car, a battered Renault Twingo the local gendarmes used when out of uniform. In theory, they were his colleagues; in fact, while some were his friends, the gendarmerie reported to the Ministry of Defense in Paris, whose interests did not always coincide with those of St. Denis. The car was being driven by the new captain he had not yet had time to get to know. He was a dour and skinny type called Duroc, from Normandy, who seemed to do everything by the book. Suddenly an alarm went off in Bruno's mind and he called Joe again.

"Stop everything now. They must be expecting more trouble after last time. That new gendarme chief has just gone by in plain clothes, and he may have arranged for the inspectors' car to be staked out. I've got a bad feeling about this."

"*Merde,*" said Joe. "We should have thought of that, but we may be too late. I told Karim to take care of it. I'll try and call him off."

Bruno called the Café des Sports, run by Karim and his wife, Rashida, very pretty and heavily pregnant. Rashida told him Karim had left the café already and she didn't think he had his cell phone with him. *Putain,* thought Bruno. He started walking briskly across the narrow bridge, trying to get to the parking lot in front of the bank before Karim got into trouble.

Since he first arrived in the town a decade ago, Bruno had known Karim as a hulking and sullen teenager, ready to fight any young Frenchman who dared take him on. Bruno had seen the type before, and had slowly taught Karim that he was enough of an athlete to take out his resentments on the rugby field. With rugby lessons twice a week and a match each Saturday, and tennis in the summer, Bruno had taught the boy to stay out of trouble. He got Karim onto the school team, then onto the local rugby team and finally into a league big enough for him to make the money that enabled him to marry Rashida and buy the café. Bruno had made a speech at their wedding.

Putain, putain, putain. If Karim got into trouble over this it could turn very nasty. The inspectors would get their boss to put pressure on the prefect, who would then put pressure on the Police Nationale, or maybe they would even get on to the Ministry of Defense and bring in the gendarmes who were supposed to deal with rural crime. A conviction for criminal damage to state property would mean an end to Karim's license to sell tobacco, and the end of his café. Karim would not name names but Rashida would be thinking of the baby and she might crack. That would lead them to old Joe and to the rest of the rugby team, who had certainly participated in the mischief, and before you knew it the whole network of the quiet and peaceful town would face charges. Bruno couldn't have that.

He carefully slowed his pace as he turned the corner by the commune notice board and passed the war memorial, moving into the ranks of cars that were drawn up like so many multi-colored soldiers in front of the Crédit Agricole. He looked for the gendarmes' Twingo and then saw Duroc standing in the usual line in front of the bank's cash machine. Two places behind him was the looming figure of Karim, chatting pleasantly to Colette from the dry-cleaning shop. Bruno closed his eyes in relief, and strode on toward the burly North African.

"Karim," he said, and swiftly added "*Bonjour,* Colette," kissing her cheeks, before turning back to Karim, saying, "I need to talk to you about Sunday's game. It will just take a moment." He grabbed Karim by the elbow, made his farewell to Colette, nodded at Duroc and steered his reluctant quarry back to the bridge.

"I think they may have the car staked out, maybe even tipped off the gendarmerie," Bruno said. Karim broke into a delighted smile.

"I thought of that myself, Bruno. Anyway, it's already done."

"You did the tires with Duroc standing right there?"

"Not at all," said Karim, grinning. "I told my nephew to take care of it with the other kids. They crept up and jammed a potato into the exhaust pipe while I was chatting with Colette and Duroc. That car won't make ten kilometers before the engine quits."

3

As the siren that sounded noon began its soaring whine over the town, Bruno stood to attention before the Mairie. At moments such as this he often wondered if this had been the same sound that had signaled the coming of the Germans. Images of ancient newsreels would come to mind: diving Stukas, people dashing for air-raid shelters, the victorious Wehrmacht marching through the Arc de Triomphe in 1940 to stamp their jackboots on the Champs-Elysées and launch the conquest of Paris. This was the day of revenge, the eighth of May, when France celebrated her eventual victory, and although some said it was old-fashioned and unfriendly in these days of Europe, the town of St. Denis remembered the Liberation with an annual parade of its venerable veterans.

Bruno had posted the ROUTE BARRÉE signs to block the side road and ensured that the floral wreaths had been delivered. He had donned his tie and polished his shoes and the peak of his cap. He had warned the old men in both cafés that the time was approaching and had brought up the flags from the cellar beneath the Mairie. The mayor himself stood waiting, the sash of office across his chest and the little red rosette of the Légion d'honneur in his lapel. The gendarmes were holding up the impatient traffic, while housewives kept asking when they could cross the road, grumbling that their bags were getting heavy and that they had to get lunch on the table.

Jean-Pierre of the bicycle shop carried the Tricolor and his enemy Bachelot held the flag that bore the cross of Lorraine, the emblem of General de Gaulle and Free France. Marie-Louise, who as a young girl had served as a courier for one of the Resistance groups and who had been taken off to Ravensbrück concentration camp and somehow survived, had the flag of St. Denis. Montsouris, the only communist council member of the town, carried a smaller flag of the Soviet Union, acknowledging one of France's wartime allies, and Monsieur Jackson held the flag of another ally, his native Britain. A retired schoolteacher, he had come to spend his declining years with his daughter, who had married Pascal of the local insurance office. Jackson had been an eighteen-year-old recruit in the last weeks of war in 1945 and was thus a fellow combatant, entitled to share the honor of the victory parade. Bruno was privately proud to have arranged this. One day, Bruno told himself, he would find a real American, but this time young Karim, as the star of the rugby team, carried the Stars and Stripes.

The mayor gave the signal and the town band began to play "The Marseillaise." Jean-Pierre raised the flag of France, Bruno and the gendarmes saluted and the small parade marched off across the bridge, their flags flapping in the breeze. Following them were three lines of the men of St. Denis who had performed their military service in peacetime but who turned out for this parade as a duty to their town as well as to their nation. Bruno noted that Karim's entire family had come to watch him carry a flag, even the reclusive old grandfather who was almost never seen in town. At the back came a host of small boys trying to march in step. After the bridge, the parade turned left at the bank and marched through the parking area to the memorial, a bronze figure of a French poilu of the Great War. The names of the fallen sons of St. Denis took up three sides of the plinth beneath the figure, more than two hundred young men from the small village. The bronze had darkened with the years, but the great eagle of victory that was perched, wings outstretched, on the soldier's shoulder gleamed golden with fresh polish. The mayor had seen to that. The plinth's fourth side was more than sufficient for the dead of the Second World War and the subsequent conflicts in Vietnam and Algeria. Happily, there were no names from Bruno's own brief experience of war in the Balkans.

The schoolchildren of the town were lined up on each side of the memorial, the smallest ones, from the nursery school, in front sucking their thumbs and holding each other's hands. In the next row, the slightly older ones in jeans and T-shirts were still young enough to be fascinated by this spectacle. Across from them, some of the teenagers of the junior high school slouched, affecting sneers and a touch of bafflement that the new Europe they were inheriting could yet indulge in such antiquated celebrations of national pride. But Bruno noticed that most of the teenagers stood quietly, aware that they were in the presence of all that remained of their grandfathers and great-grandfathers, a list of names on a plinth that said something of their heritage and of the great mystery of war, and something of what France might one day again demand of her sons.

Jean-Pierre and Bachelot, who might not have spoken for more than sixty years but who knew the ritual of this annual moment, marched forward and lowered their flags in salute to the bronze soldier and his eagle. Montsouris dipped his red flag and Marie-Louise lowered hers so far it touched the ground. Belatedly, unsure of their timing, Karim and Jackson followed suit. The mayor walked solemnly forward and ascended the small dais that Bruno had placed before the memorial.

"*Français et Françaises,*" he declaimed, addressing the small crowd. "Frenchmen and Frenchwomen, and the representatives of our brave allies. We are here to celebrate a day of victory that has also become a day of peace, the eighth of May, which marks the end of Nazism and the beginning of Europe's reconciliation and her long, happy years of tranquillity. That peace was bought in part by the bravery of our sons of St. Denis whose names are inscribed here, by our gallant allies whose flags we honor today and by the men and women who stand before you and who never bowed their heads to the rule of the invader. Whenever France has been in mortal peril, the sons and daughters of St. Denis have stood ready to answer the call, for France, and for the Liberty, Equality and Fraternity and the Rights of Man for which she stands."

The mayor stopped and nodded at Sylvie from the bakery. She pushed forward her small daughter, who carried the floral wreath. The little girl, in a red skirt, a blue top and long white socks, walked hesitantly toward the mayor to offer him the wreath, looking quite alarmed as he bent to kiss her on both cheeks. The mayor took the wreath and walked slowly to the memorial, leaned it against the soldier's bronze leg, stood back and called out, "*Vive la France, Vive la République.*"

And with that Jean-Pierre and Bachelot, old men feeling the strain of the heavy flags, hauled them to an upright position of salute, and the band began to play "Le Chant des Partisans," the old Resistance anthem. Tears began to roll down the cheeks of the two men, and Marie-Louise broke down in sobs so that her flag wavered and all the children, even the teenagers, looked sobered, even touched, by this evidence of some great, unknowable trial that these old people had lived through.

As the music faded away, the Soviet, British and American flags were marched forward and raised in salute. Then came the surprise, a theatrical coup engineered by Bruno and approved by the mayor. This was a way for the old English enemy, who had fought France for a thousand years before becoming her ally for a brief century, to take her place on the day of victory.

Jackson's grandson, a boy of thirteen or so, marched forward from his place in the town band, where he played the trumpet, his hand on a shiny brass bugle that was slung from a red sash around his shoulders. He reached the memorial, turned to salute the mayor and, as the silent crowd exchanged glances about this novel addition to the ceremony, raised the bugle to his lips. As Bruno heard the first two long and haunting notes of "The Last Post," tears came to his eyes. Through them he could see Jackson's shoulders shaking and the British flag trembling in his hands. The mayor wiped away a tear as the last pure peals of the bugle died away, and the crowd remained absolutely silent until the boy put his bugle smartly to his side. Then, they exploded into applause and, as Karim went up and shook the boy's hand, the Stars and Stripes swirling briefly to tangle with the British and French flags, Bruno was aware of a sudden flare of camera flashes.

Mon Dieu, thought Bruno. That "Last Post" worked so well we'll have to make it part of the annual ceremony. He looked around at the crowd, beginning to drift away, and saw that young Philippe Delaron, who usually wrote the sports report for the *Sud Ouest* newspaper, had his notebook out and was talking to Jackson and his grandson. Well, a small notice in the newspaper about a British ally taking part in the victory parade could do no harm now that so many English were buying homes in the commune (though it would hardly encourage them to complain less about their various property taxes and the price of water for their swimming pools).

Suddenly Bruno noticed something odd. After every previous parade, whether it was for the eighth of May, or the eighteenth of June, when de Gaulle launched Free France, or the fourteenth of July, when France celebrated her Revolution, or the eleventh of November, when the Great War ended, Jean-Pierre and Bachelot would turn away from each other without so much as a nod and walk back separately to the Mairie to store the flags they carried. But this time they were standing still, staring fixedly at one another. Not talking, but somehow communicating. Amazing what one bugle call can do, thought Bruno. Maybe if I can get some Americans into the parade next year they might even start talking. But now it was thirty minutes after midday and, like every good Frenchman, Bruno turned his thoughts to lunch.

He walked back across the bridge with Marie-Louise, who was still weeping as he gently took her flag from her. The mayor and Jackson and his family were close behind. Karim and his family walked ahead, and Jean-Pierre and Bachelot, with their almost identical wives in their dark, frumpy dresses and cardigans, brought up the rear. They marched in silence as the band played another song from the war that had the power to melt Bruno: "J'attendrai." It was the song of the women of France in 1940 as they watched their men march off to a war that turned into six weeks of disaster and five years of prison camps. "Day and night, I shall wait always, for your return." The history of France was measured out in songs of war, he thought, many sad and some heroic, but each verse heavy with its weight of loss.

The crowd thinned as the people went off to lunch, most of the parents and children heading home, though others made for Jeannot's bistro beyond the Mairie, or the pizzeria back over the bridge. Bruno would normally have gone with some friends to Ivan's café. Bruno loved telling visitors about how Ivan fell in love with a Belgian girl staying at a local campsite and, for three glorious and passionate months until she packed up and went back to Charleroi, the plat du jour was *moules-frites*. Then there was no plat du jour for weeks, until Bruno had taken the grieving Ivan out and got him heroically drunk.

Today was a special day, and the mayor had organized a *déjeuner d'honneur* for those who had played a part in the parade. Now they climbed the ancient stairs, bowed in the middle by centuries of feet, to the top floor of the Mairie, which held the council chamber and, on occasions such as this, doubled as the banquet room. The town's treasure was a long and ancient table that served council and banquet alike, and was said to have been made for the grand hall of the château of the Brillamont family itself in those happier days before their seigneur kept getting captured by the English. Twenty places were laid for lunch.

Bruno scanned the room and saw the mayor with his wife, and Jean-Pierre and Bachelot with their wives at opposite ends of the room. For the first time, Karim and Rashida had been invited, and stood chatting with Montsouris and his tall and skeletally thin wife, who was even more Left-wing than her husband. Jackson and Sylvie the baker and her son were talking to Rollo, the headmaster of the local school, who sometimes played tennis with Bruno. With them was the music teacher, who was the conductor of the town band and also the master of the church choir. Bruno had expected to see the new captain of the local gendarmes, but there was no sign of the man. The sleekly plump Father Sentout, priest of the ancient church of St. Denis, who was aching to become a monsignor, emerged puffing from the new elevator. His usual benign smile looked considerably forced as he made way for the only other passenger, the Baron, a retired industrialist of some sixty years who was the main local landowner. Bruno nodded at the Baron, who was both a fervent atheist and Bruno's regular tennis partner.

Fat Jeanne from the market appeared with a tray of Champagne glasses, swiftly followed by young Claire, the mayor's secretary, who carried an enormous tray of amuse-bouches that she had made herself. Claire, who had a *tendresse* for Bruno, had talked to him of little else for weeks, leaving the mayor's letters untyped as she thumbed through *Madame Figaro* and *Marie Claire* to seek ideas and recipes. The result was celery filled with cream cheese, olives stuffed with anchovies and slices of toast covered with chopped tomatoes. Less than inspiring, thought Bruno.

Suddenly Claire was in front of him, gazing fixedly into Bruno's eyes.

"They are Italian delicacies called bruschetta," she said. Claire was pretty enough, if overtalkative, but Bruno had a firm rule about never playing on his own doorstep. He knew, however, that his reticence on that score did not stop Claire and her mother, not to mention a few other mothers in St. Denis, from referring to him as the town's most eligible bachelor. Any sign of interest Bruno showed in any eligible young woman became a subject for gossip among the women and amusement among the married men. They teased him about it, but in fact they approved of the discretion he brought to his private life and the polite skills with which he frustrated the town's mothers and maintained his bachelorhood.

"Delicious," said Bruno, limiting himself to an olive. "Well done, Claire. All that planning really paid off." As she lingered, he suggested that the mayor's wife looked hungry. Once Claire moved on he scooped a glass of Champagne from Fat Jeanne and noticed that Montsouris and his wife were approaching him.

"Well, Bruno," boomed Montsouris, whose loud voice was more suited to bellowing fiery speeches to a crowd of striking workers, "you have made the people's victory into a celebration of the British crown. Is that what you meant to do?"

"*Bonjour,* Yves," said Bruno, starting to grin. "Don't give me that people's victory crap. You and all the other communists would be speaking German if it weren't for the British and American armies."

"The British would be speaking German if it weren't for Stalin and the Red Army," snapped Montsouris's wife in her high-pitched voice.

"Yes, and if they'd had their way, we'd all be speaking Russian today and you'd be the mayor."

"Commissar, if you please," replied Montsouris, grinning in return. Bruno knew that Montsouris was only a communist because he was a *cheminot,* a railway worker, and the Confédération Générale du Travail, the communist labor union, had those jobs sewn up for its members. Montsouris ostentatiously read *L'Humanité,* the party paper, and campaigned before each election for the communists, but most of his political views were decidedly conservative. Sometimes Bruno wondered whom Montsouris really voted for once he was away from his noisily radical wife and safe in the privacy of the voting booth. But Montsouris knew his role and in public played it to the hilt.

"*Messieurs dames, à table, s'il vous plaît,*" called the mayor, "before the soup gets warm."

Jackson gave a hearty English laugh, but stopped when he realized that nobody else was amused. Sylvie took his arm and guided him to his place. Bruno found himself sitting beside the priest, and bowed his head as Father Sentout delivered a brief grace. Bruno often found himself next to the priest on such occasions. As he turned his attention to the chilled vichyssoise, he wondered if Sentout would ask his usual question. He didn't have to wait long.

"Why does the mayor never want me to say a small prayer at these public events like Victory Day?"

"It is a republican celebration, Father," Bruno explained, for perhaps the fourteenth time. "You know the law of 1905, separation of church and state."

"But most of those brave boys were good Catholics and they fell doing God's work."

"I take your point, Father," Bruno said kindly. "But you do get to bless the meal. Most mayors would not even allow that."

"Yes, and the mayor's feast is a welcome treat after the purgatory that my housekeeper inflicts upon me. But she is a pious soul and does her best."

Bruno now watched with satisfaction as Fat Jeanne whipped away his soup plate and replaced it with a healthy slice of foie gras and some of her own onion marmalade. To accompany it, Claire served him a small glass of golden Monbazillac that he knew came from the vineyard of the mayor's cousin. Toasts were proposed, the boy bugler was singled out for praise and the Champagne and Monbazillac began their wondrous alchemy of making a staid occasion convivial. After the dry white Bergerac that came with the trout and a well-chosen 2001 Pécharmant with the lamb, it became a thoroughly jolly luncheon.

"Is that Arab fellow a Muslim, do you know?" asked Father Sentout, with a deceptively casual air, waving his wineglass in Karim's direction.

"I never asked him," said Bruno, sensing that the priest might be hoping for a convert. "If he is, he's not very religious. He doesn't pray to Mecca and he'll cross himself before a big game, so he's probably a Christian. Besides, he was born here. He's as French as you or I."

"He never comes to confession, though—just like you, Bruno. We only ever see you in church for baptisms, weddings and funerals."

"And choir practice, and Christmas and Easter," Bruno protested.

"What do you know of Karim's family?"

"Karim's religion I don't know about, and I don't think he really has one, but his father is most definitely an atheist and a rationalist. It comes from teaching mathematics."

"Do you know the rest of the family?"

"I know Karim's wife, and his cousins, and some of the nephews who play with the *minimes,* and his niece Fatima, who has a chance to win the junior tennis championship. They're all good people. I met the grandfather at Karim's wedding, which was held here in the Mairie without any priest or mullah in sight. That was before the old man moved down here."

"By chance I met the old man, too, and he seemed interested in the church, so I just wondered . . ." the priest broke off, as if looking for the right words. "He was sitting in the church, you see, while it was empty, and I think he was praying. So naturally, I was curious to know if he was a Muslim or not."

"Did you ask him?"

"No. He scurried away as soon as I approached him. It was very odd."

Bruno could only shrug. And then the mayor started tapping his glass with a knife and rose to make the usual short speech. As he listened dutifully, Bruno began to long for his after-lunch coffee, and then perhaps a little nap on the old couch in his office, to restore himself for a tiresome afternoon of paperwork.

4

Bruno always made it his business to establish good relations with each new head of the local gendarmes who arrived for his three-year tour. The gendarmerie, a station of six men and two women on the outskirts of town, was in an undistinguished modern building of red brick and brown stucco that jarred with the comforting old stone of the buildings that flanked it. There was a small yard for parking between it and the modest block of apartments where the gendarmes and their families lived. Unlike the classic military barracks that the gendarmes occupied in the big towns, the station of St. Denis had a decidedly civilian air, with washing hung out to dry on the balconies and children playing in the yard. Since the station supervised several communes in a large rural district in the largest department of France, it was run by a captain, in this case Duroc. And now, two days after the parade, a very angry Duroc, dressed in full uniform, was leaning aggressively across Bruno's untidy desk and glowering at him.

"The prefect himself has telephoned me about this. And

then I got orders from the ministry in Paris," he snapped. "Orders to stop this damned hooliganism. Stop it, arrest the criminals and make an example of them. The prefect does not want embarrassing complaints from Brussels that we Frenchmen are behaving like a bunch of Europe-hating Englishmen. He wants no more destruction of the property of government inspectors who are simply doing their job and enforcing the law on public hygiene. Since I am reliably told that nothing takes place in this town without its chief of police hearing about it, I demand your cooperation."

He said "chief of police" with a sneer. Duroc was a most unappetizing man, tall and thin to the point of gauntness, with a very prominent Adam's apple that poked out above his collar like some ominous growth. But, thought Bruno, one had better make allowances. Duroc was newly promoted, and understandably nervous after being telephoned by the prefect himself, a post established by the Emperor Napoleon to be the official representative of Paris and the French state in each of the one hundred departments of France. And since Duroc would be here in St. Denis for another three years at least, there was no sense in getting off on the wrong foot. In the best interests of St. Denis, and himself, Bruno knew he had better be diplomatic. He needed Duroc to accede to his requests that the traffic gendarmes stay at home with their Breathalyzers on the night of the rugby club dance or the hunting club dinner. If the local sportsmen couldn't have a few extra glasses of wine on a special night without getting stopped by the cops, he would never hear the end of it.

"I quite understand, *Capitaine*," Bruno said. "You're quite right and your orders are entirely proper. Nobody needs this hooliganism. We've got to work together on this. You'll have my full cooperation."

He beamed across his desk at the red-faced Duroc, who was not, alas, buying what Bruno was trying to sell.

"So, who is it?" Duroc demanded. "I want to bring them in for questioning. Give me the names—you must know who's responsible."

"No, I don't. I might make some guesses, but that's what they'd be. And guesses are not evidence."

"I'll be the judge of that," Duroc snapped. "Just give me the names and leave it to the professionals."

"Evidence will not be easy to come by, not in a small town like this where most of the people think these European laws are ridiculous," Bruno said, ignoring Duroc's attempt to pull rank and shrugging off the implied insults. Bruno had been down this road before. In time Duroc would discover how much he needed Bruno's local knowledge. "The people around here tend to be very loyal to one another, at least in the face of outsiders," he continued. "They won't talk to you—at least, not if you go around hauling them in for tough questioning."

Duroc began to interrupt, but Bruno rose, raised his hand to demand silence and strolled across to the window.

"Look out there, *Capitaine,* and let us think this through like reasonable men. Look at that scene: the river, those cliffs tumbling down to the willows where fishermen sit for hours. Look at the old stone bridge built by Napoleon himself, and the square with the tables under the old church tower. It's a scene made for the TV cameras. They come and film here quite often, you know. From Paris. Foreign TV as well, sometimes. It's the image of France that we like to show off, the France we're proud of, and I'd hate to be the man who got blamed for spoiling it. If we do as you suggest, if we go at it heavy-handed and round up kids on suspicion, we'll have the whole town up in arms."

"What do you mean, kids?" said Duroc, his brows knitted. "It's the market types doing this stuff, grown-ups."

"I don't think so," Bruno said slowly. "My experience in this commune tells me a few kids are doing this. And if you start hauling in kids, you know what the outcome will be. Angry parents, protest marches, demonstrations outside the gendarmerie. The teachers will probably go on strike in sympathy and the mayor will have to take their side and back the parents. The press will descend, looking to embarrass the government, and the TV cameras will film newsworthy scenes of the heartland of France in revolt, scenes of brutal police bullying children and oppressing good French citizens who are trying to protect their way of life against those heartless bureaucrats in Brussels. You know what the media are like. And then all of a sudden the prefect would forget that he ever gave you any orders and your boss in Paris would be unavailable and your career would be over."

He turned back to Duroc, who was now subdued, and said, "And you want to risk all that just to arrest a couple of kids that you can't even take to court because they'd be too young?"

"Kids, you say?"

"Kids," repeated Bruno. He hoped this wouldn't take too much longer. He had to do those amendments to the contract for the public fireworks for the Fourteenth of July, and he was due at the tennis club at six p.m.

"I know the kids in this town very well," he went on. "I teach them rugby and tennis and watch them grow up to play on the town teams. I'm pretty sure it's kids behind this, probably egged on by their parents, but still just kids. There'll be no arrests out of this, no examples of French justice to parade before Brussels. Just a very angry town and a lot of embarrassment for you."

He walked across to the cupboard and took out two glasses and a very old-looking bottle, its glass imperfectly shaped.

"May I offer you a glass of my *vin de noix, Capitaine*? One of the many pleasures of this little corner of France. I make it myself. I hope you'll share a small aperitif in the name of our cooperation." He poured two healthy servings and handed one to Duroc. "Now," he went on, "I have a small idea that might help us avoid any unpleasantness."

The captain looked dubious, but he was listening. He took the glass without displaying the slightest warmth.

"Unless, of course, you want me to bring in the mayor, and you can make your case to him," Bruno said. "And I suppose he could order me to bring in these children, but what with the parents being voters, and the elections on the horizon . . ." He shrugged for effect.

"You said you had an idea." Duroc sniffed at his glass and took a small but evidently pleasing sip.

"Well, if I'm right and it's just some kids playing pranks, I could talk to them myself and have a quiet word with the parents and we can probably nip this thing in the bud. You can report back that it was a couple of kids and the matter has been dealt with. No fuss, no press, no TV. No nasty questions to your boss back in Paris."

The captain took another thoughtful sip of his drink.

"Good stuff, this. You make it yourself, you say?" He sipped again. "I must introduce you to some of the Calvados I brought down with me from Normandy." He paused. "Maybe you're right. No point stirring everything up if it's just some kids, just so long as no more tires get slashed. Still, I'd better report something back to the prefect tomorrow."

Bruno smiled politely and raised his glass.

"We cops have got to stick together, eh?" Duroc said. He was now smiling and he leaned forward to clink his glass against Bruno's. At that moment Bruno's portable phone, lying on his desk, rang its familiar warbling version of "The Marseillaise." With a sigh, he gave an apologetic shrug to Duroc and picked it up.

It was Karim, breathing heavily, his voice shrill.

"Bruno, come quick," he said. "It's Grandpa, he's dead. I think—I think he's been murdered." Bruno heard a sob.

"What do you mean? What's happened? Where are you?"

"At his place. I came up to fetch him for dinner. There's blood everywhere."

"Don't touch anything. I'll be there as soon as I can." He closed his phone and turned to Duroc. "Well, we can forget about childish pranks for now. It looks like we have a real crime on our hands. Possibly a murder. We'll take my car. One minute, while I ring the firemen."

"Firemen?" asked Duroc. "Why do we need them?"

"Around here they're the emergency service. It might be too late for an ambulance but that's the way it's always done and we had better do this by the book. And you'll want to tell your office. If this really is a murder, we'll need the Police Nationale from Périgueux."

"Murder?" Duroc put his glass down. "In St. Denis?"

"That's what my caller said." Bruno telephoned the fire station and gave them directions, then grabbed his cap. "Let's go. I'll drive, you ring your people."

5

Karim was waiting for them at the end of a long unpaved lane that led through the fields to the tidy yard of a single-story stone cottage, with a carefully tended vegetable garden to one side and some magnificent rosebushes to the other. Karim was white-faced. He looked as if he had been sick. He stepped aside as Bruno and Duroc, still in his full-dress uniform, strode in.

The old man had been gutted. He lay bare-chested on the floor, intestines spilling out from a great gash in his belly. The place stank of them, and flies were already buzzing. There was indeed blood everywhere, including some thick pooling in regular lines on his chest.

"It seems to be some kind of pattern," Bruno said, leaning closer over the chest but trying to keep his shoes out of the drying pools of blood around the body. It was not easy to make out. The old man was lying awkwardly, his back raised as though leaning on something that Bruno could not see for the blood.

"*Mon Dieu*," said Duroc, peering closely. "That's a swastika carved in his chest. This is a hate crime. A race crime."

Bruno looked carefully around him. It was a small house: one bedroom, this main room—with an old stone fireplace— that was kitchen, dining and sitting room all in one, and a tiny bathroom built onto the side. It was sparsely furnished, almost spartan, with no curtains and just one elderly easy chair by the fireplace, a small table and two straight-backed chairs. Beneath the window was an old stone sink with a single tap and, beside it, a small camping stove with two burners. A meal had been interrupted; half a baguette and some sausage and cheese lay on a single plate on the table, alongside the remains of a bottle of red wine and a broken wineglass. A chair had been knocked over, and a photo of the French soccer team that had won the World Cup in 1998 hung askew on the wall. Bruno spotted a bundle of cloth tossed into a corner. He walked across and looked at it. It was a shirt, some of the buttons clearly missing, with small tears around the buttonholes, as if the garment had been ripped from the old man. There was no blood on it, so somebody quite strong had probably done it before starting to use the knife. Bruno sighed. He glanced into the bathroom and the tidy bedroom, but could see nothing out of place there.

"I don't see a cell phone anywhere, or a wallet," he said. "It may be in his trousers, but we'd better leave that until the scene-of-crime and forensics people get here."

In the distance, they heard the fire engine's siren. Bruno went outside to see if his phone could get a signal this far from town. One bar of the four showed on the screen—just enough, so he called the mayor to explain the situation. Then everything seemed to happen at once. The firemen arrived, bringing life-support equipment. Duroc's deputy drove up in a big blue van with two more gendarmes, one of them with a large old camera, the other carrying a big roll of orange tape to mark out the crime scene. Bruno went out to Karim, who was leaning awkwardly against the side of his car, his hand covering his eyes.

"When did you get here, Karim?"

"Just before I called you. Maybe a minute before, not more." Karim looked up, his cheeks wet with tears. *"Putain, putain.* Who could have done this, Bruno? The old man didn't have an enemy in the world."

Bruno knew it usually seemed that way, but it wasn't always the case.

"Have you called Rashida?" he asked.

"Not yet. I've got to pull myself together first. She loved the old guy."

"And Momu?" Karim's father was the math teacher at the local school, a popular man who cooked enormous vats of couscous for the rugby dinners. His name was Mohammed but everyone called him Momu.

Karim shook his head. "I only called you. I want to tell Papa myself, he was so devoted to him. We all were."

"When did you last see your grandfather alive? Or speak to him?"

"Last night at Papa's. We had dinner. Papa drove him home and that was the last I saw of him. We sort of take turns feeding him and it was our turn tonight, which is why I came up to get him."

"Did you touch anything?" This was Bruno's first murder, and as far as he knew the commune's first as well. He had seen a lot of dead bodies, though, and not just in his military service. It was Bruno who organized the funerals and dealt with grieving families, and he had coped with some bad car crashes, so he was used to the sight of blood. But nothing like this.

"No. When I got here, I called out to Grandpa like I usually do and went in. The door was open like always and there he was. *Putain,* all that blood. And that smell. I couldn't touch him. Not like that. I've never seen anything like it."

Karim turned away to retch again. Bruno swallowed hard. Duroc came out and told one of the gendarmes to start stringing the tape around the crime scene. He looked at Karim, still bent double and spitting the last of the bile from his mouth.

"Who's he?" Duroc asked.

"Karim is the grandson of the victim," Bruno replied. "He runs the Café des Sports. He's a good man, he's the one who called. He told me he touched nothing, called me as soon as he got here." Turning back to Karim, he asked, "Karim, where were you before you drove here to pick up your grandfather?"

"In the café, all afternoon."

"Are you sure?" snapped Duroc. "We can check that."

"That's right, we can check that," Bruno said, staring at Duroc. "Meantime, let's get him home," Bruno said calmly. "He's in shock."

"No," said Duroc. "I want him here. I called the brigade in Périgueux and they said they'd bring the Police Nationale. The detectives will want to talk to him."

Albert, the chief fireman, came out, wiping his brow. He looked at Bruno and shook his head.

"Dead for a couple of hours or more," he said. "Come over here, Bruno. I need to talk to you."

They walked down the drive and off to the side of the vegetable garden and a well-tended compost heap. It should have been a pleasant spot for an old man in retirement, the hill sloping away to the woods behind and the view from the house down the valley.

"You saw that thing on his chest?" Albert asked. Bruno nodded. "Nasty stuff, and it gets worse. His hands were tied behind his back. That's why his body was arched like that. He would not have died quickly. But that swastika? I don't know. This is very bad, Bruno. It can't be anyone from around here. I didn't know the old man but we all know Momu and Karim. They're like family."

"Somebody didn't think so," said Bruno. "Not with that swastika. Dear God, it looks like a racist thing, a political killing."

There was a shout from the cottage. Duroc was waving him over. Bruno shook hands with Albert and walked back.

"Do you keep a political list?" Duroc asked. "Fascists, communists, Front National types, activists, all that?"

"No, never have and never had to," said Bruno. "The mayor usually knows how everyone votes, and they usually vote the same way they did last time, the same way their fathers did. He can usually tell you what the vote will be the day before the election and he's never wrong by more than a dozen or so."

"Any Front National types that you know of? Skinheads? Fascists?"

"Le Pen usually gets a few votes, about fifty or sixty last time, I recall. But nobody is very active."

"What about those Front National posters and the graffiti you see on the roads around here?" Duroc's face was getting red again. "Half the road signs seem to have 'FN' scrawled on them. Somebody must have done that."

Bruno nodded. "You're right. They suddenly appeared during the last election campaign on all the roads up to Périgueux and down to Bergerac, but nobody took them very seriously. You always get that kind of thing in elections. Nobody knew who did it."

"You're going to tell me that it was kids again?"

"No, I'm not, because I have no idea about this. What I can tell you is that there's no branch of the Front National here. They might get a few dozen votes but they've never elected a single councillor. They never even held a campaign rally in the last election. I don't recall seeing any of their leaflets. Most people here vote either Left or Right or Green, except for the Chasseurs."

"The what?"

"The political party for hunters and fishermen. That's their name. Chasse, Pêche, Nature, Traditions. It's like an alternative Green Party for people who hate the real Greens as a bunch of city slickers who don't know the first thing about the countryside. They get about fifteen percent of the vote here, when they put up a candidate, that is. Don't you have them in Normandy?"

Duroc shrugged. "I don't know. I don't pay much attention to politics."

"Grandpa voted for the Chasse Party last time. He told

me," Karim said. "He was a hunter and very strong on all that tradition stuff. You know he was a Harki? Got a Croix de Guerre in the Algerian war. That's why he had to leave Algeria to come over here."

Duroc looked blank.

"The Harkis were the Algerians who fought for us in the Algerian war, in the French Army," Bruno explained. "When we pulled out of Algeria, the ones we left behind were hunted down and killed as traitors by the new government. Some of the Harkis got out and came to France. Chirac made a big speech about them a few years ago, how badly they'd been treated even though they fought for France. It was like a formal apology to the Harkis from the president of the republic."

"Grandpa was there," Karim said. "They paid his way, gave him a rail ticket and hotel and everything. He wore his Croix de Guerre. Always kept it on the wall."

"A war hero. That's just what we need," grunted Duroc. "The press will be all over this."

"You say he kept the medal on the wall?" said Bruno. "I didn't see it. Come and show me where."

They went back into the room that looked like a slaughterhouse and was beginning to smell like one. The firemen were clearing up their equipment and the room kept flaring with light as a gendarme took photos. Karim kept his eyes firmly away from his grandfather's corpse and pointed to the wall by the side of the fireplace. There were two nails in the wall but nothing hanging on either one.

"It's gone," Karim said, shaking his head. "That's where he

kept it. He said he was saving it to give to his first great-grandson. The medal's gone. And the photo."

"What photo?" Bruno asked.

"His soccer team, the one he played on when he was young, in Marseilles."

"When was this?"

"I don't know. Thirties or forties, I suppose."

"During the war?"

"I don't know," said Karim. "He never talked much about his youth, except to say he'd played a lot of soccer."

The three of them left the house for the open air. It was a relief to be away from the smell.

"You said your grandfather was a hunter," Bruno said. "Did he have a gun?"

"Not that I ever saw. He hadn't hunted in years. Too old, he used to say. He still fished a lot, though."

"If there's a gun, we'd better find it. Wait here," Duroc instructed, and went back into the house. Bruno called Mireille at the Mairie, and asked her to check whether a hunting or fishing license had been issued to Hamid Mustafa al-Bakr.

"Look under 'A' for the 'al' and 'B' for the 'Bakr,'" Bruno said. "And if that doesn't turn him up, try 'H' for 'Hamid' and 'M' for 'Mustafa.'" He knew that filing was not Mireille's strong point. A widow whose great skill in life was to make a magnificent *tête de veau,* the mayor had taken her on as a clerk after her young husband died of a heart attack.

Duroc emerged from the house shaking his head. "Now we wait for the detectives," he said derisively. The gendarmerie had little affection for the detectives of the Police

Nationale. The gendarmes were part of the Ministry of Defense, but the Police Nationale came under the Ministry of the Interior, and there was constant feuding between them over who did what.

"I'll go and see the neighbors," said Bruno. "We have to find out if they heard or saw anything."

6

The nearest house was back toward the main road, which led to a gigantic cave, a source of great pride to the St. Denis tourist office. Its stalagmites and stalactites had been artfully lit so that, with some imagination, the guides could convince tourists that a given one was the Virgin Mary and that another looked like Charles de Gaulle. Bruno could never remember whether the stalactites grew up or down and thought they all looked like pipes in giant church organs, but he liked the place for the concerts, jazz and classical, that were held there in the summer. And he relished the story that when the cave was first discovered, the intrepid explorer who was lowered in on a long rope found himself standing on a large heap of bones. They belonged to the victims of brigands who lay in wait to rob pilgrims who took this route from the shrines of Rocamadour and Cadouin to Santiago de Compostela in distant Spain.

The house he approached belonged to Yannick, the maintenance man for the cave, and his wife, who worked in the souvenir shop. They were away from home all day and their daughters were at the lycée in Sarlat, so Bruno did not expect much when he rang the doorbell. Nobody came, so he went to the back on the chance that Yannick might be working in his garden. The tomatoes, onions, beans and lettuces stood in orderly rows, protected from rabbits by a stockade of chicken wire. But there was no sign of Yannick. Bruno drove back to the main road and on to the next nearest neighbor, the so-called mad Englishwoman. Her house was a hill and a valley away from the slain man's cottage, but they used part of the same access road, so she might have seen or heard something.

He slowed at the top of the rise and stopped to admire her property. Once an old farm, it boasted a small farmhouse, a couple of barns, some stables and a pigeon tower, all built of honey-colored local stone and arranged on three sides of a courtyard. There were two embracing wings of well-trimmed poplars set back from the house, sufficient to deflect the wind in winter but too far away to cast shade over the buildings or grounds. Ivy climbed up one side of the pigeon tower and a splendid burst of bright pink early roses covered the side by an old iron-studded door. In the middle of the courtyard stood a handsome ash tree, and large terra-cotta pots filled with geraniums splashed color against the gravel. Beside the largest barn was a vine-covered terrace with a long wooden table that looked like a fine place to dine in summer. Off to its side was a vegetable garden, a greenhouse and a level area for parking. On the other side, behind a low fence covered in climbing roses, he saw the corner of a swimming pool.

From the top of the long gentle rise of the meadow, the

property looked charming in the late afternoon sunlight, and Bruno drank in the sight. He had seen many a fine house and some handsome small châteaux in his many tours through his commune, but he'd rarely seen a place that looked so completely at peace and welcoming. It came as a relief after the shock and horror of what he had found at Hamid's cottage. He felt calmer for seeing it but reminded himself that he had a job to do.

He drove slowly up the gravel road, which was lined on each side with young fruit trees that would form a handsome avenue someday, and stopped in the parking area. The Englishwoman's old blue Citroën was parked alongside a new VW Golf convertible with English license plates. He settled his cap on his head, switched off his engine and heard the familiar sound of a tennis ball being struck. He strolled around to the back of the farmhouse, past an open barn where two horses were chewing hay, and saw a grass tennis court that he had not realized was there.

Two women in short tennis dresses were playing with such concentration that they didn't notice his arrival. An enthusiastic but not very gifted player himself, Bruno watched with appreciation, for the women as much as for their play. They were both slim, their legs and arms graceful and tanned against the white of their dresses. The Englishwoman had her auburn hair tied up in a ponytail; her dark-haired opponent wore a white baseball cap. They were playing a steady and impressive baseline game. Watching the fluidity of the Englishwoman's strokes, Bruno realized that she was rather younger than he'd thought. The grass court was not very fast and the surface was bumpy enough to make the bounce unpredictable, but it was freshly mowed and the white lines had been recently painted. It would be very pleasant to play here, Bruno thought, and she could evidently give him a good game.

In Bruno's view, anyone who could keep up a rally beyond half a dozen strokes was a decent player, and this one had already gone beyond ten strokes. The balls were hit deep, and were directed toward the other player rather than to the corners. They must simply be practicing, he thought, rather than playing a serious match. When the ball was finally hit into the net, Bruno called out, "Madame, if you please?"

She turned, shading her eyes to see him against the slanting sun that was sending sparkling golden light into her hair. She walked to the side of the court, bent gracefully at the knees to put down her racket, opened the gate and smiled at him. She was handsome rather than pretty, he thought, with regular features, a strong chin and good cheekbones. Her skin glowed from the tennis, and there was just enough sweat on her brow for some of her hair to stick there in charmingly curling tendrils.

"*Bonjour, Monsieur le Policier*. Is this a business call or can I offer you a drink?"

He walked down to her, shook her surprisingly strong hand and removed his hat. Her eyes were a cool gray.

"I regret, madame, that this is very much business. A serious crime has been committed near here and we're asking all the neighbors if they've seen anything unusual in the course of the day."

The other woman came to join them, said "*Bonjour*" and shook Bruno's hand. Another English accent, another attractive woman, with that clear English skin that Bruno had been told came from having to live in the perpetual damp of their foggy island. No wonder they came to the Périgord.

"A serious crime? Here, in St. Denis? Excuse me, I'm forgetting my manners. I'm Pamela Nelson and this is Mademoiselle Christine Wyatt. Christine, this is our Chef de Police Courrèges."

Bruno nodded a greeting. "It's about the old Arab gentleman, Monsieur Bakr, who lives in that small house up the turnoff from Yannick's place. Have you seen him today, or recently, or seen any visitors?"

"Hamid, you mean? That sweet old man who sometimes comes by to tell me I'm pruning my roses all wrong? No, I haven't seen him for a couple of days, but that's not unusual. He strolls by perhaps once a week and pays me compliments about the property except for the way I prune the roses. I last saw him earlier this week. What's happened? A burglary?"

Bruno deliberately ignored her question. "Were you here all day today? Did you see or hear anything?"

"We were here through lunch and then Christine went into town to do some shopping while I cleaned the barn for some guests who arrive tomorrow. When Christine came back we had tea and then played some tennis for an hour or so until you arrived. We've had no visitors except for the postman, who came at the usual time, about ten or so."

"So *you* haven't left the property all day?" Bruno was pressing because he wondered why they were still just volleying after an hour rather than playing a game.

"No, except for my usual morning ride. But that takes me

toward the river, away from Hamid's cottage. I went as far as the bridge, and then picked up some bread and the newspaper and some vegetables and a roast chicken for lunch. I didn't notice anything out of the ordinary. But do tell me, is Hamid all right? Can I do anything to help?"

"Forgive me, madame, but there is nothing you can do," Bruno said. "And you, Mademoiselle Wyatt? What time did you do your shopping?"

"I can't say exactly. I left after lunch, probably sometime after two, and was back here soon after four." She spoke perfectly grammatical French, but with that rather stiff accent the English had, as if they could not open their mouths properly. "We had tea, and then came out to play tennis."

"And you are one of the paying guests?" She had very fine dark eyes and carefully plucked eyebrows but wore no makeup. Her hands and nails, he noticed, were well cared for. She wore no rings, and the only jewelry was a thin gold chain at her neck.

"Not really, not like the people coming tomorrow," said Christine. "Pamela and I were at school together and we've been friends ever since, so I'm not renting, but I do the shopping and buy the wine. I went to the supermarket and to that big wine cave at the bottom of the road. Then I stopped at the filling station and came back here."

"So you're here on vacation, mademoiselle?"

"Not exactly. I teach history at a university in England but I'm working on a book here. I worked on it all morning until lunchtime. I don't think I've met your Arab gentleman and I don't recall seeing another car, or anybody on the way to the supermarket and back."

"Please tell me what's happened, Monsieur Courrèges," said Pamela. "Is it a burglary? Has Hamid been hurt?"

"I'm sorry but I can't say anything at this stage, I'm sure you understand." He was feeling slightly ridiculous as he usually did when required to play the formal role of policeman. He tried to make up for it. "Please call me Bruno. Everyone does. When I hear someone say Monsieur Courrèges I look around for an old man."

"Okay, Bruno, and you must call me Pamela. Are you sure I can't offer you a drink? Some mineral water, perhaps, or a fruit juice? It's been a warm day."

Bruno accepted, and while Pamela made for the kitchen he gathered three white metal chairs by the swimming pool. Pamela emerged with a refreshing jug of freshly made *citron pressé,* and they all sat down to enjoy it. This was infinitely preferable, Bruno thought to himself, to what would now be a madhouse of squabbling gendarmes and detectives and forensic specialists at Hamid's cottage. That brought the sobering thought that his duty was not over. As a Harki, the old man had probably been a Muslim. Wasn't there something special about Muslim burial rites? He'd have to check.

"I didn't know you had your own tennis court here," he said. "Is that why we never see you at the tennis club?" Bruno was proud of the club, with its three hard courts and its single covered court where they could play in winter, and the roomy clubhouse with its bar and big kitchen. The mayor had used his political connections in Paris to get a government grant to pay for it.

"No, it's the concrete courts," Pamela explained. "I hurt

my knee skiing some time ago and the hard court is bad for it."

"But we have a covered court with a rubber surface. You could play there."

"I get quite busy here in the summer when the guests start to come. Once I have all three of the *gîtes* filled, it takes most of my time. That's why it's such a treat to have Christine here and play some tennis with her. It's not a great court, hardly Wimbledon, but if you ever want to try a grass court just give me a call. My phone number is in the book under Nelson."

"Like your famous Admiral Nelson of Trafalgar?"

"No relation, I'm afraid. It's quite a common name in England."

"Well, Pamela, I shall certainly call you and see about a game on grass. Perhaps you'd like me to bring a friend and we could play mixed doubles." He looked at Christine. "Will you be here for long?"

"Till the middle of June, when Pamela has a full house. So I've got five more weeks here, then I go back to Bordeaux to do some research in the archives."

"It's the best time, before the tourists come for the school holidays and block the roads and markets," said Pamela.

"I thought the national archives were in Paris," Bruno said.

"They are. These are the regional archives and there's a specialist archive at the Centre Jean Moulin."

"Jean Moulin, the Resistance chief? The one who was killed by the Germans?" Bruno asked.

"Yes, it has one of the best archives on the Resistance and my book is about life in France under the Vichy regime."

"Ah, that's why you speak such good French," said Bruno. "But a painful period to study, I think. Painful for France, and very controversial. There are still families here who never speak to each other because they were on opposite sides during the war—and I don't mean just the collaborators. You know Jean-Pierre, who runs the bicycle shop in town? He was in the Communist Resistance, the Francs-Tireurs et Partisans. Just across the road is Bachelot the shoemaker, who was in the Armée Secrète, the Gaullist Resistance. Or maybe it was the other way around. But they were rivals then and they're rivals now. They march in the same parades, side by side, even on the eighteenth of June, yet they never speak. And it's been decades since it happened. Memories are long here."

"What's so special about the eighteenth of June?" Pamela asked. "I don't know why that's escaped me."

"It was the day in 1940 that de Gaulle appealed to France to fight on. He was speaking over the BBC," said Christine. "It's celebrated as the great day of the Resistance, when France recovered her honor and Free France declared that it would fight on."

"'France has lost a battle, but France has not lost the war,'" Bruno quoted from the de Gaulle speech. "We all learn that in school."

"Do they tell you that it's also the anniversary of Napoleon's defeat at the battle of Waterloo?" Christine asked, winking at Pamela.

"Napoleon defeated? I can't believe it," Bruno said, entering the spirit of things. "Nobody who built the magnificent stone bridge in St. Denis could ever be defeated, least of all by the English." He grinned widely. "Did we not drive you out of France in the Hundred Years' War, starting here in the Dordogne under the great leadership of Joan of Arc?"

"But the English are back!" Christine said, grinning at him. "That was a temporary reverse, but it looks as if the English are retaking France, house by house and village by village."

"Well, we're all Europeans now," said Bruno, laughing. "And a lot of us are quite glad the English come here and restore the ruined old farms and houses. The mayor talks about it all the time. He says the whole Department of the Dordogne would be in deep depression had it not been for the English and their tourism and the money they pour in to restore the places they buy. We lost the wine trade in the nineteenth century, and now we're losing the tobacco that replaced it, and our small farmers can't compete with the big places up north. So you're welcome, Pamela, and I congratulate you on this property. You've made it very beautiful."

Bruno rose to go and the three of them started walking toward Bruno's van. As they reached it, Pamela said, "You must come again. I'll expect your call for that mixed-doubles game. And if there's anything I can do for Hamid, perhaps take him something to eat, please let me know."

"I will. And thank you for your thoughtfulness. But I think the authorities have matters in hand." He realized he was sounding formal again.

"If there has been a burglary, should I take extra precautions?" she asked, not looking in the least concerned but obviously probing.

"No, there's no reason to think you're in any danger," Bruno said. But he knew she would soon hear of the murder, so he had better say something reassuring.

"Here's my card with my cell-phone number. Feel free to call me at any time, day or night. And thank you for that refreshing drink. It's been a pleasure, mesdames."

7

Momu lived in a small modern house down by the river. It looked as if it had been built from one of the mass-produced kits that were springing up to provide cheap homes for locals who had been priced out of the market for older houses by the English with their strong currency. Like all the kit homes, it had two bedrooms, a sitting room, a kitchen and a bathroom side by side to share the plumbing, and all built on a concrete slab. The vaguely Mediterranean roof of rounded red tiles and white stucco walls looked quite wrong in the Périgord. But Bruno had spent some convivial evenings in that house, and he braced himself for the place of grief it had now become. He sighed at the tangle of illegally parked cars that almost blocked the road. One of the most obstructive belonged to the mayor, which was very unlike him. Bruno drove on for a hundred meters and then parked.

Inside the house all the lights were blazing and Bruno could hear the sound of a woman crying as he entered. He took off his hat and saw Momu slumped on the sofa, the mayor's hand on his shoulder. Momu was a burly man, not as large as his son but barrel-chested and broad in the shoulders. His hands were big, and his wrists thick like a laborer's. At first, just the look of him was enough to keep order among his pupils, but they soon kept quiet from respect. He was a good teacher, they said. Bruno had heard he made every class work out the combined weight of the local rugby team, and then of all the inhabitants of St. Denis, and then of all the people in France, and then of the whole world. He had a deep, hearty voice, always heard at rugby matches on Sunday afternoons, cheering on his son. Momu rose to greet Bruno and they touched cheeks.

"I'm very sorry for your loss, Momu. The police won't rest until we find who did this, believe me," Bruno said. He shook hands with the mayor and the other men in the room, all Arabs except for Momu's boss, Rollo, the headmaster. Rollo held up a bottle of Cognac and offered Bruno a glass, but he looked around to see what others were drinking and took an apple juice like the Arabs. This was their home, their time of grief, so he would abide by their rules.

"I just came from the cottage," he said. "We're still waiting for the detectives and forensic men from Périgueux. Nothing more will happen until they arrive, and the police doctor releases the body. The gendarmes have sealed the place off, but when the detectives are done, I'll have to ask you to go up there and take a good look around to see if you notice anything missing or stolen. When the police are through, they'll take the body to the funeral home, but I need to know what you want to do then, Momu. I don't know if you have any religious rules or special customs."

"My father gave up religion a long time ago," Momu said solemnly. "We'll bury him here in the town cemetery, in the usual way, as soon as we can. What about Karim? Is he still up there?"

Bruno nodded. "Don't worry. It's routine. The detectives have to talk to the person who found the body but they probably won't keep him long. I just wanted to come and pay my condolences here and find out about the funeral and I'll go right back up there and keep an eye on Karim. He's had a very bad shock."

When he had called back at Hamid's cottage earlier, Duroc had been busy placing angry phone calls to demand why the Police Nationale were taking so long to get there, and still he insisted on keeping Karim at the scene. That was about all Duroc had done. It was left to Bruno to call the public works and arrange for a portable generator and lights to be taken up to the cottage, which had only basic electricity and no outdoor light. He also arranged for the local pizzeria to deliver some food and drink for the gendarmes.

The sound of crying had stopped, and Bruno noticed Momu's wife peering around the door. Bruno had always seen her in Western dress, but today she wore a black scarf on her head which she held across her mouth as though it were a veil. Perhaps it was her mourning dress, he thought.

"What can you tell us?" Momu asked. "All I know for sure is that the old man has been killed, but I still can't believe it."

"That's all we know at this stage, until the forensics team do their work," Bruno said.

"That's not what I heard at the fire station," said Ahmed, one of the drivers for the public-works department, who also volunteered as a fireman. There were two professionals at the small fire station and the rest were local volunteers, summoned as needed by the howl of the old wartime siren they kept on top of the Mairie. And since the firemen were also the emergency medical team and the first people called out to any sudden death or crisis, it was impossible to keep anything quiet. The volunteers talked to their wives and the wives talked to each other and the whole town knew of fires or deaths or road accidents within hours.

"It was a brutal killing, a stabbing. That's all we really know so far," said Bruno cautiously. He had a good idea of what Ahmed must have heard from the other firemen, but he wanted to find out precisely.

"It was racists, fascists," Ahmed said angrily. "I heard what was carved on old Hamid's chest. It was those Front National swine, taking on a helpless old man."

Putain. This bit of news had become public even faster than Bruno had feared, and it would spread more poison as it traveled.

"I don't know what you heard, Ahmed, but I know what I saw, and I couldn't tell if it was meant to be some kind of pattern or if they were wounds he received when he put up a fight," he said levelly, looking Ahmed in the eye. "Rumor has a way of exaggerating things. Let's stick with the facts for the moment."

"Bruno is right," said the mayor quietly. A small, slim man whose mild-mannered looks were deceptive, he had a way of making himself heard. Gérard Mangin had been mayor of St. Denis long before Bruno had taken up his job a decade earlier. Mangin had been born in the town, into a family that had been there as long as anyone could remember. He had won scholarships and competitive examinations and gone off to one of the *grandes écoles* in Paris where France educates its élite. He worked in the Finance Ministry while allying himself with a rising young star of the Gaullist party named Jacques Chirac and launching his own political career. He had been one of Chirac's political secretaries, and was then sent to Brussels as Chirac's eyes and ears in the European Commission, where he had learned the complex art of securing grants. Elected mayor of St. Denis in the 1970s, Mangin had run the party for Chirac in the Dordogne, and was rewarded with an appointment to the Senate to serve out the term of a man who had died in office. Thanks to his connections in Paris and Brussels, St. Denis had thrived. The restored Mairie and the tennis club, the retirement home and the small industrial zone, the swimming pool and the agricultural research center had all been built with grants the mayor had secured. His mastery of the planning and zoning codes had eased the construction of the commercial center with its new supermarket. Without the mayor and his political connections, St. Denis might well have died, like so many other small market towns of the Périgord.

"My friends, our Momu has suffered a great loss and we grieve with him. But we must not let that loss turn into anger before we know the facts," the mayor said in his precise way. He gripped Momu's hand and pulled him to his side before looking round at Ahmed and Momu's other friends. "We who are gathered here to share our friend's grief are all leaders of our community. And we all know that we have a responsibility here to ensure that the law takes its course, that we all give whatever help we can to the magistrates and the police, and that we stand guard together over the solidarity of our town. I know I can count on you all in the days ahead. We have to face this together."

He went first to Ahmed, and then shook hands with each of the others and gestured to Bruno to leave with him. Then, gently gripping Bruno's arm, he propelled him into the night, along the driveway and out of earshot of the house.

"What is this about a swastika?" he asked.

"It isn't clear, but that's what the gendarmes and the firemen thought was carved into Hamid's chest. They're probably right, but I told the truth in there. I can't be sure, not until the corpse is cleaned up. He was stabbed in the belly and then eviscerated. There could have been the *Mona Lisa* painted on that chest and I couldn't swear to it." The mayor's grip tightened on his arm.

"It was a butchery," Bruno went on after a moment. "The old man's hands were tied behind his back. It looked like he was interrupted while having his lunch. Two things were missing, according to Karim. There was a Croix de Guerre he won while fighting for France as a Harki, and a photo of his old soccer team. The neighbors don't seem to have seen or heard anything unusual. That's all I know."

"I don't think I ever met the old man, which probably makes him unique in this town," said the mayor. "Did you know him?"

"Not really. I met him at Karim's wedding last year just before he moved here. I never spoke with him beyond pleasantries and never got much sense of the man. He kept to himself, always seemed to eat on his own or with his family. I don't recall ever seeing him in the market or the bank or doing his shopping. He was a bit of a recluse way out there in the forest. No TV and no car. He depended on Momu and Karim for everything."

"That seems strange," the mayor mused. "These Arab families tend to stay together—the old ones move in with their grown children. But a Harki and a war hero? Maybe he was worried about reprisals from some young immigrant hotheads. You know, these days they think of the Harkis as traitors to the Islamist cause."

"Maybe that's it. And because he wasn't religious perhaps some of these extremists could see him as a traitor to his faith," Bruno said. Yet why would Muslim extremists want to carve a swastika into someone's chest? "But we're just guessing, sir. I'll have to talk to Momu about it later. It must have been a chore for him and Karim, driving over every day to pick up the old man for his dinner and then taking him home again. Maybe there's more to Hamid than meets the eye, and perhaps you could ask Momu if he remembers any details about that old soccer team his father played on. Since the photograph has disappeared, it might be significant. I think they played in Marseilles back in the thirties or forties."

The mayor nodded. "I know you understand how delicate this could be," he said. "We'll probably have a lot of media attention, maybe some politicians posturing and making speeches and organizing marches of solidarity and all that. Leave that side of it to me. I want you to stay on top of the investigation and keep me informed, and also let me know in good time if you hear of any trouble brewing or any likely arrests. Now, two final questions: First, do you know of any extreme Right or racist types in our commune who might conceivably have been guilty of this?"

"No, sir, not one. Some Front National voters, of course, but that's all, and I don't think any of our usual petty criminals could have carried out an act of butchery like this."

"Right. Second question: What can I do to help you?"

"Two things." Bruno sounded as efficient as his mayor, aware of a sense of both duty and real affection as he did so. "First, the Police Nationale will need somewhere to work, with phone lines and desks and chairs and plenty of space for computers. You might want to think about the top floor of the tourist center where we hold the art exhibitions. There's no exhibition there yet, and it's big enough. If you call the prefect in Périgueux tomorrow you can probably persuade him to pay some rent for the use of the space, and there's room for police vans, too. It might be useful for people to see a reinforced police presence in the town. And if we do that, they're on our turf, which means they cannot bar us access."

"And the second thing?"

"Most of all, I'll need your support to stay close to the case. It would help a great deal if you could call the brigadier of the gendarmes in Périgueux and also the head of the Police Nationale, and ask them to order their men to keep me fully in the picture. There's good reason for it, with the political sensitivities and the prospect of demonstrations and tension in the town. You know our tiny Police Municipale does not rate very high in the hierarchy of our forces of order. Would you be comfortable calling me your personal liaison?"

"Right. You'll have it. Anything else?"

"You could probably get hold of the old man's military and

civil records and the citation for his Croix de Guerre faster than I'll get them through the gendarmes. We know very little about the victim at this stage, not even whether he owned his house or rented it, what he lived on, how he got his pension or whether he had a doctor. His family will help, but I think we should investigate independently, too."

"You can check the civic records tomorrow," said the mayor. "I'll call the defense minister's office—I knew her a bit when I was in Paris, and there's someone in her cabinet I went to school with. I'll have Hamid's file by the end of the day. Now, you go back up to the cottage and stay there until you can get Karim back to his family. Any trouble, just call me on my cell phone, even if it means waking me up."

Bruno went off comforted, feeling as he had in the Army when he had a good officer who knew what he was doing and trusted his men enough to bring out the best in them. It was a rare combination. Bruno acknowledged to himself, although he would be reluctant to admit it to another soul, that Gérard Mangin had been one of the most important influences in his life. He had sought Bruno out on the recommendation of his son, who happened to be an old comrade in arms of Bruno's from that hideous business in Bosnia. Ever since, Bruno had felt like a member of a family, for the first time in his life, and for that alone the mayor had his complete loyalty. He got into his van and drove back up the long hill toward Hamid's cottage, wondering what arts of persuasion he might muster to extricate poor Karim out of the custody of the tiresome Captain Duroc.

8

The regional headquarters of the Police Nationale had sent down their new chief detective, Jean-Jacques Jalipeau, inevitably known as J-J. Bruno had worked amicably with him once before, on the one bank robbery in St. Denis in recent memory. J-J had cleared that up and even got some of the bank's money back. That had been two promotions ago. Now he had his own team, including the first young female inspector that Bruno had met. She wore a dark blue suit and a silk scarf at her neck, and had the shortest hair he had ever seen on a woman. She sat in front of a freshly installed computer in the exhibition room, while around them other policemen were plugging in phones, claiming desks, booting up other computers and photocopiers and setting up the murder board on the wall. Instead of the usual gentle Périgord landscapes and watercolors by local artists, the room was now dominated by the long whiteboard with its grisly photos of the murder scene, including close-ups of Hamid's bound hands and cleaned-up chest where the swastika could clearly be seen.

"Okay, here we go. Our rogues' gallery of the extreme Right. I hope your eyes are in good shape because we have got hundreds of photos for you to view," said Inspector Perrault, who had told Bruno with a briskly efficient smile to call her Isabelle. "We'll start with the leaders and the known activists and then we'll go to the photos of their demonstrations. Just shout if you recognize anyone."

Bruno knew the first three faces from TV, party leaders in publicity shots. Then he saw one of them again at a public rally, standing on a podium to address the crowd. Then came random photos of crowds: ordinary French men and women being addressed by party officials, each photo identified by the name and position of the official, including various regional chairmen, secretaries and treasurers, executive committee members, known activists and local councillors. Bruno pursed his lips at the thoroughness of the research that had gone into this.

"Just that one," he said, pointing to a tough-looking man. "I know him through rugby. He plays for Montpon, and we've seen him here once or twice."

She made a note and they continued. Isabelle's short hair smelled pleasantly of shampoo. She looked fit, as though she ran or worked out every day. Her legs were long and slim and her shoes looked too flimsy for a police officer and far too expensive, even on an inspector's salary.

"Who collected all these pictures?" he asked, looking at her hands, nails cut short but her fingers long and elegant as they danced over the computer keys.

"We got them from different places," she said. She had no regional accent he could discern, but was well spoken, sounding cool but affable, a bit like a TV reporter. "Some from their Web sites, election leaflets, press photos and TV footage. Then there are some from the Renseignements Généraux that we're not supposed to know about, but you know how computer security is these days. We take photos of Right-wing marches and rallies, just so we know who they are. We do the same for the far Left. It seems only fair." The Renseignements Généraux is the intelligence arm of the French police.

She was screening images of what looked like a pre-election rally in the main square of Périgueux, shot after shot of the crowd, taken from a balcony. There were dozens of faces in each shot and Bruno tried to scan them conscientiously. He stopped at one face, but it was only a reporter he knew from *Sud Ouest,* standing to the side of the rally squinting against the smoke from his cigarette, and holding a notebook and pencil. Bruno rubbed his eyes and signaled Isabelle to continue.

"You sure you don't want to take a break, Bruno?" she asked. "It can drive you crazy, staring at these screens all the time, especially if you're not used to it."

"I'm not," he said. "We don't have much use for computers down here. I mainly use them for typing and e-mails." Nor did he much like to, he added to himself. They tended to get in the way of the kind of police work he understood, which was mainly about getting to know people. And his time in the military had left him with a healthy skepticism of the kind of official records that computer systems usually offered.

She stopped, told him to look out the window to rest his

eyes and came back with some sludgy coffee from a hot plate that had been rigged up in the corner.

"Here," she said, handing him a plastic cup and juggling her own as she fished one-handed for a cigarette and lit a Royale.

"This coffee's terrible," said Bruno. "But thanks for the thought. If we can spare five minutes there's a café on the next corner."

"You must have forgotten what a slave driver J-J can be," she said, and smiled. "When I first started working for him I didn't even dare go to the toilet. I'd go in the morning and then just wait. I'll probably pay for it when I'm older."

"Well, this is St. Denis. Everything stops for lunch. It's the law," Bruno said, wondering if she would take this as an invitation. He wasn't sure that he had enough cash in his wallet to pay for them both.

"I think we're too pressed for time," she said kindly, and turned back to the screen.

There were more photos of the same event in the same square, taken from another vantage point. Bruno looked at each face one by one until suddenly he recognized a central-heating salesman from St. Cyprien to whom he had once given a ticket for obstructing traffic. Again, Isabelle made a note then went on scrolling. There were more photos of the same rally, yet another vantage point, but no familiar face except those that he'd seen in the previous photos.

"Okay, that's it for the Périgueux rally. On to the one in Sarlat," said Isabelle, clicking her way expertly through the computer screens. In Sarlat the rally was smaller. He spotted a couple of people he knew from rugby, and one from a tennis tournament, but nobody from St. Denis. Then Isabelle brought up the photos from a campaign meeting in Bergerac, and at the third shot he gave a small gasp.

"Seen someone? I can blow the faces up a bit if you want."

"I'm not sure. It's that group of young people there."

She enlarged the image but the angles were wrong, so she scanned through the rest of the photos, looking for shots from a different viewpoint. And there, close to the stage, were two youngsters he knew well. The first was a pretty blond girl from Lalinde, about twenty kilometers away, who had reached the semifinals of the St. Denis tennis tournament the previous summer. And the boy with her, looking at her rather than at the stage, was Richard Gelletreau, the only son of a doctor in St. Denis.

"We may get lucky here," Isabelle said, after she had printed out the photos and scribbled down Richard's name. "The party branch in Bergerac is two doors down from a bank, and it has a security camera. Don't ask me how, but somehow the RG got hold of the tape and made some mug shots of everyone coming in and going out during the campaign."

"I would say that's borderline legal," said Bruno.

She shrugged. "Who knows? It's not the kind of stuff that can be used in court, but for an investigation . . . well, it's just the way it is. If you think this is something, wait till you see the stuff the RG has on the communists and the Left, archives going back to before the war."

The Renseignements Généraux was part of the Ministry of the Interior, and had been collecting information on threats to the French state, to its good order and prosperity, since

1907. It had a formidable, if shadowy, reputation, and Bruno had never come across its work before. He was impressed, even though the shots of the people entering and leaving the Front National office were not very good. It was too far for a clear focus, but he could pick out young Richard easily enough, holding hands with the girl as they went in and putting his arm around her waist when they left.

They went through the rest of Isabelle's mug shots, but Gelletreau provided the only clear connection to St. Denis.

"What can you tell me about the boy?" Isabelle said, swiveling her chair and picking up a notepad from the desk.

"He's the son of the chief doctor at the clinic here, and they live in one of the big houses on the hill. The father is a pillar of the community, been here all his life, and the mother used to be a pharmacist; I think she still owns half of the big pharmacy by the supermarket. The girl is from Lalinde. She played tennis here last year and I can get her name from the club easily enough. The boy went to the usual schools here and is just finishing his first year at the lycée in Périgueux. He stays there during the week and comes home on weekends. He'd be about seventeen by now, a normal kid, good at tennis, not much involved in rugby. His parents are well-heeled, so they'd go skiing. And of course he was in Momu's mathematics class—that's the teacher who is the son of the dead man."

"Local knowledge is a wonderful thing. I don't know what we'd do without it." Isabelle smiled at him. "Thanks, Bruno. Just stay here and I'll go and tell J-J. It may be nothing, just coincidence, but so far it's the only lead we have."

The forensics team was still working, and the fingerprints report had yet to come in, but the preliminary report that lay on Isabelle's desk was clear enough. Hamid had been hit hard in the face, probably to stun him, and then tied up for some time. The burns on his wrists where he had tried to work himself loose of his bonds, the rough red twine that farmers use, were a clear indication that he had been alive for more than a few minutes. He had been stabbed deep into the lower belly by a long, sharp knife, which was then pulled up and across "like a Japanese ritual suicide," said the report. There was no sign of a gag, the report went on. Traces of red wine were found in his eyes and his thinning hair, as though someone had thrown a glass of it in his face. The time of death was put between noon and two p.m., most probably around one o'clock. Indications were that the swastika had been scored into his chest postmortem. Bruno took some small relief from that.

There was no sign of a theft, except for the missing photo and medal from the wall. Hamid's wallet was found in the back pocket of his trousers. It contained 40 euros, an ID card, a newspaper photo of himself standing in a parade by the Arc de Triomphe in Paris, another of Karim scoring a try in a rugby match, and some old bills and postage stamps. There was a checkbook from Crédit Agricole in a drawer with some pension slips, and some previously unopened mail from the bank, mainly showing deposits from a military pension. The old man had over 20,000 euros in the bank. Bruno raised an eyebrow at that. He knew from the Mairie's records that Momu and his father had bought the small house a year ago for 78,000 euros in cash (not a bad deal given the predatory way the local agencies were pricing up every tumbledown ruin to sell to the English and the Dutch).

The old man had had no luxuries in the cottage, not even a refrigerator. He kept his supplies in a small cupboard—wine, pâté, cheese, fruit and several bags of nuts. There were two liter bottles of cheap *vin ordinaire,* and one very good bottle of a Château Cantemerle '98. At least sometimes the old man had cared about what he drank. There was cheap ground coffee in an unsealed bag on the shelf above the small stove, which was fueled, like the hot water, by gas canisters. This was routine in rural homes; Bruno cooked and heated his own water in the same way. He continued to run his eye down the list: Hamid had no gun and no hunting license, but he did have an up-to-date fishing license and an expensive fishing rod. He had no TV, just a cheap battery radio tuned to France Inter. There were no newspapers or magazines, but a shelf of books on war and history whose titles were listed in the report. There were books on de Gaulle, the Algerian war, the French war in Vietnam, World War II and the Resistance, and two books on the OAS, the underground army of the French Algerians who had tried to assassinate de Gaulle for giving the colony its independence. That might be significant, Bruno thought, although he could see no connection to a swastika. Apart from the books of an old soldier revisiting his campaigns, all the evidence suggested a rather lonely and even primitive life.

At the back of the file, Bruno found a new printout showing details about Hamid's military pension. Until almost two years ago, he had been living in the north, spending over twenty years at the same address in Soissons until his wife,

Allida, died. Then he moved to the Dordogne. Bruno did the calculation. The old man had settled in St. Denis the month after Karim's marriage, probably to be with the only family he had left. His profession was listed as *gardien,* or caretaker. Bruno scanned the pension printout. He had worked at the military academy, where he'd had a small flat. Yes, Bruno thought, they would do that for an old comrade with a Croix de Guerre. And with a caretaker's flat, he'd have paid no rent, which would account for the savings. There was no sign on the pension form of any medical problem.

That reminded him: He rang Mireille at the Mairie to see if the Ministry of Defense information had arrived yet. It hadn't, but she told him that Hamid was not named on any local doctor's list of patients, or at the clinic, or with any of the pharmacies in town, and no medical claims were registered in the social security records. Evidently Hamid was a healthy person, an athlete in his youth. Why had that photo disappeared along with the medal?

"*Salut,* Bruno. Robbed any banks lately?" shouted J-J, striding into the room with Isabelle at his heels. Then he grinned. "I always thought you must have been the brains behind that job. It was too smart for those idiots we put away."

"It's good to see you, J-J." Bruno smiled with genuine pleasure as they shook hands. The last time he had seen J-J they had been taken to a magnificent celebration dinner at Le Centenaire in Les Eyzies at the end of the robbery case by the bank's regional manager. Two Michelin stars, a couple of bottles a head of some of the best wine Bruno had ever tasted, and a chauffeur to take him home afterward. He'd had to take off from work the next day. "I see you're a big shot now, top cop in the *département*," he added.

"And there's not a day goes by that I don't sit back and feel a twinge of envy for the life you have here, Bruno." J-J gave him an affectionate slap on the back. "That's what intrigues me about this vicious little murder. It's so out of character for this place. Isabelle tells me you think we might have a lead in this doctor's son."

"I'm not sure I'd call it much of a lead, but he's the only local from St. Denis that I saw in the photos. This is a weekday. He should be at school in Périgueux."

Isabelle shook her head. "I just checked. He didn't turn up on Monday. He called in sick, and they got a note signed by his dad the doctor."

"Gelletreau writing a sick note for his son? I think we'd better verify that," said Bruno, impressed at her speed of action but wary that she'd gone elsewhere to make the calls rather than do so in his presence. Maybe Isabelle was not quite a team player. "He doesn't like writing sick notes at all, old Gelletreau. He accuses half his patients of malingering. He told me I just had a cold once, and it turned out to be pneumonia. And doctors are notoriously tough on their own families." He reached for the phone.

"You see why I like this guy?" J-J said to Isabelle. "Local knowledge. Invaluable."

"Madame Gelletreau?" Bruno said into his phone. If Isabelle could move fast, so could he. "Could I speak to Richard, please? It's Bruno about the tennis, or is he too sick? He's at school in Périgueux, you say. Oh, my mistake, I'd heard he was at home sick. Very well, it's not urgent." He rang off.

"This looks a little more interesting," said J-J. "A false note to school, and he's at neither place."

Bruno drove down to the tennis club with Isabelle and checked the records. The semifinalist from Lalinde was named Jacqueline Courtemine. Bruno called Quatremer, his counterpart in Lalinde, a young ex-serviceman whom he knew only slightly. He asked for an address and some information about the family. Bruno explained that they were looking for a young man who might be in her company, and that Quatremer might want to keep an eye on the house until the Police Nationale turned up.

Then he called Quatremer's predecessor, an old hunting friend named René who had retired the previous year. He put the same question and elicited a volley of information. Jacqueline's parents were separated, perhaps divorced. The mother was living in Paris on money from the wealthy father, who had inherited a family furniture store and expanded it into a profitable chain that now stretched across the region. Between his business and his mistresses he was rarely at home, and Jacqueline had the large house on the outskirts of town pretty much to herself, as well as her own car. René thought she would be going to university in the fall. He also said she had a reputation as a wild one. Bruno scribbled quick notes on how to find the house, and then suggested to René that Quatremer might need some support and advice. "And warn your mayor," Bruno added, before hanging up.

Isabelle was already downstairs, waiting in her car. She

drove down to the main road leading to Bergerac and pulled in to wait for J-J. She fished in the backseat for the magnetic blue light, and as she clamped it onto her roof J-J's big black Citroën drew up, flashing its lights, with another police car close behind. The small convoy now raced toward Lalinde.

9

The police convoy drew up to a large detached house that stood on the low hill that rose above Lalinde with a sweeping view of the Dordogne River. The river was wide and shallow here on its descent from the high plateau and into the flat farmlands that had for a century produced tobacco for the dark Gauloises cigarettes. The house was designed in the traditional Périgord style, with a steep tile roof, tall chimneys, and turrets like witches' hats, and it gleamed with a brightness of stone that showed it had been newly built. Four cars, a motorbike with a German Army–style helmet hanging from the handlebars and two small Mobilette scooters were parked untidily in the broad gravel forecourt. Behind the house was a large garden, and then the land rose gently again to the hill that stretched all the way to Bergerac. Noisy rock music came from the open windows, and an empty bottle of wine lay on its side in the hallway.

"Very welcoming," said J-J as they approached the house and caught the distinctive whiff of marijuana. "A wide-open door and grass. We can hold her on a possession charge if we have to." He directed the second carload of detectives to go around to the back, knocked quietly on the open wooden door, waited for a moment and then strode in.

Several teenagers wearing vacant expressions were sprawled around a table in the big dining room, which opened onto a patio and swimming pool at the rear. A large bar ran along the side of the room. Cans of beer and bottles of wine stood on the table, along with dirty plates, a cheese board and a bowl of fruit. Through the window, Bruno could see three young men with shaven heads and tattoos playing in the pool with two bare-breasted girls. J-J went over to the impressive stereo and pulled the electric wire from its socket in the wall. The music came to a blessed halt. Bruno could see no sign of Richard Gelletreau at the table or in the pool.

"Mademoiselle Courtemine?" J-J asked. There was no response. "Is Mademoiselle Courtemine or the owner of this property present? This is a police inquiry."

One of the girls at the table put her hand to her mouth and glanced at the wide staircase. J-J gestured with his head and Isabelle went quickly up the stairs.

"Seize that," J-J told another detective, gesturing to the bag of grass and rolling papers on the table. "Then get all their names and IDs. Bring the local gendarme in from the front gate. He should know most of them. What's his name again, Bruno?"

"Quatremer."

"Good, now we'll try again," said J-J, facing the young people around the table. "I'm looking for Richard Gelle-treau."

No response. The girls in the pool had their hands over their breasts. The guys were looking around, probably considering running for it, Bruno thought, but at that moment more police came from the side of the house to block any possible exit. Bruno tried to focus on the faces. The youths in the pool looked vaguely familiar, perhaps from the surveillance photos he had seen. His eyes kept drifting back to the half-naked girls. His own teenage years had never been like this.

"J-J," called Isabelle from upstairs. "Here." J-J motioned Bruno to come with him. They walked side by side up the wide and handsome staircase. The landing above was the size of an average living room. Straight ahead was a corridor with a series of closed doors to rooms that would have faced the town. As Isabelle called again they followed the sound of her voice to a second wing that must have stretched toward the garden. They walked into a large room that probably would have been bright and airy had the curtains been open, but was now dark except for some low lighting and the flickering of a TV. On the tangled bed were two young people, hauling themselves from sleep. The girl was trying to pull the sheet up to cover them. The boy could not move; his wrists were tied to the bedposts with silk scarves.

Bruno raised his eyes from the couple on the bed to two posters on the wall. One was of Jean-Marie Le Pen, the leader of the Front National; the other was what looked like an original cinema placard for the film *The Battle of Algiers*. The boy on the bed turned his head away from the sudden light and groaned. It was Richard. He looked around, recognized Bruno and groaned again.

"Who the fuck are you?" the girl screamed. "Get out."

"Check out the TV, J-J," said Isabelle. "Nazi porn."

On the screen, two men in black uniforms with swastika armbands and SS lapel pins were being serviced by two young women, one white and blond and evidently willing, one black and in manacles.

J-J moved quickly as the girl covered herself with the sheet and squirmed to the side of the bed. He caught her wrist in his strong hand and yanked it behind her back as she yelped. He held her firmly while he looked at the bedside table for which she had been reaching. A razor blade lay next to a small mirror on which sat some grains of white powder.

"You've been a naughty girl," J-J said, still holding her firmly. "Coke. That's three years, right there." He took a pen from his pocket and poked the lid of a small box beside the mirror. He shook his head at the pile of small white pills inside and then looked at the girl, who was now silent. She had stopped squirming and the bedsheets had fallen away to reveal that she was wearing black stockings, supported by a black garter belt.

"All this and Ecstasy, too," said J-J quietly. It appeared to Bruno that J-J looked genuinely shocked. "I think we have enough here for trafficking charges. That could be ten years in prison, mademoiselle. I hope you enjoy the company of tough old lesbians. You are going to be spending a lot of time with them."

He turned to Isabelle. "Put the cuffs on her, and then let's take some photos of this scene. I want another forensics team to go through this room and check out every knife in the house. The Périgueux boys are still in St. Denis so you may have to call more in from Bergerac, and then let's get the narcotics people here. We could do with some extra manpower for the search. It's a big property."

He looked at Bruno. "Bruno, can you help us track down this girl's parents? They'll have to be informed, and you'd better do the same with the boy's father. Then tell my men to organize a search of the premises as soon as they have all the young thugs downstairs arrested, charged with possession of illegal drugs and in police cells where we can question them. I take it this is indeed the young Richard?" Bruno nodded. "Isabelle, I want a lot of shots of the pair of them and make sure you get the focus just right. Then you can start checking out all the other videos and films in Mademoiselle Courtemine's collection."

"Including her own," Isabelle said drily, pointing at the back wall. Neither Bruno nor J-J had yet noticed the small video camera on its tripod, pointing at the bed, a red light on its side still blinking.

As evening began to fall, more carloads of police arrived, along with two vans to take away a total of eight young people. Jacqueline waited in handcuffs; Richard was finally untied once the police photographers had finished with the bedroom and the forensics team had taken their samples. He and Jacqueline were then each given a set of the plastic white overalls the forensics team used, handcuffed again and taken to police headquarters in Périgueux. Bruno had tracked down the families. Jacqueline's father was on a business trip to Finland and would fly home the next day. Her mother was driving down from Paris. Richard's father would meet them in Périgueux. Lawyers had been arranged, but the search had already found four shoe boxes of Ecstasy pills in one of the outbuildings.

"Street value of twenty thousand euros, they tell me," said J-J, lighting an American cigarette. He and Bruno were standing on the wide terrace in front of the house. "They just found another shoe box in her car, hidden under the spare tire. Lots of fingerprints. And those tattoo-covered boys in the pool turn out to be members of the Front's Service d'Ordre, its own private security guard. They had photos of themselves with Le Pen at some party rally. There were drugs in their cars and very large amounts of cash in their wallets."

"Have you told Paris yet?" asked Bruno. "Most of the politicians will love it. Front National types involved in a drug-running gang, perverting our French youth."

"Sure, sure," said J-J, "but it's the murderer I'm after. I don't much care about the politics, except that I hate that Nazi crap. My God, after what this country went through in the war, to see these young kids getting caught up in Third Reich nonsense. . . . Do you have kids?"

"No kids, J-J, and no wife as yet," said Bruno, a note of sadness in his own voice. Where had that come from? He changed the subject. "And straight sex was always good enough for me."

"Well, I certainly can't say that porno film would turn me on," said J-J. "Mind you, at my age there's not much that does light my fire."

"Yet in the old days, there wasn't much that didn't get you going. Your reputation still precedes you, J-J. I'm surprised that Isabelle isn't wearing armor."

"Not necessary with these new regulations, Bruno. They can fire you these days if you so much as look at a female colleague. You're lucky to be out of it, down here in your little commune."

"We have that as well. We aren't insulated from what goes on everywhere else. Hamid's death made that clear," said Bruno. "Maybe I was fooling myself when I thought we were different down here, with our little weekly markets and all the kids playing sports and staying out of trouble. A good place to raise a family, you'd think, and now this. You know, J-J, this is my first murder."

"So when are you going to start your own family, Bruno? Or do you have your own little harem among the farmers' wives?"

Bruno grinned. "I wish. Have you seen the farmers' fists?"

"No, and I haven't seen the farmers' wives either," J-J said with a grin. "But seriously, aren't you planning to settle down? You'd make a good father."

"I haven't found the right woman," said Bruno, shrugging. He could have made a joke of it, as he usually did to keep his privacy, but suddenly the memory of the woman he had loved and lost in Bosnia, rescued and then failed to save, was very much with him. Perhaps it was the violence he had seen now in St. Denis as he had seen it in Bosnia. It was nobody's business but his own. "I suppose I came close to it a couple of times."

"I remember that pretty brunette who worked for the railway—Josette. You were seeing her when we worked together."

"They moved her up north to Calais to work on the Eurotunnel service because she spoke good English. I miss her," said Bruno. "We got together once in Paris for a weekend, but somehow it wasn't the same."

J-J grunted, a sound that seemed to acknowledge many things, from the power of women to the corrosive effects of time and the inability of men to ever quite explain or comprehend them. As darkness spread over the river below them, they stood in silence for a moment.

"I guess I'm lucky, really, having something close to an ordinary family life," said J-J. "Most cops' marriages don't work out, what with the strange hours and the things you can't talk about, and it's not easy making friends outside the police. Civilians get nervous around us. But you know that. Or maybe it's different for you down here."

"Yes and no," said Bruno.

"The only thing she gives me grief about now is grandchildren," J-J went on, as if he hadn't heard Bruno. "She goes on and on about why our kids aren't married and breeding." He sighed. "I suppose your folks are getting at you about the same thing."

"Not really," Bruno said shortly. "I thought you knew I was an orphan."

J-J turned away from the view to scrutinize him. "I remember somebody telling me that, but it slipped my mind."

"I never knew them," Bruno said, looking into the distance. "I know nothing at all of my father, and my mother left me in a church when I was a baby. It was the priest who christened me Benoît, the blessed one. You can understand why I call myself Bruno instead."

J-J smiled weakly.

"I was in a church orphanage until I was five," said Bruno, "and then my mother committed suicide. But first she wrote a note to her cousin in Bergerac naming the church where she'd left me. Those cousins raised me, which wasn't easy since they never had much money. That's why I went off to the Army as soon as I left school. I don't have great memories of childhood. Besides which, they have five kids of their own, so there's no pressure on me."

"Do you still see them?"

"Weddings and funerals, mostly. I'm close to one of the kids because he plays rugby. I've taken him out hunting a few times, and I tried to talk him out of going into the Army. He sort of listened; joined the Air Force instead."

"I thought you enjoyed your time in the service. I remember you telling some stories, that night we went out to dinner."

"Bits of it were fine. Most of it, really. I try to forget the bad times."

"You mean Bosnia?"

Yes, he meant Bosnia. He'd been there with the U.N. peacekeepers, but he quickly found there wasn't much peace to be kept. They'd had over a hundred dead, a thousand wounded, but nobody even noticed at the time. They were being hit by snipers and mortars from all sides, Serbs, Muslims and Croats. He'd lost friends, but the U.N. ordered the peacekeeping troops not to fight back. They could hardly even defend themselves. After that, he'd chosen to live here, in the quiet heart of rural France. At least it used to be quiet before a man was found dead with a swastika carved in his chest. Bruno told J-J some of this, but not all.

"Well, you turned out okay," J-J said. "And I'm a prying old fool. I suppose it goes with the job. Still, I meant it about my wife, she's a good woman. I'm lucky." J-J paused. "You know she's got me playing golf?"

Bruno chuckled, grateful for the change of subject, and of mood.

"She started playing with a couple of her girlfriends, then she insisted I take some lessons, said we had to have some common interests for when I retire," J-J said. "I enjoy it; a nice stroll in the open air, a couple of drinks after, some decent people in the clubhouse. We're planning on going down to Spain this summer on one of those special golfing vacations, play every day, get some lessons. Look, forget all this, I need a drink. Stay here. I'll be right back."

Bruno turned and looked back at the house. All the lights were on and white-garbed figures crossed back and forth behind the windows. The last time he had seen this many police was at the big parade when he completed his training course.

"Well, it looks like we have our chief suspect for the poor old Arab," J-J said as his silhouette loomed out of the light in the house, offering him a glass. A Ricard, mixed just right, not too much ice. The furniture tycoon would hardly miss a couple of drinks.

"It's circumstantial, unless forensics comes up with some traces or we find the weapon," Bruno said. "You know you're going to lose control of this case once Paris gets involved, J-J. There's too much politics."

"That's why I want to wrap it up fast," said J-J. "They're sending down a special magistrate from Paris, along with something they call a media coordinator to handle the press. They'll be spinning everything for the evening news and the minister's presidential ambitions. I'd be surprised if he doesn't come down here himself, maybe even for the funeral."

"The mayor is already worried enough about the impact on tourism this summer without having ministers making headlines. I can just see it now." Bruno shook his head. "St. Denis: The little town of hate."

"In your shoes, I'd try to keep out of the way of those *mouettes* from Paris, those damn seagulls who fly in with a lot of noise, crap on us all from a great height and then fly off again. Let the big boys do their thing and then try and sweep up the mess when they go. That's the way it works."

"Not with my mayor, it doesn't," said Bruno. "Don't forget he used to be on Chirac's staff in Paris. He can play politics with the best of them. He's been good to me, helped me, taught me a lot. I don't want to let him down."

"You mean, like the father you never had?"

The remark stung. Bruno stared intently at J-J then told himself to relax. "You must have been reading some paperback on psychology," he said, more curtly than he had intended.

"*Merde,* Bruno, I didn't mean anything by it." J-J leaned forward and punched his arm gently. "I was just talking, you know."

"Forget it, maybe you're right," Bruno said. "He *has* been like a father to me. But it's not just the mayor. It's the town itself and the damage all this mess could do. It's my home and it's my job to defend it."

10

It was raining, a thin persistent drizzle that would last for a couple of hours. The four men hurried across the wet grass to the covered court of which Bruno was so proud. It looked like a disused hangar on an old airfield, with a corrugated roof in translucent plastic and tarpaulins for walls. But the court was sound inside, and boasted an umpire's chair, a scoreboard and benches for spectators. An array of small placards, advertising local businesses and the *Sud Ouest,* hung on the metal frame.

Bruno partnered with the Baron. Xavier, the deputy mayor, and Michel, who ran the public-works department, took the other side, as they usually did, and they began to hit the ball back and forth across the net, not too hard and none too skillfully, for the pleasure of the game and of the weekly ritual. When Bruno took the ball to serve, the Baron stayed alongside him at the back of the court. He preferred playing the backcourt, letting "young Bruno" take the volleys at the net. As always, each man was allowed to have his first serve of the day as many times as he required to get the ball in. And, as usual, Bruno's hard first serve went long but his second was decently placed. After a double fault, a missed volley and one accidentally excellent serve that made Bruno think he might one day be able to play this game, they changed ends.

"Have you caught the bastard yet?" Michel asked as they passed each other at the net. He was a powerful man physically, though not tall, compact with a small but firm paunch. He was even more powerful in the life of the town, and his signature was needed on any planning permission. Sixteen men served under him and he supervised a motor pool of trucks, ditch-diggers and a small bulldozer. He came from Toulon, where he had served twenty years in the Navy engineers.

Bruno shrugged. "It's out of my hands. The Police Nationale are running the show, and Paris has got involved. I don't know much more than you do, and if I did, you know I couldn't talk about it."

But of course he knew his companions wouldn't let him get away with that. These four were the town's shadow government. The Baron owned the land, and was rich enough to make the donations that helped the tennis and rugby clubs to keep functioning as they did. Michel was a man of real influence and Xavier did most of the administrative work and ran the day-to-day business of the Mairie. He had worked in the sub-prefecture in Sarlat until he came home to St. Denis, where his father ran the Renault dealership and his father-in-law owned the big local sawmill. Along with Bruno and the mayor, these men ran the business of the town. They had learned to be discreet and they expected Bruno to keep them informed, above all at these ritual Friday matches.

Michel had a classic serve, a high toss of the ball and a good follow-through, and his first service went in. Bruno's forehand return hit the lip of the net, and rolled over to win the point.

"Sorry," he called out, and Michel waved acknowledgment, then bounced the ball to serve again. When they reached deuce, two men entered the court, wiping the raindrops from their faces. Rollo, the school headmaster, always arrived a little late. He waved a greeting, and he and Dougal, a Scotsman who was the Baron's neighbor and drinking chum, sat on the bench to watch the end of the set. It was not long before Rollo and Dougal rose to take their turn. This was the usual rule. One set, and then the extra men played the losers. Bruno and the Baron sat down to watch. Rollo played with more enthusiasm than skill and loved to attack the net, but Dougal had once been a decent club player and his ground shots were always a pleasure to watch.

"I suppose you can't say much," the Baron began, in what he thought was a low voice.

"Not a thing," replied Bruno. "You understand."

"It's just I heard there were some arrests over in Lalinde last night and that you were involved. A friend of mine saw you there. I just want to know if there was a connection to our Arab."

"Our Arab, is he now?" Bruno asked. "I suppose he is, in a way. He lived here, died here."

"Our Arab I said, and I mean it. I know Momu and Karim as well as you do. I know the old man was a Harki, and I have a very special feeling for the Harkis. I commanded a platoon of them in the Algerian war. I spent the first month wondering when one of them would shoot me in the back, and the rest of the war they saved my neck on a regular basis."

Bruno turned and looked at the Baron curiously. In the town, he had a reputation as a true Right-winger, and it was said that only his devotion to the memory of de Gaulle kept the Baron from voting for the Front National.

"I thought you were against all this immigration from North Africa," Bruno said, breaking off to applaud as Michel served an ace.

"I am. What is it now, six million, seven million Arabs and Muslims over here, swamping the place? You can't recognize Paris anymore. But Harkis are different. They fought for us and we owed them—and we left too damn many of them behind to have their throats cut because we wouldn't take them in. Men who fought for France."

"More than just a Harki, our victim got a medal. He fought for us in Vietnam, too, that's where he won it," Bruno said.

"In that case, he wasn't a Harki. They were irregulars. He sounds like he was in the regular Army, probably a Zouave or a Tirailleur. That's what most of those colonial regiments were called. They were allowed back into France when it was over, but most of the Harkis were refused entry. And those who made it to France were put in camps. It was shameful. Some of us did what we could. I managed to bring some of my men back on the troopship, but it meant leaving their families, so the bulk of them decided to stay and take their chances. Most of them paid the price."

"How did you find out about who was killed?" Bruno wanted to know.

"I stayed in touch with the men I brought over, helped them get jobs, that sort of thing. I took some of them on in my business. They had ways of keeping contact through their families. You know I'm not much of a churchgoing type, but every time I heard one of my Harkis had been killed, I used to go and light a candle." He cleared his throat and sat up. "So tell me about our Arab, a good soldier of France. Do you know who killed him?"

"No. We're just starting the investigation, and I'm not even really involved. As I said, the Police Nationale are handling it. They've set up a temporary office in the exhibition rooms."

"What about Lalinde?"

"There may not even be a connection. It seems to have been more of a drug bust," Bruno said, careful not to tell his friend an outright lie.

The Baron nodded, his eyes still fixed on the game. Rollo had just served two double faults.

"Did I ever tell you how we left Algeria?" he asked suddenly. Bruno shook his head.

"We were in Oran, at the harbor. It was chaos. De Gaulle had signed the peace deal at Evian and then half the Army in Algeria launched that crazy coup d'état.

"Anyway, I got our unit down to the troopship, and on the way we picked up those of my old Harkis that we could find, or who were smart enough to know they had better get out fast. My sergeant had been with me all through the war and he liked the Harkis, so he helped. We scrounged some uniforms—no shortage of them—and we just let them board with us. There were no lists, nothing organized, because there were so few officers, so I just bullied them all aboard."

"And when you got to France?" Bruno asked. "How did you get them ashore?"

"They couldn't put us all into the naval base at Toulon, where at least there was some kind of control system, so we docked at Marseilles, at the commercial port, and the Army had dozens of trucks to drive us to the nearest bases. But there was no system for which unit went to which base, so we all just boarded the first trucks we saw and Harkis jumped off them at every corner. We had found some civilian clothes for them and a few francs. Apart from that, all they had was my name and address."

"I knew the Algerian war ended in a mess, but I didn't know about that," Bruno said.

"Game and set," called Dougal, and on the court they began collecting the tennis balls.

"The thing I remember best," said the Baron, "was the very last moment when we left Algiers. I stayed at the foot of the gangplank, trying to be sure I had all my men. And one of the Algerian dockworkers was standing by me, ready to cast off the ship's rope. He looked me straight in the eye, and he said, 'Next time, we invade you.' Just like that. And he kept his eyes fixed on me until I turned and boarded the ship. I'll never forget it. And when I look at France these days, I know he was right."

As always after their game, the group of men walked back to the clubhouse. The rain had eased. They showered and then brought in the ingredients of their ceremonial Friday lunch from their cars. Bruno provided eggs from his hens and herbs from his garden. In early spring, he picked *boutons de pissenlit,* the tiny green buds of the dandelion, but now it was young garlic and flat-leaf parsley. He also had some of his own truffles, which he had stored in oil since the winter. Michel brought pâté and rillettes, made from the pig they had gathered to slaughter in February, in happy defiance of the European Union regulations. Dougal supplied bread and cheese and the bottle of Scotch that they took as an aperitif after their first thirst-quenching beers from the tap at the clubhouse bar. Rollo brought steaks and Xavier the salad and a *tarte aux pommes,* and the Baron provided the wine, a St. Emilion '98 that was tasted and judged to be at its best

Bruno cooked, as he always did, and when they had set the table and prepared the salad the men gathered at the hatch between the kitchen and the bar. Usually they joked and gossiped, but this time there was only one topic on their minds.

"All I can say is that we don't yet have any firm evidence, and so no obvious suspect," Bruno told them as he broke the dozen eggs, lit the grill for the steaks and threw a stick of unsalted butter into the frying pan. He began to slice the truffle very thin. "We have some leads that we're following. Some point one way and some another, and some of them I don't know about because I am on the fringes of this investigation. That's all I can say."

"The doctor's son has been arrested, along with a bunch of Front National thugs," said Xavier. "That we know."

"It may not be connected," said Bruno.

"It looks connected," said Michel. "Front National thugs and a swastika carved into the poor old bastard's chest. Who else would do that?"

"Maybe the murderer did that to cast suspicion else-where," said Bruno. "Have you thought of that?"

"Which doctor's son?" asked Rollo.

"Gelletreau," said Xavier.

"Young Richard?" said Rollo, startled. "He's still at the lycée."

"He wasn't there this week. He forged a note from his dad saying he was sick," said Bruno, tossing the whipped eggs into the sizzling butter and the fresh garlic. As the base of the omelette began to cook, he threw in the sliced truffle and twirled the pan.

"In the Front National? Richard?" Rollo had disbelief in his voice. "I never had any idea when he was in school." He paused. "Well, I suppose there was one thing, a fight with one of Momu's nephews, but nothing serious. Two bloody noses and some name-calling, the usual thing. I suspended them both from school for a day and sent a note to the parents."

"A fight with one of Momu's nephews, and then Momu's dad gets killed?" said the Baron. "That sounds significant. What was the name-calling? *Sale beur*—dirty Arab—that kind of thing?"

"Something like that," Rollo said stiffly. "Look, I didn't mean . . . it was just one of those tussles that boys get into. It happens all the time. I should never have mentioned it."

They fell into a silence, all eyes on Bruno as he lifted and tilted the heavy iron pan, gave two strategic pushes with his wooden spoon and tossed the herbs into the runny mix before folding the giant omelette over onto itself. Without a word, they all trooped to the table and sat. The Baron poured the wine and Bruno served the perfect omelette, the earthy scent of the truffle just beginning to percolate as he divided this opening course onto six plates.

"One of your best, Bruno," said the Baron, savoring his first mouthful and slicing the big country loaf against his chest with a Laguiole knife he took from the pouch at his belt. He was not trying to change the subject, since all the men understood that something significant had been said and the matter could not be allowed to rest.

"But you did mention it, Rollo," the Baron went on. "And now you must satisfy not just our curiosity but the judicial questions this must raise. Our friend Bruno may be too delicate to insist, but you understand what is at issue here."

"It was just boys," Rollo said. "You know how they are. One gets a bloody nose, the other gets a black eye and then they're the best of friends." He looked from one to the other, but none was meeting Rollo's eyes.

"Well, were they?" asked Michel.

"Were they what?" snapped Rollo. Bruno could see he hated the way this was going.

"Did they become the best of friends?"

"They didn't fight again."

"Friends?"

"No, but that doesn't mean anything. They got on. Momu even invited the boy back to his home, sat him down to dinner with the family so he could see for himself they were just another French family. No difference. Momu told me he liked the boy. He was bright, respectful. He brought flowers."

"That would have been his mother's idea," said Xavier.

"She's on the Left, isn't she?" Michel asked.

"Green," said Xavier, who followed such allegiances

closely. "She got involved in that campaign against the pollution from the sawmill. Thirty jobs at stake and those daft Ecolos want to close it down."

"What I mean is that Richard wouldn't have heard any of this anti-immigrant stuff at home. His mother is a Green and the doctor doesn't seem to have any politics," Michel continued. "So where did he pick it up?"

"In bed, I think," said Bruno. "I think he fell for that girl from Lalinde who got to the tennis semifinals last year, and she was in the Front. She's a pretty thing and he was besotted with her."

"Then that's that," said Rollo. "This fight took place three years ago. And Richard didn't meet the girl until the tournament last summer." He took his glass as if he were about to gulp the wine, but remembered himself and took an appreciative sniff of the St. Emilion and then a sip. "When he left my care, he was a fine boy, a good pupil, a credit to the town. I thought he might go on to Paris, the Sciences-Po or the Polytechnique."

"Instead, it looks like it could be prison for your fine boy," said the Baron, using a chunk of bread to mop up every last trace of buttery egg from his plate.

11

Bruno did not normally drink in the mornings, but Saturday was the exception. It was the day of the small market of St. Denis, usually limited to the open space beneath the Mairie where the stallholders set out their fruit and vegetables, their homemade breads and their cheeses between the ancient stone pillars. Stéphane, a dairy farmer from the rolling country upriver, parked his custom-made van in the square to sell his milk and butter and cheeses. He always arranged a small *casse-croûte,* a breaking of the crust, at about nine a.m., an hour after the market opened. For Stéphane, who rose at five to tend his cows, it was like a mid-morning snack, but for Bruno it was always the first bite of his Saturday, and he drank a small glass of red wine with the thick hunk of bread stuffed with Stéphane's rabbit pâté. The wine came from young Raoul, who had taken over his father's business selling wines at the various local markets. This day he had brought along a young Côtes de Duras, best known for its whites, but he thought this red was special. It was certainly an improvement on the Bergerac Bruno normally drank on Saturday mornings.

"What does that one sell for?" he asked.

"Normally five euros, but I can let you have a case for fifty, and you should keep it three or four years," said Raoul.

Bruno had to be careful with his money, since his pay was almost as modest as his needs. When he bought a wine to store, it was usually to share with friends on some special occasion, so he preferred to stay with the classic vintages that they would know. Mostly he bought a share of a barrel with the Baron from a small winemaker they knew in Lalande de Pomerol, and they bottled the three hundred liters themselves on a well-lubricated day to which they both looked forward and which, inevitably, by evening had become a large party for half the village at the Baron's château.

"Have you seen the doctor?" Stéphane asked.

"Not yet," said Bruno. "It's out of my hands. The Police Nationale are involved and everything is being handled over in Périgueux."

"He's one of us, though," Stéphane said, avoiding Bruno's eye and taking a large bite of his bread and pâté.

"Yes, and so are Karim and Momu," Bruno said firmly.

"Not quite the same way," said Raoul. "The doctor's family has been here forever and he delivered half the babies in town, me and Stéphane included."

"I know that, but even if the boy is not involved in the murder, there's still a serious drug case being investigated," said Bruno. "And it's not just some weed, there are pills and hard drugs—the kind of things we want to keep out of St. Denis if we can."

Bruno felt uneasy about the spreading word of mouth. Half the town seemed to know about Gelletreau's arrest, and everybody knew the doctor and his wife. There were not many secrets in St. Denis, which was usually a good thing for police work, but not this time. Naturally people would talk about the arrest of a schoolboy, the son of a prominent neighbor, but there were layers to this rumor, about Arabs and Islam, that were something new both for him and for the town. There were six million Muslims among a French population of sixty million people. Most of them came from North Africa and too few of them had jobs, probably through no fault of their own, Bruno felt. He knew about the riots and the car burnings in Paris and the big cities, about the number of votes the Front National had won in the last election, but he had always felt that that was something remote from St. Denis. There were fewer Muslims in the Dordogne than in any other department of France, and those in St. Denis were like Momu and Karim: good citizens with jobs and families and responsibilities. The women did not wear the veil and the nearest mosque was in Périgueux. When they married, they performed the ceremony in the Mairie like good republicans.

"I'll tell you what we also want to keep out of St. Denis," said Raoul, "and that's the Arabs. There are too many here already."

"What, half a dozen families, including Momu, who taught your kids to count?"

"Thin end of the wedge," said Raoul. "Look at the size of the families they have—six kids, seven sometimes. Two or three generations of that and we'll be outnumbered. They'll turn Notre Dame into a mosque."

Bruno put his glass down on the small table behind Stéphane's van, buying a little time to settle on what he wanted to say.

"Look, Raoul. Your grandmother had six kids, or was it eight? And your mother had four, and you have two. That's the way it goes, and it will be the same for the Muslims. Birth rates fall just as soon as the women start to get an education. Look at Momu—he only has two kids."

"That's just it. Momu is one of us. He lives like us, works like us, likes his rugby," said Raoul. "But you look at the rest of them, six and seven kids, and the girls don't even go to school half the time. When I was a kid there were no Arabs here. Not one. And now there's what, forty or fifty, and more arriving and being born every year. And they all seem to have first call on the public housing. This is our country, Bruno. We've been here forever, and I'm very careful about who I want to share it with."

"You want to know why the Front National gets the vote it does?" said Stéphane. "Just open your eyes. It's not just the immigrants, it's the way the usual parties have let us down. It's been coming for years, that's why so many people vote for the Greens or for the Chasse Party. Don't get me wrong, Bruno. I'm not against the Arabs, and I'm not against immigrants; not when my own wife is the daughter of a Portuguese who immigrated here before the war. But they are like us. They are white and European and Christian, and we all know the Arabs are something different."

Bruno shook his head. He understood what these people were saying, what they feared. But it was all totally, dangerously wrong. He knew that this kind of conversation, this kind of sentiment, had existed even in quiet little St. Denis for a long time. Now it was out in the open.

"You know me," he said after a pause. "I'm a simple man,

simple tastes and simple pleasures. I follow the law, and not only because it's my job. And the law says anybody who is born here is French, whether they are white or black or brown or purple. And if they're French, they're just the same as everybody else in the eyes of the law, and that means in my eyes. And if we stop believing that, then we are in for real trouble in this country."

"We already have trouble. We've got a murdered Arab and one of our own under arrest, and now a load of drugs floating around," said Raoul. "Nobody is talking about anything else."

Bruno bought some butter and some of the garlic-flavored canaillou cheese from Stéphane, a pannier of strawberries and a big country loaf from the organic baker in the market and took them up the stairs to his office in the Mairie before walking down the hall to the mayor's office. His secretary didn't work Saturdays, but the mayor was usually in, smoking the big pipe his wife wouldn't allow around the house and working on his hobby, a history of St. Denis. It had been under way for fifteen years already; he never seemed to make much progress, and he was usually glad of an interruption.

"Ah, my dear Bruno," Mangin said, rising and moving across the thick Persian rug, which glowed in soft reds against the dark wooden floorboards, to the small corner cupboard where he kept a few bottles. "Let's have a glass and you can tell me your news."

"Not very much news, sir, just what J-J could tell me on the phone this morning. You know young Gelletreau was arrested, and he has a lawyer; so does the young girl from Lalinde. So far they are saying very little except that they know nothing at all about the killing of Hamid. We're still waiting for the forensics, but there's nothing obvious to connect them. No fingerprints, no blood traces."

The mayor nodded grimly. "I had hoped everything might be settled quickly, even if it meant one of our local boys is responsible. The mood will turn sour very fast. I just wish there was something we could do to speed things up. By the way, that reminds me." He picked up a sheet of paper from his desk. "You asked me about the old man's photograph of his soccer team. Momu remembers it well. It was an amateur team that played in a youth league in Marseilles. All the players were young North Africans. The coach was a former professional player for Marseilles named Villanova, and he was in the photo along with the rest of the team. They won the league championship in 1940. Momu remembers that because his father held a soccer ball in the photo with the words 'Champions, 1940,' painted in white. But that's all he remembers."

"Well, it's a start, but it doesn't tell us why the killer might want to take the photo away, or the medal," said Bruno. "By the way, I had to tell J-J about some school-yard fight that Gelletreau got into with Momu's nephew, which is probably meaningless but it is a connection. Of course the boy is still in big trouble because of the drugs and the politics, and J-J says he expects Paris to send down some big shot to make a big political case of it to discredit the Front."

The mayor handed Bruno a small glass of his *vin de noix,* which Bruno had to admit was probably just a little better than his own—but then, Mangin had had more practice. The mayor perched on the edge of his large wooden desk, piled high with books, files bound with red ribbon and an elderly black telephone on the corner. Neither a computer nor even a typewriter graced the remaining space, only an old fountain pen, neatly capped and resting on a page of notes.

"I also heard from Paris today, from an old friend in the justice ministry and then from a former colleague in the Elysée, and they said much the same thing," the mayor told Bruno. The Elysée Palace was the official home, as well as the personal office, of the president of France. "They see some political opportunities in our misfortune, and I have to say that, in their place, I might look at things the same way."

"I'm not too sympathetic to their point of view. I'm worried about the damage this could do to St. Denis," said Bruno.

"Well, I used to be in their place when I was young and ambitious, so I understand their motives and their concerns. But you're right, of course." He turned to a window that overlooked the small market square and the old stone bridge. "If this thing drags on and becomes a nasty confrontation between Arabs and whites and the extreme Right, we will get lots of publicity and we are likely to have a lot of bitterness that could last for years. And tourists will stay away."

Bruno was worried about the same things, and the mayor's responsibilities were far greater: he had a duty to almost three thousand souls, to a history that went back centuries, and to their forebears who had built this Mairie and the serene old room where they now talked. Bruno remembered his first visit, to be interviewed by this same man, who still had a political career and a seat in the Senate at the time. He had been awed then, in his first meeting with the mayor, by the heavy dark beams on the ceiling and the wood paneling on the walls, the rich rugs and the desk that seemed made for the governance of a town far grander than St. Denis.

"Indeed, the law must do as it must," said the mayor. "And for the moment the course of the law seems to be based in Périgueux, and in Lalinde. I know it's not nice to say, but if there is to be trouble, I would much rather it took place in Périgueux and Lalinde than here. You understand me, Bruno? It won't be easy to deflect attention from St. Denis, but we must do what we can. I told Paris that they might want to focus on Périgueux rather than here, but I'm not sure they quite got the point. Or maybe they got it too well."

He sighed, and continued. "There's another problem. Montsouris is planning to hold a small demonstration here at lunchtime on Monday. A march of solidarity, he calls it." Bruno could sense his irritation. "France in support of her Arab brethren under the red flag seems to be his idea. He has asked for my support with Rollo to get the schoolchildren marching against racial hatred and extremism. What do you think?"

Bruno began to calculate how many people might be involved and what the route might be, and wondering whether he would have to block the road. And recalling the conversation he had just had in the market with Stéphane and Raoul, a march of solidarity might not be altogether popular.

"We certainly can't stop it, so we will just have to keep it as low-key as possible," he said.

"You know as well as I do that Montsouris and his wife

will call all the newspapers and TV and get some of the trade unions involved, all publicity we don't need."

"Well, I think it's better if we are known as a town that stands up for racial harmony than if we're seen as a center of race hatred," said Bruno. "As the Americans say, if they give you lemons, make lemonade. And if we have to have such a march, it might be better that it take place with you at the head and all the council and responsible people, rather than leave it to the red flags."

"You could be right," the mayor said, still not pleased.

"If you take charge, and set the route, perhaps we could limit it? You could say the route will be from the Mairie to the war memorial, because old Hamid was a veteran and a war hero," said Bruno. "He won the Croix de Guerre, so you could make it a patriotic march, nothing to do with Arabs or Muslims and the extreme Right, but the town commemorating the tragic death of a brave soldier of France."

"You're becoming quite a canny politician," the mayor said. It was meant to be a compliment. The mayor raised his glass and they drank.

Their mood was suddenly shattered by the braying sound of the siren on a gendarmerie van. The sound grew, and then stayed, as if right beneath the window. The two men moved as one toward the window and saw blue uniforms and gray suits scrambling amid the market stalls. They were closing in upon an agile boy who was darting between them and ducking beneath the stalls, delaying the inevitable moment of his capture.

"*Merde*," said Bruno. "That's Karim's nephew." And he dashed for the stairs.

By the time Bruno reached the covered market, the boy's arm was held firmly by a self-congratulatory Captain Duroc. The two men in gray suits, Bruno knew, were the hygiene inspectors from Brussels, civil servants working on a Saturday. One of them held a large potato above his head in triumph.

"This is the culprit," said his partner. "We caught him red-handed."

"And this is the potato, just like the one he used on our car on Tuesday," said the one holding it.

"Leave this to me, gentlemen," Duroc said emphatically, and glanced triumphantly around at his audience—market people and shoppers who were gathering to enjoy the scene. "This kid is going to prison."

"*Mon Capitaine,* perhaps it would help if I came along," said Bruno, suppressing the anger he felt for this buffoon, and for himself. If only he had thought ahead and stopped this nonsense of slashing tires. "I can ensure that we inform the parents, *mon Capitaine.* You know the regulations about minors, and I think I have their number in my phone. You can take the statements of complaint of these two gentlemen at the gendarmerie while I contact the boy's family."

Duroc paused, and pursed his lips. "Ah, yes. Of course."

"What about my eggs?" shrilled old Madame Vignier, pointing to the mess of shells and yolks on the ground beside her overturned stall. "Who's going to pay for them?"

One of the inspectors bent down to retrieve a shell, and came up staring at her.

"No date stamp on this egg, madame. You know that's strictly against the regulations? Such eggs may be consumed for private use but it is an offense under the food-hygiene law to sell them for gain." He turned to Captain Duroc. "This woman is to be fined, Officer."

"Well, you had better find a witness to confirm that these eggs were being sold," said Bruno. "Madame Vignier is known for her generosity, and makes a regular donation of her surplus eggs to the poor. And if she has any left over after the Saturday market, she gives them to the church. Is that not so, madame?" he said courteously to the old hag who was staring at him, her mouth agape. But her brain moved fast enough for her to nod assent.

The old woman was dirt poor, since her husband drank the farm away. She bought the cheapest eggs at the local supermarket, rubbed off the date stamps, rolled them in straw and chicken shit and sold them to tourists as farm-laid for a euro apiece. No local ever bought anything from her except her eau-de-vie, since her one useful legacy from her husband had been his ancestral right to eight liters a year and she naturally made a lot more than that.

"I'm sure the local priest would testify to Madame Vignier's good character," Bruno went on. "Our Father Sentout is a very important man, you know, about to be made a monsignor."

"No, no," said the inspector. "No need to bother the good Father. The lady may go. We are only concerned with this boy and his damage to state property, namely, our car."

"You saw him damage your car today?" inquired Bruno politely. He had to find a way out of this for the boy. And he was damned if these two gray men were going to get away with this.

"Not exactly," said the inspector. "But we saw him hanging around our car and we called the gendarmes, and when we pounced he had a potato in his hand."

"Forgive me, but this is a vegetable market with hundreds of potatoes on sale. What's so unusual about a boy holding a potato?"

"He used a potato to immobilize our car at the Tuesday market, that's what. The engine gave up on the road to Périgueux."

"Somebody threw a potato at your car? Was the windscreen broken?" Bruno was beginning to enjoy this.

"No, no. The potato was stuffed into the exhaust pipe to block the escaping gases, and the engine died. We had to wait two hours for a repair truck."

"Did you see this boy do this on Tuesday?"

"Not exactly, but Captain Duroc told us when we complained that he thought it must have been some boy, and so we came back today to see if we could see one—and we caught him."

"Isn't it unusual that you are on duty today, on a Saturday?" Bruno asked. "I presume you are on duty."

"Not exactly," the inspector repeated, "but since our duties bring us to the Dordogne this week and next, we decided to stay over and make a weekend of it."

"So, you are not exactly on duty today. Yes or no?" Bruno had taken on a serious air.

"Er, no."

"Let me get this clear, monsieur," said Bruno coldly. "Your car was allegedly damaged by a person or persons unknown on Tuesday, and it is not yet established that any damage was inflicted by the potato rather than by other causes. And now because you find a boy holding a potato, in a vegetable market, somewhere near your unharmed car of today—a day when you are not on duty and thus I presume not empowered to enforce the hygiene rules that you tried to deploy against the kindly Madame Vignier—you are now proposing to take the very serious step of arresting and bringing charges against a minor?"

"Well, yes."

Bruno drew himself up to his full height, frowned and continued in his most formal tone of voice.

"I suggest that while I telephone the boy's parents to inform them of the forcible detention of their son for being in suspicious possession of a potato"—he paused to let the absurdity of this sink in—"I am also bound as an officer of the law to inform the parents of their right to file a formal complaint against persons responsible for what may be the wrongful arrest of a minor. So, at this time I would advise that you might want to contact your own superiors in order to establish what exactly is your personal authority and responsibility in such matters, and whether your department will defray any legal expenses that you are likely to incur. This will include any liability that you may have unfortunately brought upon the gendarmes if unlawful arrest is indeed established. I'm sure that you would not want to implicate Captain Duroc and his men, who clearly acted in the finest and most efficient traditions of the gendarmerie, if such is the case."

Somebody in the crowd let out a long, appreciative whistle for the speech. Then Bruno solemnly opened his shirt pocket and drew out the pencil and notepad on which he had written his morning shopping list.

"I had better make a formal record of this notification," he said. "So, gentlemen, might I see your identity cards, please, along with any documents that testify to your lawful authority? And Captain Duroc," he went on, "we shall obviously need a camera to take photographs of that young boy's arm and shoulder which you have been gripping so tightly. Just a formality, you understand, to protect you personally against any malicious charges of ill-treatment as a result of your being suborned into what seems very likely to be a case of wrongful arrest."

There was a long silence, and then the captain let go of the boy's arm. The boy burst into tears, scurried over to Bruno and buried his face in the policeman's freshly laundered shirt.

"Well, we may have been a little hasty," began one of the inspectors. "But the damage to our car is a serious matter."

"Indeed it is, sir, which is why we should proceed according to the letter of the law," said Bruno. "We will all go to the gendarmerie where you will file your complaint, and I will bring the boy's parents, and probably their legal representative, and there will be no need for further witnesses since the mayor and I saw the arrest and forcible seizure of this young boy from the window of the mayor's office."

"My chief of police is absolutely right," said the mayor from behind Bruno's shoulder. "We saw the whole thing, and I must say that I am deeply disturbed that an underage member of our community can be seized in this way on what seems like the flimsiest of evidence. As mayor of St. Denis and a senator of the republic, I reserve the right to bring this matter to the attention of your superiors."

"But unless we file charges, we'll be liable for the damage to the car," bleated the younger inspector.

"Shut up, you fool," hissed his partner, and the two inspectors turned away to whisper to each other and then the elder of them spoke.

"*Monsieur le Maire, Monsieur le Chef de Police, mon Capitaine,* allow me to congratulate you on the efficiency and good sense you have brought to ease this little misunderstanding. I think it might be advisable for all of us to let this matter rest, and we shall get on with our duties elsewhere in the region."

He bowed slightly, and the two inspectors then turned and marched toward their car, leaving Duroc nonplussed.

"Bloody Gestapo," said the mayor, and Duroc's eyes widened.

Bruno leaned down and ruffled the boy's hair. "Where did you learn that trick with the potato?" he asked.

"From my great-grandpa. He told me it was what they used to do to the German trucks in the Resistance."

12

Bruno's garden had been planned for the long term. The first time the mayor had shown him the small stone cottage, with its roof just beginning to collapse, Bruno had looked at the sheltering trees on the hill above and the great sweep of the view to the south across the plateau, and known that this place would suit him well. The old shepherd who had lived here had died almost a decade earlier. His heirs, who had long since moved to Paris, had neglected to pay the modest taxes, so it had fallen into the hands of the commune, which meant into the disposition of the mayor. He and Bruno had walked over the wide stretch of rough turf that would become Bruno's lawn and his terrace, poked around the overgrown vegetable garden and a collapsed henhouse, and carefully lifted the rotting wooden cover from the well. The stonework was still sound and the water fresh. The beams of the old barn behind the cottage were solid chestnut and would last forever, and the cart track leading up from the road, although rutted and overgrown, was easily passable. They had paced out the dimensions of the house, twelve meters long and eight deep. Inside, there was one large room and two small, and the remains of a ladder that went up to the attic beneath the roof.

"It comes with four hectares but it will take a lot of work," the mayor had said.

"I'll have the time," Bruno had replied, already imagining how it could be and wondering whether his mustering-out pay from the Army would be sufficient to buy this home of his own.

"The land stretches to the brow of the hill behind, in those woods, about a hundred meters to the right and down to the stream below us," the mayor explained. "We cannot legally sell the place unless it is habitable, which means that the commune will have to install electricity, but you would have to fix the roof and put in some windows before we can make a contract. That's your risk. If I'm voted out of office in the elections, you might have done the work for nothing. I cannot promise that my successor would honor the deal, but we might be able to reach a long leasehold agreement, tied to the post of chief of police."

Bruno, just a few months into the job as the municipal policeman of St. Denis, was confident that the mayor would be reelected in St. Denis as long as he was breathing, and probably even if he was not, so they shook hands on the bargain and he set to work. It was springtime, so Bruno gave up the small apartment he had been renting and moved into the barn with a cot, a sleeping bag and a camping stove. The briskness of his morning shower, a bucket of water from the well poured over his head, a quick soaping and then another bucket to rinse himself off, was nothing new to him. It was the way he had kept clean on Army exercises. He spent his first days off and all his evenings clearing the old vegetable garden and building a new fence of chicken wire to keep out the rabbits. Then, with a happy sense of mission, he began planting potatoes, zucchini, onions, lettuce, tomatoes and herbs.

Bruno explored the copse of trees behind the vegetable garden and found wild garlic. Later, in the autumn, he discovered big brown cèpe mushrooms, and under one of the white oaks he saw the darting movement of the tiny fly that signaled the presence of truffles on his land. Below the turf that stretched out generously to the front of his new home were hedges of raspberries and black currants, and three old and distinguished walnut trees.

By the time the electricity was connected, he had put new tiles on the cottage roof and installed insulation. He had bought ready-made windows from Bricomarché, making them fit by building his own wooden frames. The doorway was of an unusual size, so he built his own door of planks and beams, and to fulfill an idea he had harbored ever since he had first seen a horse staring curiously over a half door in the cavalry stables at Saumur, he made the door so that the top half could open separately, and he could lean on the half door inside the cottage and gaze out at his property. Michel had brought up a mechanical digger from the public-works depot to repair the old car track, dig a hole for the septic tank and lay trenches for the pipes. He stayed to help install the electricity and run cables to the barn. René from the tennis club had put in the plumbing, and someone else had brought a cement mixer up the newly leveled track to help him lay a new floor, and then showed him how to make foundations for the additions that Bruno was planning, a large bedroom and bathroom. Without really thinking about it, Bruno assumed that someday there would be a wife here and a family to house.

By the end of the summer, the foundations of the new wing were laid and Bruno had moved out of the barn and into the big room of the house with its view over the plateau. He could take a hot shower in his own bathroom with water from the gas heater, fueled by the big blue containers that Jean-Louis sold at the garage. He had a gas cooker, a refrigerator, a sink with hot and cold running water, wooden floors and a very large bill at the Bricomarché that he would be paying off with one-fifth of his monthly paycheck for the following two years.

He signed the contract of sale in the mayor's office, the town notary on hand to ensure that all was legal. There was enough of his Army mustering-out pay left to cover the first year of property taxes and to buy a wood-burning stove and a hundred liters of good Bergerac wine and throw himself a housewarming party. He dug the pit for the fire to roast the lamb and made his couscous in a giant *fait-tout* enamel pot he borrowed from the tennis club and served the meal on trestle tables and benches loaned by the rugby club. In one glorious evening, he feasted all his new friends, showed off his house and became an established man of property.

He had not expected so many gifts. His colleagues at the Mairie had chipped in to buy him a washing machine. Joe, his predecessor as chief of police, brought him a cockerel and half a dozen hens. It seemed that every housewife in St. Denis had prepared him jars of homemade pâté or preserved vegetables and jams, salamis and rillettes. Not a pig had been killed in St. Denis over the past year without some of it reaching Bruno's larder. The tennis club brought him a set of cutlery and the rugby club brought him crockery. The staff of the medical clinic gave him a mirror for his bathroom and a cupboard with a first-aid kit that could have equipped a small hospital. Fat Jeanne from the market gave him a mixed set of wine and water glasses that she had picked up at the last *vide-grenier* jumble sale, and the staff at the Bricomarché had donated a set of cooking pots. Michel and the others from the public-works depot gave him some old spades and garden tools that they had managed to replace by juggling the following year's budget. The gendarmes bought him a big radio, and the fire department gave him a shotgun and a hunting license. The children in the tennis and rugby clubs whom he taught to play had put together their centimes and bought him a young apple tree, and everyone who came to his housewarming brought him a bottle of good wine to lay down in the cellar that he and Joe had built under the new wing.

As the night wore on, Bruno had drunk a small toast with virtually every one of his guests. Finally, when wine and good fellowship overcame him sometime toward dawn, he fell asleep with his head on one of the outdoor tables. The friends who had stayed the course carried him into his house, took off his shoes, laid him on the big new bed that René had built and covered him with the quilt that the firemen's wives had sewn.

But Bruno had one more gift. It was curled up peacefully asleep on an expanse of old newspaper, and as Bruno rose with an aching head, it woke up and came across to lick his feet and then scrambled up into his lap to burrow into the warmth and gaze at its new master with intelligent and adoring eyes. This was the mayor's gift, a basset hound from a litter of his own renowned hunting dog, and Bruno decided to name him Gitan, or Gypsy. But by the end of the day, when Bruno had already come to delight in his puppy's long, velvet ears, outsized feet and seductive ways, it had been shortened to Gigi. For Bruno it had been the most memorable evening of his life—his formal baptism into the fraternity of the Commune of St. Denis.

Dressed in shorts and sandals, Bruno was staking his young tomato plants when he heard a car coming up the road. Its driver was one of the celebrants from that first happy night years ago. But there was no cheer this day in Dr. Gelletreau as he levered himself from the elderly Mercedes, patted the welcoming Gigi and lumbered up the path to the terrace. Bruno rinsed his hands under the garden tap and went to welcome his unexpected guest.

"I drove to your house earlier, but there was no one there," Bruno told him.

"Yes, thanks, Bruno. I found your note on the door. We were in Périgueux, with the lawyer and then at the police station." The doctor had taped Bruno's broken ribs after a rugby game, tended his influenza and signed his annual certificates of health after a casual glance up and down the policeman's healthy frame. But he was not a regular visitor to Bruno's home and he looked in even worse shape than usual.

Gelletreau was overweight and far too red in the face for comfort, a man who ignored the sound advice he gave to his patients. With his white hair and heavy mustache, he looked almost too old to have a teenage son, but there was a daughter even younger.

"Any news?" Bruno asked.

"No. My son is being held pending drug charges. But it's the murder they are interested in," Gelletreau said.

"I can't talk about that, Doctor, not with you," said Bruno, as Gigi came to nuzzle his leg. Automatically, he reached down to scratch behind his dog's ears.

"Yes, yes, I understand that. I just wanted you to know that I'm strongly convinced he's innocent of that crime. He's my son, and I'm bound to say that, but I believe it in my bones. There's no cruelty in the boy, Bruno, you know that. You've known him long enough."

Bruno nodded. He had known young Richard since he was little more than a toddler, had taught him to hold a tennis racket, and then how to serve and hit a ball with topspin. Richard was a careful player rather than an aggressive one. Bruno doubted the boy had anything of the killer in him. But who knew what people could do under the sway of drugs or passion or political fervor?

"Have you seen Richard?" Bruno asked.

"They gave us ten minutes with him, just us and our lawyer. The mayor recommended some bright young fellow named Dumesnier from Périgueux, so we hired him. Apparently they didn't even have to let us see him, but the lawyer fixed it. They let us give him a change of clothes, after they searched every seam. My son is terrified and ashamed and confused. You can imagine. But he says he knows nothing of the killing. And he keeps on asking after that damn Jacqueline. He's besotted with her."

"His first girlfriend?" asked Bruno.

"She's his first lover, I think, and she's a pretty little thing. Pure poison, but certainly pretty. He's seventeen this week. You remember how we were at that age, all those hormones raging. She's all he can think about. He's infatuated."

"I understand."

"Can you tell them that?" Gelletreau asked eagerly. "Can you speak for him, just to explain that? I know you aren't running this business, Bruno, but they'll listen to you."

"Doctor, sit down, and let me get you a glass. It's hot and I need a beer and you can join me." He steered Gelletreau to one of the green plastic chairs on his terrace and went inside to get two cans from the refrigerator and two glasses. When he emerged he was surprised to see the doctor drawing on a yellow Gitane.

"You made me give those things up," Bruno said, pouring the beers.

"I know, I know. I haven't smoked in years, but you know how it is."

They raised their glasses to one another and drank in silence.

"You've done a great job with this place, Bruno."

"You said that when you were here last year for the barbecue, Doctor. I think you're changing the subject. Let me try to answer what you said before." Bruno put his glass down and leaned forward, his elbows on the green table.

"I'm not really part of the case," he began. "It's a matter for the Police Nationale, but they consult me whenever they want some local knowledge. I haven't seen all the evidence. I haven't seen the full forensic report on the murder, or on the house where Richard was arrested, and they probably won't show them to me. But I can tell you that the detective running the investigation is a decent man and he'll go with the evidence. In a case like this, he'll want to be sure that the evidence is very clear before he makes any recommendation to the magistrate. I wouldn't be surprised if they send some ambitious hotshot down from Paris because of the politics that are mixed up in all this. This is the sort of case that can make or break a career, and the magistrate will want to be very certain before he makes formal charges. If Richard is innocent, I'm confident he'll be cleared."

"The mayor just told me the same thing," said the doctor.

"Well, he's right. And you have to concentrate on being a support for your wife and family, and for Richard. You've got a good lawyer, which is very important at this stage. Other than that, what you have to focus on is telling Richard you love him and believe in him. He needs that right now."

Gelletreau nodded. "We'll give him all the support we can, you know that. But the question I keep asking myself is whether I really know my son as I thought I did. We had no idea he was getting involved with the Front National. He never showed any interest in politics."

"It may have been the girl who drew him in. That's one of the things the detectives are looking at. They'll get to the bottom of it. And I don't know about you, but at that age if my first lover had been a raging communist I'd have carried a red flag and marched wherever she asked me to." Bruno emptied his glass. "Another beer?"

"No thanks. I haven't finished this one. And you don't

want to have a second after being out in this sun." Gelletreau managed a smile. "That's your doctor speaking."

"There's one more thing." Bruno twirled his empty glass, wondering how best to put this. "You'd better start thinking about what to do if and when he's cleared and released. It wouldn't be a good idea to keep him in a local school. It would be difficult, with the gossip and the relatives of the old man. You should think about sending him to stay with a relative or to boarding school; maybe send him abroad where he can make a fresh start and put all this behind him. Perhaps you could even suggest that he go into the military for a while. It did me no harm, and it would be the kind of clean break the boy will need."

"It did me no harm either, although I just did three years as a medical orderly in West Africa, enough to save me a year of medical school. But I don't think the boy is cut out for that kind of life, that kind of discipline. Maybe that's the problem," said the doctor with a sigh. "Still, he respects the military. In the cell today he asked us how anyone could think he would kill someone who'd won a Croix de Guerre. But getting him out of here when all this is done is a good thought, Bruno. Thanks for the advice."

As the doctor drove off, Bruno was already wondering how on earth Robert had known about the Croix de Guerre. . . .

13

Less than an hour later, with the sun sinking fast and the heat easing so that he had donned a T-shirt, Bruno was watering the garden when he heard another vehicle lumbering up the road. He emptied the watering can and turned to see Isabelle in her unmarked car. She got out, waved and opened the rear door to bring out a supermarket bag.

"Hi, Bruno. I came to invite you to supper, unless you have plans."

"It looks like you made the plans already, Isabelle," he said, coming forward to push the enthusiastic Gigi out of the way and kiss the young woman on both cheeks. She was looking distinctly appealing in her jeans and red polo shirt, with a brown leather jacket slung loosely over her shoulders. She stood just a fraction below his height.

"Pâté, steak, baguette and cheese," she said, standing back to brandish her bag. "That's what J-J said you liked to eat. And wine, of course. What a wonderful dog—is this the great hunting dog J-J told me about?"

"J-J asked you to come?" She was not the first woman to come here alone bearing food, but she was the first to descend on him uninvited, and his immediate instinct was to approach this unexpected visit as if she were here as a professional colleague. "Not exactly," said Isabelle, down on her knees and making much of the eager Gigi, who liked women. "Can basset hounds really hunt wild boar?"

"That's what they were bred for, by Saint Hubert himself, according to legend. They aren't fast but they can run all day and never tire, so they exhaust the boar. Then one hound goes in from each side and grabs a foreleg and pulls and the boar just sprawls flat, immobilized until the hunter comes. But I use this one mainly to hunt *bécasse*. He's good with game birds; he has a very gentle mouth."

"J-J said I should brief you on the day's developments," she said, prizing herself free from the dog's attentions. "He left me in charge at St. Denis, but all the action has moved to Périgueux. I got bored and so I thought I'd pay you a visit. It just happened I remembered that J-J told me what you liked to eat. As if I couldn't guess."

"Well, I'm curious to know the latest and you're more than welcome. And congratulations on finding the house."

"Oh, that was easy," she said. "I just asked the woman in the Maison de la Presse when I went to pick up *Le Monde*. They ran a small piece about a racist murder in the Périgord, with the Front National involved. Half of the Paris press corps will be down here by Monday."

The whole of St. Denis would know by now that Bruno had a new lady friend. Some might even be staking out the bottom of the road to see if she left at a decent hour. He resolved privately that she would.

"He's called Gigi," said Bruno, as his dog signaled complete devotion by rolling onto his back and baring his tummy to be scratched.

"Short for Gitan. J-J told me. He's a great fan of yours and he told me all about you on our first drive down here. He didn't explain why you gave a male dog a girl's name."

"How else do you shorten Gitan into a nickname? And Gigi is the sort of sound dogs recognize easily even when you whisper. That's important for a hunting dog."

"I suppose J-J wouldn't know that," she said. "He's not a country type."

"He's a good man and a fine detective," said Bruno. "Hand me that bag and come and sit down. What would you like to drink?"

"A *petit* Ricard for me, lots of water, please, and then can you show me round? J-J said you'd been in the engineers in the Army and you built the whole place yourself."

She was trying very hard to please, thought Bruno, but he smiled and invited her through the main door and into the living room, where he had built a large fireplace. They went into the kitchen and he made the drinks while she leaned against the high counter where he normally sat when he ate alone. He poured some Ricard into two tall glasses, tossed in an ice cube and filled the glasses from a jug of cold water from the refrigerator. He handed one to Isabelle, raised his glass in salute, sipped and turned to work.

He unwrapped the beefsteaks she had brought and made a swift marinade of red wine, mustard, garlic and salt and pepper. Then he hammered the steaks with the flat of a cleaver until they were the thinness he liked, and put them in the marinade.

"Your own water?" she asked.

"We put an electric pump in the well. My friends from the town built this place more than I did—the plumbing, electricity, foundations, all the real work. I was just the unskilled labor. Come on, there's not much more to see."

He showed her the small utility room by the door, where he kept the washing machine and an old sink, his boots and coats, fishing gear and his shotgun. The ammunition was locked away. She hung her leather jacket on a spare hook and he showed her the big bedroom he had added on and a smaller spare room that he used as a study. He watched her make a fast appraisal of the double bed with its plain white sheets and duvet, the bedside reading lamp and the shelf of books. A copy of *Le Soleil d'Austerlitz,* one of Max Gallo's histories of Napoleon, lay half open by the bed, and she moved closer to look at the other books. She ran a finger gently down the spine of his copy of Baudelaire's poems and turned to raise a speculative eyebrow at him. He half smiled, half shrugged, but said nothing. She turned to him again after studying a print of le Douanier Rousseau's *Soir de Carnaval* that hung on the wall opposite the bed. He bit his lip when he saw her looking at the framed photographs he kept on the chest of drawers. There were a couple of happy scenes of tennis-club dinners, one of him scoring a try at a rugby game and a group photo of men in uniform around an armored car, Bruno and Captain Félix Mangin with their arms around each other's shoulders. Then, inevitably, she focused on the photograph of Bruno, in uniform and laughing, lounging on an anonymous riverbank with a happy Katarina, pushing her long, fair hair back from her dark eyes. It was the only picture he had of her.

Isabelle said nothing. She brushed past him to look into the spartan bathroom.

"You're very neat," she said. "It's almost too clean for a bachelor."

"That's only because you caught me on cleaning day," he said with a smile, relieved that the inspection was over.

"Where does Gigi sleep?"

"Outside. He's a hunting dog and supposed to be a watchdog."

"What's that hole in the ceiling?"

"My next project, when I get around to it. I'm going to put a staircase and a couple of windows in the roof, and make an extra bedroom or two up there."

"Where's your TV?" she said.

"I only have a radio. Come and see the outside and I'll get the fire going for the steak."

She admired the workshop he had made at one end of the barn, all the tools hanging neatly on a Peg-Board on the wall, and the jars of pâté and preserves standing in military ranks on the shelves. He showed her the chicken run, where a couple of geese had joined the descendants of Joe's original gift. She made a point of counting the number of tomato plants and the rows of vegetables.

"Do you eat all that in a year?"

"A lot of it, and we have dinners and lunches down at the tennis club. Any extra I can always give away. I put some into cans for the winter."

He picked up a stack of dried branches from last year's grapevine and stacked them in the brick barbecue, then he shook a bag of wood charcoal onto the top, thrust a sheet of old newspaper underneath and lit it. Back in the kitchen, he put plates, glasses and cutlery on a tray and opened the bottle of wine Isabelle had brought, a decent Cru Bourgeois from the Médoc. He opened the jar of venison pâté she had brought, put it on a plate with some cornichons and arranged a wedge of Brie on a wooden board.

"Let's eat outside," he said, taking the tray. "If you pick a lettuce from the garden you can make the salad while I do the steak, but we have time to enjoy our drinks before the barbecue is ready."

"There's no sign of a woman here," Isabelle remarked, when they had sat down at the green plastic table on his terrace and were watching Gigi licking his lips in anticipation. The dog knew what it meant when the barbecue was lit.

"Not at the moment," said Bruno.

"No woman, no TV, no pictures on your walls except photos of sports teams. No family photos, no pictures of adoring girlfriends, except that one when you were in the Army. Your house is impeccable—and impersonal—and your books are mostly nonfiction. I would have to say that you are a very self-controlled and organized man."

"You haven't seen the inside of my van," he said with a smile.

"That's your public life, your work. This home is the private Bruno, and very anonymous it is, except for the books. That's quite a library, the sign of an educated man."

"I'm not an educated man," he said. "I left school at sixteen."

"And went into the Army youth battalion," she said. "Yes, I know. And then into the combat engineers, and you did paratroop training and were promoted. You served in some special operations in Africa before you went to Bosnia and won a medal for hauling some wounded men from a burning armored car. They wanted to make you an officer but you refused. And then you were shot by a sniper when you were trying to stop some Serb paramilitaries from burning a Bosnian village, and they flew you back to France for treatment."

"So. You read my Army file." Of course, she couldn't know what the official files left out. She did not seem to have made the connection between the names of his captain in Bosnia, Félix Mangin, who wrote that approving report, and the mayor of St. Denis. He wondered if she was curious that the report didn't mention why Bruno had tried to save that particular Bosnian village.

Félix had been with him when they first found the decrepit motel that the Serbs had turned into a brothel for their troops, and had rescued the Bosnian women who had been forced to service them. They had relocated the women into what was supposed to be a safe house in a secure Bosnian village and brought in Médecins Sans Frontières to care for them. They had used their own money to buy the women new clothes and decent soaps and cosmetics. The official files made no mention of that.

"J-J got hold of your dossier on the day after the arrests at Lalinde when we realized that this was going to blow up into a political matter. It was routine, the kind of standard background check we'd do on anybody involved in something as sensitive as this. He showed it to me. I was impressed. I just hope my superiors write equally good things about me in my performance reviews." She smiled. "I even saw your magazine subscriptions, your surprisingly poor scores on the

Gendarmerie pistol range given that your Army file rated you as a marksman. And your savings account is in better shape than mine."

"I don't have much to spend my salary on," he said, as if that might explain something.

"You're rich in friends and reputation, from what I see," she said, and finished her Ricard. "I'm not here as a cop, Bruno, and I'm not probing." She remained silent for a few moments. "Sorry, I am probing," she said. "I'm curious about the woman in the photo."

He rubbed the back of his neck but said nothing. She picked up the wine and poured herself a glass, twirled it and sniffed.

"This is the wine J-J ordered when he took me to lunch my first day when I was posted down here," she said. He nodded, still with half of his Ricard to finish.

"And what did J-J tell you to brief me about?" he asked, determined to shift the conversation back onto safe ground.

"He hasn't got very far. No fingerprints and no forensics that put the boy or the girl anywhere inside Hamid's cottage, nor any of the other young fascists we found at her house. They both deny knowing him or ever visiting him. So all we have so far is the drugs and the politics, and while we can convict the girl on the drugs, I'm not sure about the boy, since he was tied up. A lawyer can say that makes him noncomplicit, and since he's under eighteen he counts as a juvenile."

"That sex looked pretty consensual to me," said Bruno.

"Yes," she said briskly. "I suppose it was, but that was the sex, which is not illegal, even for juveniles, and it's not evidence of drug use. We may have to release him. If it had been up to me, I'd have put pressure on the boy through the girl. I feel sure they had some involvement in the murder, even though there's no forensic evidence."

Bruno glanced behind him at the embers. Not ready yet. He finished his Ricard and Isabelle poured him a glass of Médoc.

"There's one new development, from that patch of mud on the path that leads to the cottage," she said. "We took casts of the tire prints, and there's one set that could match Jacqueline's car—except they're Michelins, and they match thousands of cars."

"Yes, and the path leads to several houses."

"True. And some ambitious young magistrate arrives from Paris on Monday to take over the case, at which point we simply become the investigators following the leads he chooses. My friends in Paris say there's some political jockeying over who gets the job. J-J stays in charge of the case, probably because there's so little evidence. If we were close to proving anything, some Paris brigadier would have been down to take the credit." She gave a short laugh and shrugged. "I'll go make the salad."

He rose to turn on the terrace light and Isabelle came back from the vegetable patch with a perfect young lettuce. In the kitchen he pointed her to the olive oil and the wine vinegar. He put a pot of water on to boil and began to peel and slice some potatoes, then he flattened some cloves of garlic, took a frying pan and splashed in some oil. When the water boiled, he tipped in the sliced potatoes, aware that she was watching, and turned over his egg timer, a miniature hourglass, to blanch them for three minutes.

"When the timer goes, drain them, dry them on a paper towel and fry them in the oil for a few minutes with the crushed garlic. Add salt and pepper and bring it all out," he said. "Thanks. I'll go and do the steaks."

The embers were just right, a fine gray ash over the fierce red. He put the grill close to the coals, arranged the steaks, and then under his breath sang "The Marseillaise," which he knew from long practice took him exactly forty-five seconds. He turned the steaks, dribbled some of the marinade on top of the charred side, and sang it again. Then he turned the steaks for ten seconds, pouring on more of the marinade, and then another ten seconds. Now he took them off the coals and put them on the plates he'd left to warm on the bricks that formed the side of the grill. Soon Isabelle appeared, the frying pan in one hand and the salad in the other, and he brought the steaks to the table.

"You waited," she said. "Another man would have come in to see that I was doing it *his* way."

Bruno didn't quite know what to say to that so he shrugged, handed her a plate and said, "*Bon appétit.*" She shared out the potatoes and left the salad in the bowl. That scored points with Bruno. He liked to soak up the juices from the meat in his potatoes rather than mix them with the oil and vinegar of the salad.

"The potatoes are perfect," he said.

"So is the steak."

"There's one thing that nags at me," said Bruno. "I saw Richard's father, and somehow the kid knew that Hamid had won the Croix de Guerre. Now, unless you or J-J told him that during the questioning, I don't know how he would have known about it if he hadn't seen it on the wall or been in the cottage. Were you in on all the interrogation sessions?"

"No. J-J did that in Périgueux. But the sessions are all on tape, so we can check. I don't think J-J would have tripped up like that. Is it something he could have heard at school from one of Hamid's relatives?"

"Possibly, but as I told you, he didn't get on too well with them. There was that fight in the playground."

"Too long ago to mean much, don't you think?" He watched with approval as she wiped the juices from her plate with a piece of bread and then helped herself to salad and cheese. "That steak was just right."

"Yes, well, the credit is all yours for bringing dinner, and the wine. Thank you." He helped himself to some salad. "The boy's father says he's absolutely sure Richard didn't do it."

"What a surprise!" she said. "Don't you have a candle, Bruno? With this electric light, I won't be able to see the stars, and they must be brilliant here."

"I know the boy, too, and I think the father may be right." Bruno went inside and brought out a small oil lamp. He took off the glass case, lit the wick, replaced the glass and only then turned off the terrace light.

"That would mean we have no suspect at all," she said. "And the press and politicians baying at our heels."

"And the public. Hang on a moment," he said. He went into the house for a sweater, and came back with her leather jacket and his mobile phone. "In case you get cold," he said, giving her the jacket and thumbing in a number.

"Momu," he said. "Sorry to bother you, but it's Bruno. Something has come up in the case. You remember when young Richard had that fight in the playground and you invited him to your home for dinner?"

Isabelle watched Bruno as he spoke on the phone. Without looking in her direction, he knew while he listened to Momu that she was appraising him. He sensed she was making up her mind about going or staying, if she was asked. The call ended, but he held the phone to his ear and delayed returning to the table, trying to fathom her intentions. He assumed that she liked him, and she was bored in St. Denis just as she was bored in Périgueux. She probably thought he might make an amusing diversion. But she was out of her depth here in the country. Had this been Paris, she would have known the ways to signal whether or not she was ready to stay, but she was smart enough to understand that the social codes were different here, the mating rituals more stately, more hesitant. She would probably find that interesting in itself, to flirt a while with a stranger in this strange land they called *la France profonde,* deepest France.

"Another dead end," said Bruno, turning off his phone. "Momu—that's the son of the murdered man—had Richard over to dinner when he was thirteen years old, and told him how proud the family was that his father had won the Croix de Guerre fighting for France. That's how he knew about the medal." He sank down on his chair. "Some coffee, Isabelle?"

"No thanks. I'd never sleep, and I have to get up early to check on those tires. J-J will be coming down tomorrow to make sure everything is in order for the guy from Paris."

He nodded. "By the way, there's some demonstration being arranged for Monday at noon, a march of solidarity organized by our communist councillor, but the mayor will probably lead it. I don't expect many people, mainly school-children."

"I'll tell J-J, make sure the RG are there with their cameras," she said, with a nervous laugh. "Just for the files. But I think we both know how much the official files can never know and explain." She stood. "I should go," she said, but didn't move.

"Isabelle, thank you for this unexpected but very pleasant evening, and Gigi thanks you for the dinner he's making from the scraps. Let me walk you to your car." When they reached it, he opened the car door for her. She kissed him briefly on both cheeks, but before she could close her door Gigi darted past Bruno's legs and put his paws on her thighs and stretched, trying to reach her face. She leaned over to pet him and he licked her face. She gave a start, then laughed, and Bruno pulled his dog away.

"Thank you, Bruno," she said. "I really enjoyed the evening. It's lovely here. I hope you'll let me come again."

"Of course," he said. He wondered if she felt disappointed to be leaving. "It would be my pleasure," he added, and was surprised by the brilliant smile she gave him in return, a smile that seemed to transform her face.

Isabelle closed the door, started the engine and drove off, watching him in her rearview mirror standing there waving farewell, Gigi at his knee. As the lights of her car disappeared he looked up and gazed at the great sweep of the stars twinkling in the black night above him, his thoughts jumbled and starting to race the way they sometimes did on those rare occasions when he could not sleep. He sighed and went back into the kitchen to wash the dishes, but feeling the tug of memory as he went about the familiar task. It had not just been the presence of Isabelle, the prospect she represented of a new woman in his life, it was her direct touch on the memory of his lost love.

What strange feminine alchemy had inspired Isabelle to run her finger down the spine of the slim volume of Baudelaire's poems? It was a gesture that had been characteristic of Katarina, a gentle touch of greeting to a well-remembered friend. And what intuitive force had led Isabelle's finger to the very book that Katarina had given him, the only tangible memory he had of her? He had half expected her to open the book and inevitably to read the inscription, but somehow she had let it be.

A snuffling at his feet brought him back to awareness of his surroundings. He blinked his eyes and kneeled to caress Gigi, who was waiting amiably at his feet, hoping that perhaps not all the scraps from dinner were gone. Bruno cradled the dog's head in his hands, scratching those soft spots behind its ears, then bent his own head so that their foreheads met and he made an affectionate noise deep in his throat, hearing its echo as his dog responded. Gigi twisted his head to lick Bruno's face, clambering up so that his front paws rested on his master's shoulders, the better to lick his ears and nuzzle into his neck. Bruno relished the contact and the affection, and hugged his dog before patting its shoulders and getting to his feet.

Time for bed, he told Gigi, for both of us, and he led the hound out into the yard. He took a last attentive look at the fence around his henhouse. An owl was hooting far off in the woods. He checked that nothing was left on the table, splashed water on the ashes in the barbecue and saw Gigi to his kennel, realizing as he watched his dog settle that he now deeply regretted his tame acceptance of Isabelle's departure. Why had he not kissed her and invited her to stay?

Bruno went back into his house, turned off the lights and, once in his bedroom, picked up the photo of a younger Bruno, beaming broadly at the camera, Katarina graceful and smiling beside him. That summer in Bosnia had been the only time they had together, a small chapter of happiness that he had known between the horror of the spring and the even deeper anguish of the winter that followed. His hand reached down to touch the scar at his waist from the sniper's bullet, a wound that had yet to be inflicted when the photo was taken. He felt again the sudden confusion of memories, of noise and flames, the world spinning as he fell, the glare of headlights and blood on the snow. It was a sequence he could never get straight in his mind, the events and images all jumbled. Only the soundtrack remained clear, a discordant symphony of helicopter blades in low rhythm against the counterpoint chatter of a machine gun, the slam of grenades, the squealing clatter of tank tracks and the shouting of men.

He replaced the photo and picked out Katarina's book from the shelf, and on an impulse opened it at random and raised it to his face to see if some elusive scent of her or of that summer might still remain. Whatever might have lingered was long gone. He turned to the flyleaf, to read yet again her inscription to him and to stare at the flowing signature. He could almost hear her voice, reading the poems aloud to him in that charmingly liquid French that she had taught her schoolchildren before the war came.

It was more than ten years since the summer of Katarina, and yet he felt her memory so strongly that it almost became her presence, each time a new woman began to stir his interest. Partly from courtesy, partly from a wish to protect his own privacy, he always put Katarina's photo away in a drawer when there was a chance that a new lover might see it. But this time he had been taken unawares by Isabelle, who had not only seen the photograph but read his Army files. She knew enough to put him into a wider context than the placid life of a village policeman. And some instinct had steered her hand to Katarina's book, to touch it but to leave it closed and in its place. It had been, Bruno concluded as he composed himself to sleep, an acknowledgment but not an invasion.

14

It was a lovely May morning as the Baron drove his big old Citroën up the lane beside Yannick's house. As they passed, Bruno glanced quickly up the side road that led to Hamid's lonely cottage, now sealed with police tape. They approached Pamela's farmhouse and the Baron slowed his car to a halt, gazed at the scene in solemn approval and then climbed out to stand and take a longer look. Bruno opened his door and joined him, enjoying the Baron's reaction to the surroundings and pleased that it matched his own. They looked in silence, until a drumming noise came from behind them and they turned to see two women on horseback, their hair flowing free, cantering toward them along the ridge and spurring into a near gallop as they saw the car and the two men.

Pamela was wearing a white shirt open at the neck, with a green silk scarf that flowed into her auburn hair, and some jeans stuffed into her riding boots. The Baron let out a low whistle of admiration that only Bruno could hear, and raised his hand in salute.

"We'll just be a moment, Bruno. And welcome to your friend," called Pamela as she reined in her snorting brown mare to a quick trot. Christine rode on at speed, lifting a hand briefly in greeting before bending over her horse's neck and racing on down the slope. Pamela turned back to call, "We'll take the saddles off and change and see you on the court. You can use the *cabane* by the swimming pool if you need to change."

"Two handsome women riding fast on horseback. *Mon Dieu*, but that's a magnificent sight," said the Baron, and Bruno knew that whatever happened on the tennis court, the day would be a success.

He had warned the Baron that the two women played in tennis dresses, so both men wore white shorts and T-shirts. It struck Bruno that their four white-clad figures looked almost formal as they met on the court and made introductions. The Baron bowed as he presented Pamela with a bottle of Champagne "to toast your victory, mesdames." She took it quickly to the *cabane,* where an ancient refrigerator purred noisily, and by the time she rejoined them, the Baron had invited Christine to be his partner and Bruno was sending forehands over the net to each of them in turn.

"It looks like you're stuck with me," he said as Pamela came onto the court, bringing a can of tennis balls.

"I always prefer to have the law on my side, Bruno," she said with a smile, and they put two balls in play, with Bruno sending his to Christine and the Baron sending backhands to Pamela. The women played well and with careful control, placing each ball deep, and Bruno found himself responding in kind and getting into a rhythm of forehand after forehand.

The first set went to four all, with Bruno barely holding serve. Pamela and Christine knew the strange ways of the grass court. They used their experience to position themselves while Bruno and the Baron tired themselves scrambling after each wayward bounce. The women still looked cool and fresh and in control, while the men were mopping their brows and flapping the fronts of their shirts.

At set point, Bruno waited for the crucial serve, swaying gently on the balls of his feet, knowing the Baron's game well enough to expect a slice. But the Baron fooled him, serving a fast ball to his forehand, and Bruno played it down the line back to Christine. She returned it to him, and he played the same shot back to her from the baseline. Five strokes, six and then eight, then Christine suddenly changed tactics and hit her next forehand hard to Pamela. She played it back to the Baron, and it was their turn to exchange strokes from the baseline. Then Pamela's sixth shot hit some bump in the grass surface and the ball bounced high and just within the sideline. The Baron scrambled after it but he barely reached the net with his flailing return. Game and set.

"What a magnificent rally," called Pamela, with an enthusiasm so warm that Bruno could not think it quite genuine. "Well done, Baron, and hard luck on that very unfair last bounce. I think you had us but for that."

"I need a drink," said Christine, running forward to shake Bruno's hand and then going back to kiss the Baron on both cheeks. "And I need a shower," Pamela said, laughing, "and then a drink. And thank you for the game and that last rally. I can't think when I played one that went so long."

Bruno admired the easy skill of the women in smoothing

bruised male egos. He and the Baron had been outplayed. Dripping with sweat, they looked as if they had been through three hard sets of singles instead of a single set of mixed doubles. The Baron, usually grim-faced and brooding when he lost, was almost purring with pleasure at their attention.

"You'll find a shower and towels in the *cabane*," Pamela told them. "We'll take our showers inside and see you out here in twenty minutes for the Champagne. Meanwhile, there are bottles of water in the refrigerator. Help yourselves."

Bruno mopped his neck with his towel, and put away his racket as the Baron limped up smiling.

"What charming girls," he said.

Bruno grinned a weary assent. They were indeed charming, and yes, they were also girlish, and if they could twist the cynical old Baron around their little fingers so easily, they were two very formidable women. After Bruno had drunk a liter of water, showered and changed, he sauntered out to the table by the pool, where four Champagne flutes and an ice bucket stood ready, beside a bottle of dark purple cassis. He looked discreetly at the label. It was a bottle of the real stuff from the Bourgogne, not the industrial black-currant juice they sold in supermarkets.

Pamela and Christine had changed into jeans and blouses when they reappeared carrying trays—with plates, knives and napkins on one, pâté, olives, cherry tomatoes and a fresh baguette on the other. The Baron uncorked his Champagne, poured a splash of cassis into each glass and then filled them carefully with the wine.

"Next time, you must let me partner you, Bruno," said

Christine. "Unless the Baron would like to help me take our revenge."

"I'm not changing a winning team," said Pamela. "I'll stick with Bruno."

"We are at your disposal, ladies," said the Baron. "Perhaps we might invite you to play at our club tournament later this summer. You would do very well, partnering each other or in the mixed doubles."

"Sorry, but I only have until mid-June," said Christine. "Then it's back to England to write up my research before the end of my sabbatical."

"That reminds me," said Bruno. "You know something of the archives here and the local wartime history. How would I go about researching a soccer team in Marseilles, around 1939?"

"Start with the local newspapers, *la Marseillaise* or *le Provençal,* or the sports paper, *l'Equipe,*" Christine said. "Contact the local sports federation to see if they have any records. If you have the names of the players, or of the team, it should be quite straightforward."

"I only have one player's name, but not the name of the team or any other information. The team played in an amateur youth league, and won a championship in 1940, but I think their coach had been a professional player. I have his name."

"It could be a long search, Bruno," Christine said. "Regional papers like *la Marseillaise* tend to keep microfiche records, but I'd be surprised if they have been digitized, and so you can't do an electronic search. You may have to go through all the issues for 1940. But if they won a championship, that would probably be at the end of the season, in the springtime, March or April. You might try just looking for those months. Is this to do with that murder inquiry you refused to tell us about when you were last here? We saw the reports in *Sud Ouest*."

"Yes. Hamid. Nothing seems to have been taken except his wartime medal and this old photo, so I'm curious to see if it might shed some light on the affair. It's just a chance—he may have taken the things down from the wall himself or thrown them away. We might be following a false trail, but so far we don't have much to go on."

"I thought I heard on Radio Périgord that some suspects had been detained, in Lalinde, was it not?" asked Pamela. "They didn't give any names."

"They're under eighteen, juveniles, so their names can't be released. Some local young people involved in the Front National have been the subject of police investigation, but so far there's no real evidence to connect them to Hamid's killing, or even to connect them with Hamid."

"I don't know too many young people around here," said Pamela thoughtfully. "Some of my guests have teenage children and it's always a good thing to introduce them to some young locals. We did that a bit last summer with a young French couple who played tennis on the court here. Rick and Jackie, I think they were called."

"Rick and Jackie?" Bruno said sharply. "Could that have been Richard and Jacqueline?"

Pamela shrugged. "I just knew them by those names. An attractive young couple, about sixteen or seventeen. She's a pretty thing, blond hair, a very good tennis player. He's slim, maybe sixty kilos. I think he said his father is a doctor around here. Why? Do you know them?"

"How did you meet them, Pamela? And when was this, exactly?"

"They said they'd been walking in the woods and noticed my tennis court. They said they'd never played on grass before and asked if they could give it a try. I had an English family with some teenage children and they spent the afternoon playing tennis. They seemed very pleasant and polite, but I got the impression they had been courting pretty energetically in the woods, rather than just walking. It must have been late August, maybe early September, last year. Rick and Jackie came two or three times. I think she had a car, but I haven't seen them this year."

"You say they came out of the woods and down to your property. Which woods, exactly?"

"Those over that hill." She pointed. "Over toward Hamid's place. From the hill, you can see both my place and his."

"Did they ever mention Hamid, or meet him, or see him here when he came to tell you how to prune your roses?"

"Not that I can recall."

"When they came to visit you again, did they come the same way, from the woods?"

"No, they came up the road by car. I remember it well because she drove too fast and I had to tell her to slow down."

"Did they go walking off into the woods again?"

"Yes, I think they did, teenage passion and all that. You're sounding very policeman-like and serious, Bruno. Do you think they could be connected to Hamid's murder?"

"I don't know, but it suggests that they may have known the old man, or seen him, or at least had the opportunity to do so, and other than that there is nothing to connect them with Hamid."

"They didn't seem like Front National types. They weren't skinheads or thuggish in any way. They seemed pretty well educated and had good manners, always saying please and thank you. They even brought me some flowers once. They spoke quite a bit of English, got on well with the English kids. They were really very pleasant—I enjoyed meeting them."

"Well, it may be nothing, but since we have so few leads, we have to follow them all. So I had better get back to work, but I want to stroll up to those woods and see whatever's to be seen before I go."

It was perhaps a kilometer to the first thin trees. Another three hundred meters through the woods and over the ridgeline, and there was Hamid's cottage, fifteen hundred meters or so away and the only building in sight. He walked along the fringe of the woods and found a small clearing of soft turf, sheltered and private but with a glorious view over the plateau. It was a perfect place for a romantic rendezvous in the open air, thought Bruno. He looked carefully around and found some old cigarette stubs and a broken wineglass under a bush. He would have to send the forensics team up here.

He walked briskly back to Pamela's house, where the Baron had drunk what was left of the Champagne. As Bruno approached, he rose, and they thanked the women for the game and strolled back to the Baron's car. They made no plans to play together again, but Bruno felt that they would. Now would not be a good time, Bruno thought, not with the knowledge that the suspects had visited Pamela, enjoyed her hospitality and played on the same tennis court where they had spent such an agreeable morning.

15

The magistrate, a dapper and visibly ambitious young Parisian named Lucien Tavernier, who might just have reached the age of thirty, had arrived on an early morning flight down to Périgueux. Bruno took an instant dislike to him when he noticed the predatory way he looked at Isabelle at the first meeting of the investigative team. It was just after eight a.m. and Isabelle had woken him with a phone call at midnight to say his presence would be required. Bruno had not wanted to go; he had a parade to organize for midday and he was not a member of the investigative team, but J-J had specially asked him to be there to explain the new evidence that put Richard and Jacqueline in the vicinity of Hamid's cottage. Without Bruno's phone call to J-J on the previous day, Richard would already have been released.

"What he said is that he used to go to the woods to have sex, and he hadn't even noticed Hamid's house since he had other matters on his mind," said J-J. With his hair awry and his shirt collar undone, he looked as if he'd barely slept as he gulped at the dreadful coffee they served at the police station. After one sip, Bruno had abandoned his plastic cup and was drinking bottled water instead. There was a bottle, a notepad, a pencil and a report on J-J's last interrogation sessions in front of each person at the conference table.

"Neither Richard nor Jacqueline have any alibi for the afternoon of the killing except one another, and they claim to have been in bed at her house in Lalinde," J-J went on. "But we know that she used her credit card to fill her car at a garage just outside St. Denis at eleven-forty in the morning. So they're both lying, and she at least could have been at the murder scene. This strengthens the evidence from the tire tracks on the way to Hamid's place, and we're awaiting the forensic report on the cigarette butts and wineglass and the used condoms found in the woods. But there's still no clear evidence from the house itself to demonstrate that they ever went into the place. So far, it's only circumstantial evidence, but in my view it points clearly to them. They were in the vicinity, if not necessarily at the murder scene. I should add that we have no traces of blood on their clothes or in her car. But I think we have enough cause to continue to detain them."

"I agree," said Tavernier briskly. "We have a clear political motive, and the opportunity, and they are lying—quite apart from the drugs." Tavernier studied them all through his chic black eyeglasses. His suit was black and clearly expensive, as was his knitted silk tie, and he wore a shirt with thick purple and white stripes. Lined up neatly on the conference table before him were a black leather-bound notebook and a matching Montblanc pen, the slimmest cell phone that

Bruno had ever seen and a computer small enough to fit into his shirt pocket that seemed to deliver his e-mails. Phone and computer had come from black leather pouches on his belt. To Bruno, Tavernier looked like an emissary from an advanced and probably hostile civilization.

"That's quite a strong case," Tavernier continued. "We have no other suspects at all, and my minister says it is clearly in the national interest that we resolve this case quickly. So if the forensic evidence from the woods places them there, I think we might be able to file formal charges—unless there are any objections."

He looked severely around the table, as if daring any of those present to challenge him. J-J was pouring more coffee, Isabelle was quietly studying her notes. A police secretary was taking minutes. Another bright young thing from the prefecture was nodding sagely, and the media specialist from police headquarters in Paris, a smart woman with blond streaks in her hair and sunglasses pushed back above her brow, raised a hand.

"I can schedule a press conference to announce the charges, but we'd better fix the timing to catch the eight p.m. news. Then we have the anti-racism demonstration in St. Denis at noon. You'll want to be there, Lucien. No?"

"Have you confirmed that the minister will be there?" he asked.

She shook her head. "Just the prefect and a couple of deputies from the National Assembly, so far. The Minister of Justice is stuck with meetings in Paris, but I'm waiting for a call from the interior ministry. The minister has a speech in Bordeaux in the evening, so there's a suggestion he might fly here first."

"He will," said Tavernier, obviously pleased at being first

with the news. "I just received an e-mail from a colleague in the minister's office. He's flying into Bergerac and plans to be at the mayor's office in St. Denis at eleven-thirty. I'd better be there." He looked at J-J. "You have a car and driver ready for me?" He turned to Isabelle with a smile. "Perhaps the inspector?"

"An unmarked police car and a specialist gendarme driver are at your disposal for the length of your stay. Inspector Perrault will be engaged in other duties," J-J replied, his tone studiously neutral. J-J had been bitter when he called Bruno on his cell phone earlier in the morning, as Bruno was driving to Périgueux from St. Denis. The young hotshot, as J-J called him, had been magistrate for only three months. The son of a senior Airbus executive who had been at the Ecole Nationale d'Administration at the same time as the new Minister of the Interior, Tavernier had gone straight from law school to work on the minister's private staff for two years and was already on the executive committee of the youth wing of the minister's political party. A glittering career evidently loomed. He would want this case prosecuted, tried and convicted with maximum dispatch and to his minister's entire satisfaction.

"I'm heading back to St. Denis after this meeting, so I could give you a lift," said Bruno.

Tavernier looked at Bruno, the only person there wearing a uniform, as if not sure what this ordinary policeman was doing in his presence.

"And you are?"

"Benoît Courrèges, chief of police of St. Denis. I'm attached to the inquiry at the request of the Police Nationale," he replied.

"Ah yes, our worthy *garde champêtre,*" Tavernier said, using the old term for the Police Municipale, dating back to the days when country constables had patrolled rural France on horseback.

"It might help your inquiries if I briefed you on the local background, and on some of the odd features about this case."

"It looks very straightforward to me," said Tavernier, picking up his little computer and flicking his thumb on a small knob as he studied the screen.

Bruno had learned from similar situations to ignore the arrogance and stick to his point. "Well, there's the question of the missing items, the military medal and the photograph of Hamid's old soccer team," he said. "They disappeared from the wall of the cottage where they'd always been kept. It might be important to find out where they went or who took them."

"Ah yes, the Croix de Guerre," Tavernier said, still studying his screen. He looked up and focused on Bruno and, adopting a patient and kindly tone as if he were addressing someone of limited intelligence, said, "It's the Croix de Guerre that persuades me that we have the right suspects. These young fascists from the Front National would detest the idea of an Arab being a hero of France. They probably threw it away in a river somewhere."

"But why take the photo of the old soccer team?"

"Who knows how these little Nazis think," Tavernier said airily. "A souvenir, perhaps, or just something else they wanted to destroy."

"If it were a souvenir, they'd have kept it and we'd have found it by now," said J-J.

"I'm sure you would," said Tavernier. "Now, when do we get the forensic report on that little love nest in the woods?"

"They promise to have it by the end of today," said Isabelle.

"Ah yes, Inspector Perrault," said Tavernier, turning to give her a wide smile. "How do *you* feel about our two prime suspects? Any doubts?"

"Well, I haven't attended all the questioning, but they look like very strong candidates to me," Isabelle said firmly, looking directly at Tavernier. Bruno felt a small bud of jealousy begin to uncurl inside him. Isabelle would not have a difficult choice to make between a lowly country cop and a glittering scion of the Parisian establishment.

"Naturally I'd like some firm evidence, or a confession," she went on. "I'm sure we all would. They both come from backgrounds that can afford them good lawyers, so the more evidence we have, the better. And maybe we should also be looking harder at those thugs from the Service d'Ordre, the security squad of the Front National. They are no strangers to violence. But again, we need evidence."

"Quite right," said Tavernier with enthusiasm. "That's why I'd like the forensics people to take a second look at the murder scene and at the clothes and belongings of our two suspects. Could you arrange that please, mademoiselle? Now that they know what they are looking for, the forensics experts might come up with something that puts them at the killing ground. Wouldn't that calm your doubts about circumstantial evidence, Superintendent? Or would you like me to call down some experts from Paris?"

J-J nodded. "Some of my doubts, yes, it would. But our

forensics team is very competent. I doubt that they'll have missed anything."

"You have other doubts?" Tavernier's question was silkily put, but there was irritation behind it.

"I don't quite get the motive," J-J said. "I see the obvious political motive, but why kill this Arab, at this particular time, in this particular way, tying up and butchering the old man as if he were a pig?"

"Why kill this one? Because he was there," said Tavernier. "Because he was alone and isolated and too old to put up much resistance and it was a remote and safe place to commit this murder. Then they took his medal to demonstrate that their victim was not really French at all. Yes, I think I have their measure. Now it's time for me to question these two young fascists myself. I'll have two hours with them before I have to leave for this little town called—what is it?—ah yes, St. Denis."

J-J's office was in spartan contrast to the man. J-J was overweight and looked scruffy inside his crumpled suit, but his desk was clean, his books and documents all neatly filed, and his newspaper precisely aligned with the edges of the low table where he sat, drinking some decent coffee that Isabelle had made in her own adjoining room. J-J had kicked off his shoes and smoothed his hair, and was riffling through a slim file that Isabelle had brought him. She was with him, looking cool and very efficient in a dark trouser suit with a red scarf at her neck, and what looked like expensive and surprisingly elegant black flats with laces. She looked at Bruno, who was also there, with a disinterested smile, and he felt a touch of embarrassment at the fantasies of her he had conjured up after she left his home.

"There's something odd about this military record of the victim," said J-J. "He first appears on the payroll of our First Army on 28 August 1944, listed as a member of the Commandos d'Afrique. That unit was part of something called Romeo Force, which had taken part in the initial landings in southern France on 14 August 1944, and they seized a place called Cap Nègre. Our man is not, apparently, listed as a member of the original assault force for the invasion. He just appears suddenly on 28 August at a place called Brignoles."

"I spoke with someone at the military archives," Isabelle said. "He told me that it wasn't uncommon for members of Resistance groups to join up with the French forces and stay with them throughout the war. The Commandos d'Afrique were a Colonial Army unit, originally from Algeria, and most of the rank and file were Algerians. We had taken heavy casualties at a place called Draguignan and took on local Resistance volunteers to fill our ranks. Since Hamid was Algerian, he was signed up and stayed with them for the rest of the war. In the fighting in the Vosges mountains in the winter, he was wounded and spent two months in the hospital and was promoted to corporal. And then, when they got into Germany, he was promoted to sergeant in April 1945, just before the German surrender."

"And he stayed in the Army after the war?" Bruno asked.

"He did," said J-J, reading from the file. "He transferred to the twelfth regiment of the Chasseurs d'Afrique, with whom he served in Vietnam, where he won his Croix de Guerre in a failed attempt to rescue the garrison at Dien Bien Phu. His unit was then posted to Algeria until the war ended in 1962 and the Chasseurs d'Afrique were formally retired from the French Army. But before that, along with some of the other long-serving sergeants, he was transferred to the training battalion of the regular Chasseurs, where he remained until he retired in 1979 after thirty-five years' service. He was hired as a caretaker at the military college at Soissons after one of his old officers became the commander."

"What's so strange about all of this, J-J?" Bruno asked.

"What's strange is that we can't find any trace of him in the Resistance groups around Toulon, where he was supposed to have been before joining the Commandos. Isabelle checked with the Resistance records. Since it was useful after the war to be able to claim a fighting record in the Resistance, most of the unit lists were pretty thorough. And there's no Hamid al-Bakr."

"It might not mean much," Isabelle said. "There aren't many Arab names in any of the Resistance groups and not many Spanish names either, although Spanish refugees from their civil war played a big part in the Resistance. But the records for the two main groups, the Armée Secrète and the Francs-Tireurs et Partisans, tend to be fairly reliable. He could have been in another group or he might have slipped through the net. He might even have used another name in the Resistance—it wasn't uncommon."

"It just nags at me a bit, like a loose tooth," said J-J. "Once Hamid was in the Army, the records are impeccable, but we can't track him before that. It's as if he just turned up out of nowhere."

"Wartime," Bruno said. "An invasion, bombing, records get lost or destroyed. And I can tell you one thing from my own military service: The official records may all look very neat and complete because that's how they have to be and how the company clerks file them. But a lot of the paperwork is pure invention, or just making sure the books balance and the numbers add up. What we know is that he served for thirty-five years and fought in three wars, his officers respected him enough to take care of him and he was a good soldier."

"Yes, all that is true," said J-J. "Which is why I had Isabelle look back a bit further."

"We asked the Marseilles and Toulon police to run a check, but there's not much left of the files before 1944 and they had nothing," Isabelle said. "The date and place of birth that he listed in Army records was Oran in Algeria on 14 July 1923. The guy at the archives said a lot of the Algerian troops listed Bastille Day as a birth date because they didn't know their real birthday and that was the easiest date to remember. Birth registers for Algerians were pretty hit and miss in those days, even if we could get access to the Algerian records. And we don't have a date for his arrival in France. As far as we can tell, he had no official existence until he turned up with the Commandos d'Afrique."

"I've been pushing this, Bruno, because I'm not sure about our two suspects," said J-J. "I talked with each of them separately for a long time, and I just don't feel confident that they did it. So I had Isabelle check back into Hamid's history to see if there were any clues there that might open other possibilities."

"Our friend Tavernier seems happy to go ahead and press charges," Bruno said.

"Yes, and I'm certainly not comfortable with that, not with the evidence we have so far," said J-J.

"Me neither," said Bruno, "but there doesn't seem to be much other evidence of any kind, either to incriminate them or to steer us anywhere else."

"See if you can get anything more on our mystery man from his family. He must have told them something about his childhood and growing up," said J-J. "Otherwise, we're stuck."

16

The mayor was quietly furious. Less than an hour remained before the parade was to begin and two of his most reliable standard-bearers had decided they would boycott it. It was the first time in living memory that they had turned him down. To reject a mayoral request in St. Denis was unheard of, and to decline his invitation when a minister of the republic and two generals were to grace the town's proceedings was close to revolution.

"Unless you can find somebody else you'll have to carry the flag of France, Bruno," the mayor said testily. "Old Bachelot and Jean-Pierre refuse to take part. They made it quite clear that they don't approve of Muslims, Algerians or immigrants in general and do not intend to honor them."

"What will Montsouris be carrying?" Bruno asked. "We can't have the red flag since there is no sign that Hamid had any politics at all, least of all communist."

"I think he's planning an Algerian flag," said the mayor, sounding tired of it all. "I've already had to do two interviews this morning, including a long one with France-Inter, and there's a woman from *Le Monde* who wants to see me this afternoon. All this attention, of the worst possible kind. I don't like it at all, Bruno. And now you say the magistrate seems convinced that young Richard is going to be formally charged with murder?"

"Tavernier is his name, very modern, a go-getter, very determined," said Bruno. "And very well connected."

"Yes, I think I knew his father from the Ecole Nationale." Bruno was not much surprised; the mayor seemed to know everybody who mattered in Paris. "And his mother wrote one of those dreadful books about the New Woman when feminism was all the fashion. I'll be interested to see how the boy turned out. You'd better go and make sure that everything is organized. We don't want chaos in front of all these media types. Quiet and dignified, that's the style."

Outside in the town square, two TV cameras were taking shots of the Mairie and the bridge, and a knot of what Bruno assumed were reporters had taken over two outdoor tables at Fauquet's café, all interviewing each other. At the bar inside were some burly men drinking beer, probably Montsouris's friends from the Confédération Générale du Travail. Bruno waved away a reporter who thrust a tape recorder toward him as he climbed into his van, and drove off to the school where the march was to begin, noting some buses parked in the lot in front of the bank. Montsouris must have organized a bigger turnout than expected.

Rollo had half the school lined up in the courtyard already, some of them leaning on homemade placards that said NO TO RACISM and FRANCE BELONGS TO ALL OF US. Rollo wore a small button in his lapel that read TOUCHE PAS À MON POTE, HANDS OFF MY BUDDY, a slogan that Bruno vaguely recalled from some other anti-racist movement of twenty years before. Some of his tennis pupils called out "*Bonjour,* Bruno," and he waved at them as they stood in line, chatting and looking reasonably well behaved and soberly dressed for a bunch of teenagers. Or perhaps they were intimidated by the presence of the entire St. Denis rugby squads, both the first and the A team, about thirty big men in uniform tracksuits who were there for Karim's sake, and as a guarantee against trouble.

Bruno looked around, but there was no sign of Montsouris, the man who had come up with the idea of the solidarity march. He would probably be in the bar with his friends from the union, but Montsouris's dragon of a wife was in the school yard with Momu, along with Ahmed from the public-works department. Just about all the immigrant families in town had turned out, and to Bruno's surprise, several of the women were wearing head scarves, something he had not seen before. He supposed it was a symbol of solidarity for the march. He hoped it was no more than that; St. Denis had so far been spared the arguments over Muslim identity that had been triggered by the government's ban on head scarves in schools.

"We'll leave here at eleven-forty, and that'll get us to the Mairie by midday," said Rollo. "It's all arranged. Ten or fifteen minutes for a couple of speeches and then we march to the war memorial with the town band, which gives us time to give the kids lunch before classes start again this afternoon."

"There may be more speeches than we expected," said Bruno. "The Minister of the Interior is turning up, and with all these TV cameras he'll certainly want to say a few words. And you'll have to carry the Tricolor. Bachelot and Jean-Pierre have decided to boycott the event since they have apparently developed strong feelings about immigrants."

"The bastards," snapped Madame Montsouris, who had somewhere found a small flag that Bruno assumed was the national emblem of Algeria. "And that bastard Minister of the Interior. He's as bad as the Front National. What right does he have to be here? Who invited him?"

"I think it was arranged with the mayor," Bruno told her calmly. "But the program doesn't change. We want an orderly commemoration of an old war hero, along with a show of solidarity with our neighbors against racism and violence. Quiet and dignified."

"We want a stronger statement than that," Madame Montsouris said loudly enough for the teachers and school-children to hear. "We have to stop this racist violence now, once and for all, and make it clear that there's no place for fascist murderers around here."

"Save it for the speeches," Bruno said. He turned to Momu. "Where's Karim? He ought to be here by now."

"On his way," said Momu. "He's borrowing a Croix de Guerre from old Colonel Duclos so he can carry the medal on a cushion at the war memorial."

"Don't worry, Bruno," said Rollo. "We're all here and everything's under control. I can carry the Tricolor if you want to stop the traffic. We'll start as soon as Karim arrives."

And no sooner had he said it than Karim's Citroën turned into the parking lot in front of the school and he came out in his rugby club tracksuit, holding a velvet cushion in one hand

and brandishing the small bronze medal in the other. Rollo formed them up, Momu and Karim and the family at the front with half a dozen of the rugby team, and then the school students in columns of three, each class led by a teacher and all flanked by the rest of the rugby team. Rollo shepherded a schoolboy with a small drum on a sash around his neck into the column beside him, and the boy started to beat out the cadence of a march with single taps of his drumstick.

Bruno stood back to let them get started and then went out to the main road to stop traffic. It looked like it was going to be a brave and dignified parade, until Montsouris's wife produced a bullhorn from a bag she was carrying and began chanting, "No to racism, no to fascism." Fine sentiments, but not quite the tone that had been planned. He was about to intervene when he saw Momu step back to have a word with her. She stopped her chanting and put the bullhorn away.

Two TV cameras were filming them as they marched along the Rue de la République, past the supermarket and the farmers' co-op, past the Crédit Agricole branch and over the bridge, lined on both sides with townspeople, to the town square and the Mairie. There, the mayor and the other dignitaries stood waiting on the low platform that was normally used for the music festival. With irritation, Bruno noticed that the town's small force of gendarmes was lined up with Captain Duroc in front of the podium. He had asked Duroc to post his men in twos at different spots around the square as a precaution. As the church bells began to ring out noon, the siren on top of the Mairie sounded, and the entire parade squeezed into the remaining space. There was already quite a crowd. The bar was empty and a third TV camera had joined the media group. The siren faded away and the mayor stepped forward.

"Citizens of St. Denis, *Monsieur le Ministre, mes généraux,* friends and neighbors," the mayor began, his practiced politician's voice carrying easily over the square. "We are here to show our sympathy with the family of our local teacher Mohammed al-Bakr at the tragic death of his father, Hamid. We are here to salute Hamid as a fellow citizen, as a neighbor, and as a war hero who fought for our dear native land. We all know the brutal circumstances of his death, and the forces of order are working tirelessly to bring justice to his family, just as we in our community are here to show our revulsion against all forms of racism and hatred of others for their origin or their religion. And now I have the honor to present *Monsieur le Ministre de l'Intérieur,* who has joined us today to bring the condolences and support of our government."

"Send the Arab bastards back where they came from," came a shout from somewhere at the back, and everybody turned to look as the minister stood uncertainly at the microphone. Bruno began to move through the crowd, looking for the idiot who had called out.

"Send them back! Send them back! Send them back!" A chant had begun, and with a sinking heart Bruno saw three flags of the Front National lift from the crowd and start to wave. *Putain!* Those buses he'd seen had not been full of Montsouris's union friends after all. He felt a flurry in the crowd behind him and a knot of rugby men with Karim at their head began pushing their way through toward the flags.

Then came a howl from a bullhorn and another amplified

chant began of "Arabs go home! Arabs go home!" Montsouris's wife joined in with her own bullhorn, calling, "No to racism!" and the first volley of rotten fruit, eggs and vegetables began sailing through the air toward the stage. This has been well organized, thought Bruno. He had seen three buses in the parking area, say thirty or forty men in each, so there were probably as many as a hundred of them here—and only thirty men from the rugby club and a handful of Montsouris's union men to stop them. This could be very nasty, and all on national television. One of the Front National flags went down as the rugby men reached it, and groups of men began punching each other as women started to scream and run away.

There was not much Bruno could do as a lone policeman, but he began pushing his way back toward the stage. His priority now was to get the schoolchildren clear. He'd leave the gendarmes to look after the dignitaries. A sudden charge by some burly men, Montsouris among them, nearly knocked him down, and as he scrambled for balance, a cabbage hit the back of his head and knocked his cap off. Quickly he bent to grab it, otherwise the schoolchildren might not know who he was. He found Rollo already trying to steer the children into the shelter of the covered market. A handful of the older boys slipped aside and joined in the charge against the groups of Front National supporters.

Amplified howls of "Send them back! Send them back!" battled against bullhorn slogans of "No to racism! No to fascism!" as the dignitaries put their hands over their heads against the volleys of tomatoes and scampered into the Mairie past a protective gauntlet of otherwise useless gendarmes. Captain Duroc went into the Mairie with the mayor, the minister and the two generals, the gold braid of whose dress uniforms looked the worse for wear after the barrage of old fruit and smashed eggs.

Bruno, Momu and Rollo managed to get the schoolchildren into the market. Shouting to make himself heard over the din of chanting protesters, Bruno told Rollo and Momu to get the youngest children into the café and tell Fauquet to make sure the door was locked and the shutters down; then to call the firemen and tell them on his behalf to get their fire engines into the square *now,* with their sirens going and their water hoses ready to send out some high-pressure jets to clear the area.

Bruno took in the scene around him. In the confused mêlée in front of the hotel, flags and placards were being turned into clubs and lances. Another smaller fight was under way beside the steps that led to the old town, and a group of St. Denis women, Pamela and Christine among them, were trying to escape up the steps as some skinheads grabbed at them. The crowd was thinning and Bruno pushed his way through, seized the first of the thugs by the collar, kicked his feet from under him and shoved him into the legs of two of his cronies. That made enough space for Bruno to reach the foot of the steps and get between the thugs and the women.

"Get out of here!" he shouted at the women as the thugs closed in, trying to grab him. Bruno was moving automatically into a fighting stance now, his eyes scanning the scene for threats and targets. He dropped his arms, ducked and rammed his head into the stomach of his nearest assailant, seized the leg of another and pulled him off balance, and then thumped his fist into the throat of the next, who sank to his knees, choking.

That stopped the first rush, and he knew from his training that now was the time to attack, when they had lost their momentum. Bracing himself on the steps, he jumped at one youth who was brandishing a length of wood, with a Front National poster attached. He slammed the heel of one hand into the base of the youth's nose, then spinned to ram a vicious elbow into the solar plexus of another. He used the turn to kick yet another on the side of his knee and he was back at the base of the steps, three men down before him.

One of the women stepped down beside Bruno and deliberately kicked the choking skinhead in the testicles. It was Pamela, who was drawing back her foot to do it again. He stretched out his arms to hold her back and keep the thugs away from the rest of the women when he felt a thudding blow on the side of his face. Then he was punched hard in the kidneys and kicked in the knee and someone else was grabbing at his ankle. He knew that the first rule of brawling was to stay on your feet, but he was dazed and he felt himself start to go down. He tried to turn, to brace his arm against the stone wall, but someone was holding tight on to his leg and two more men were coming at him. He flailed at the first one and tried to kick the man holding his leg, then pulled hard on his hair, and the grip on his ankle slackened. But there were too many . . .

And then there was Isabelle, leaping into the air, kicking out one lethal foot aimed straight at the belly of the man in front of Bruno. She dropped, pirouetted and launched a second high kick into the throat of another thug, and then landed and delivered two hard, short punches to the nose of the man holding Bruno's ankle. Suddenly free to move, he turned to where the first blow to his head had come from and saw a middle-aged stranger backing away. Bruno grabbed an arm and twirled the man, seizing the back of his jacket and hauling it upward to imprison his arms, then tripped him and planted his boot hard on the back of his prisoner's neck. The others retreated.

"Thank you," he said to Isabelle. She smiled and nodded and darted off to the brawl still under way in front of the hotel. Bruno released his foot from his prisoner. The man groaned, shook his head and began to crawl away. Bruno ignored him.

He climbed the steps to get a clearer view, and saw what he had to do next. He trotted back to the small squad of gendarmes milling outside the Mairie. As he heard the sound of windows being smashed he shouted, "Follow me—and start blowing your whistles."

The Front National bullhorn seemed to be just in front of the hotel, and that was where he headed. Four or five men were down on the cobblestones. The rugby men knew what they were doing. They had organized themselves into pairs, and fought back-to-back. Karim picked up a heavy metal garbage can, which he raised over his head and threw into the knot of men guarding the Front National flags. The flag fell and the "Send them back!" bullhorn squealed in electronic pain and went silent. Then Bruno led the gendarmes into the resulting confusion and started handcuffing the ones on the ground. All of a sudden, it appeared to be over. Men were still running, but running away.

Bruno shouted to the burliest of the gendarmes, a decent man he had known for years and who was his best friend among the local cops, "Jean-Luc! There are three buses in the bank parking lot. Go and immobilize them—that's what these bastards came in and that's how they'll try to get out. Take a couple of your men with you and handcuff the drivers if you have to. Or get some cars to form a blockade to keep the buses from leaving."

Then the fire trucks arrived, two of them taking up most of the square, and the firemen climbed out and began to help. The first casualty they found was Ahmed. He was unconscious, his face bloodied from a smashed nose, and one of his front teeth was missing. A smaller red command truck then screeched to a halt beside Bruno, its siren wailing, and Morisot, the professional fireman who ran the local station, asked Bruno what his men could do.

"Start with first aid for those who need it, then round up anyone you don't recognize and lock them in your truck," Bruno said. "We'll sort it all out later at the gendarmerie."

Then he bent to check on young Roussel, a fast winger on the rugby team but too slim and small for this kind of fighting. He was dazed and winded and would have a magnificent black eye, but he was otherwise okay. Beside him, Lespinasse, short and squat and tough as they come, was on his knees and retching. "Bastards kicked me in the balls," he grunted. Now a TV camera and a microphone were in Bruno's face, and a concerned voice asked him what had happened.

"We were attacked in our hometown by a bunch of outside extremists. That's what happened." Bruno said angrily. He was composed enough to know you always get your side of the story out first because that would define the subsequent coverage.

"We were holding a quiet and peaceful parade and a meeting to commemorate a dead war hero and some jerks began chanting racist taunts and throwing crap and beating people up," he said. "Mainly schoolchildren were gathered here in our town square, but these extremists didn't seem to care. They had organized this attack. They hired buses to get here and brought their banners and bullhorns and they came with one intention—to wreck our town and our parade. But they didn't reckon with the people of St. Denis."

"What about casualties?"

"We are still counting."

"What about your own injuries?" he was asked. "That blood all over your face?"

He put his hand to his face and it did indeed come away bloody. "I hadn't noticed," he said.

The camera then turned away as an ambulance blared its way into the square. In front of the smashed plate-glass window of the Hôtel St. Denis, Dr. Gelletreau was kneeling beside one of the prone bodies.

"A couple of broken legs, a cracked collarbone and a few broken noses. Nothing much worse than a good rugby match," Gelletreau said.

Bruno looked around the town square. He saw fire engines and ambulances, broken windows, cobblestones littered with smashed fruit, eggs and vegetables, and frightened young faces peering from behind the stone pillars of the market. He glanced up to the windows of the Mairie and spotted some shadowed faces peering out from the banqueting chamber. So much for today's lunch, he thought, and began organizing the transfer of those arrested over to the gendarmerie. That idiot Duroc, thought Bruno; this is *his* job.

17

Dougal, Bruno's Scottish pal from the tennis club, almost never interfered in the official business of St. Denis, even though the mayor had twice asked him to join his list of candidates for election to the local council. After selling his own small construction company in Glasgow and taking an early retirement in St. Denis, Dougal had become bored and started a company called Delightful Dordogne that specialized in renting out houses and *gîtes* to tourists in the high season. A lot of the foreign residents in the area had signed up with him, taking their own vacations elsewhere in July and August and showing a handsome profit from the tenants to whom Dougal rented their homes. With the handymen, cleaners, gardeners and swimming-pool maintenance staff that he hired to service the holiday homes, Dougal had become a significant local employer. Bruno thought it made sense, with so many foreigners moving into the district, to have one of them on the council to represent their views. Dougal had always declined, pleading that he was too busy and his French too flawed. But the day after the disturbances he was in the council chamber with the rest of the delegation of local businessmen. Speaking a serviceable French, he stated the obvious—how bad the TV news reports of the previous evening had been.

"I've had three cancellations today, all from good and regular customers, and I'm expecting more. It even made the English papers. Look at this," he said, and tossed a stack of newspapers onto the table. Everybody had already seen them. Bruno's picture was on the front page of *Sud Ouest,* his arms outstretched as he had tried to shelter Pamela and Christine and the other women, just before he had been knocked down. The headline read ST. DENIS—THE FRONT LINE. The photo should have been of Isabelle, he thought.

"All credit to you, Bruno, you did a great job, but this is very bad for business," Dougal said. There were murmurs of agreement around the council table.

"How long is this going to go on?" demanded Jérôme, who ran a small theme park of French history where Joan of Arc was burned at the stake twice a day and Marie Antoinette was guillotined every hour, with medieval jousting in between. "It is up to the police to end this quickly, arrest somebody and get it over with. Interviewing suspects with no real result is going to spark more trouble from the Right and more counterdemonstrations from the Left and more bad publicity on TV. It will ruin our season."

"Listen," said the mayor. "There's been a hideous racist murder and passions have been aroused on both Left and Right. We've been assigned extra gendarmes to keep order and we have over forty people charged with riot and assault, so they're unlikely to bother us again. This is an isolated event. It may well hurt our business this year, but the effects won't last. We just have to grit our teeth and wait this process out."

"I'm not sure I'll still be in business next year," said Franc Duhamel, who ran one of the biggest campgrounds. He said this every year, but this time he might be proved right. "I borrowed a lot of money to finance that big expansion and the new swimming pool, and if I have a bad season I'm in real trouble. If it hadn't been for all those Dutch guys who came down for the motocross rally, I'd have been in trouble already."

"I've talked to the regional managers of the banks," said the mayor. "They understand that this is a temporary problem, and they won't be closing anybody down—not if they want to get any business from this commune again. And not unless they want to make an enemy of the Minister of the Interior. You all saw the report of his speech last night, about the whole of France standing firmly with the brave citizens of St. Denis."

The politician had been trying to put the best possible face on what had for him been a humiliation, shouted down from speaking and pelted with fruit and eggs. To be seen on TV presiding helplessly over a riot was not a good image for a Minister of the Interior, so naturally he had tried to spin it differently in his scheduled speech in Bordeaux. Bruno doubted very much that he would lift a finger to help any troubled businessman falling behind on his bank loans. He would never be able to hear of St. Denis again without an instinctive shiver of distaste. But such assurances were what the businessmen needed to hear from their mayor.

"We need some temporary tax relief for this year to help us get through this bad patch," said Philippe, the manager of the Hôtel St. Denis, who usually acted as spokesman for the town's business community. "We know taxes have to be paid, but we want the council to agree to give us some time, so that rather than pay in June, we can pay in October when the season is over. If we go down, the whole town goes down, so we see this as a sort of investment by the town in its own future."

"That's a useful idea," said the mayor. "I'll put it to the council."

"The other thing on our minds is that new head of the gendarmes," said Duhamel. "He was useless, totally useless. If it hadn't been for Bruno taking charge it could have been a lot worse. We'd like you to ask for Captain Duroc to be transferred. Nobody in town has any respect for him after yesterday."

"I'm not sure that's fair," said Bruno. He had felt less angry at Duroc when he arrived at the bank parking lot after the riot and saw the three buses blocked by a dozen of the gendarmes' motorbikes, a burly cop standing guard at each door, and the captain taking the names and addresses of the forty-odd men detained inside. Two blue gendarmerie vans were parked beside the buses.

"His immediate reaction was to ensure that the mayor and distinguished guests were secure," Bruno went on. "Although he is obviously new in the town and a bit short of experience, I'm not sure we have anything to reproach him with."

"Bruno could be right," the mayor chimed in. "I'd rather we used the sympathy we now have in official circles to get some financial help than squander whatever influence we have in a fight with the defense ministry to get the captain removed."

"That could have gone a lot more disagreeably," said the mayor when he and Bruno were left alone. "Are you sure you should be at work? You looked pretty bad on TV last night with that blood running down your face."

"I used to get worse on the rugby field every week. Did you see how Inspector Perrault rescued me, by the way?"

"Yes," the mayor said. "The Minister of the Interior was most impressed with her martial skills. I suspect the inspector will find herself promoted back to a staff job in his Paris office with that karate black belt of hers, or whatever it is she has. An elegant and very dangerous woman—they love that sort of thing in Paris. I'll make you a bet that Inspector Perrault will soon be in a position to help us if needed."

"I'm not sure she'd take such a job if it were offered. She's an independent sort of woman."

"You're certainly in a better position to know than I am." The mayor knew more than he let on, Bruno always assumed. "What's going on with those goons who were arrested? I assume that's being handled by the Police Nationale in Périgueux?"

"It should be. I'll find out."

Bruno had barely got back to his own office and opened his mail when the mayor burst in, muttering, "*Merde*. That fool woman . . . one of the phone calls Mireille sat on while we were chatting was from the Café des Sports. I told her to interrupt me for anything urgent. Captain Duroc has apparently arrested Karim for assault. Can you find out what's going on?"

"Assault? It was self-defense." Bruno conjured up the image of Karim picking up the garbage can and hurling it at the knot of Front National men. He winced. It had seemed a good idea at the time, but if that crucial moment of the brawl had been caught by the TV cameras, Karim could be in trouble.

"Do you remember seeing Karim throw the garbage can?" he asked the mayor.

"Yes, it helped turned the tide. But I suppose it could be seen as assault with a weapon. Still, I think the minister and the generals and I could testify that Karim did the right thing."

"Yes, but there's another witness—the TV cameras. Front National has access to clever lawyers and they would relish filing a complaint against an Arab. Even if the police decide not to press charges upon their urging, the victims could do so."

"*Putain!*" The mayor slammed a fist into the palm of his other hand. He paced back and forth before Bruno's desk. "How do we fix this?"

"I'll see what I can do with the police in Périgueux," said Bruno. "But if there's a magistrate being assigned to bring charges against the Front National, he'd also be the one to decide about charges against Karim, and that's way above my head. If that's the case, you'll probably have to see what influence you can bring to bear. It should be a local magistrate, so you might be able to get the prefect to have a quiet word with somebody. A lot will depend on the statements taken by the police, so depositions by you and the minister and the generals would be very useful."

The mayor took a pad and pen from Bruno's desk and began to scribble some notes.

"The first thing is to find out exactly on what grounds the gendarmes arrested Karim, and whether charges have been filed by the Front," Bruno said. "I'll do that."

"Is it possible that the FN is charging Karim so they'll have some leverage? If we drop the charges against them, they'll drop the charges against Karim? They can hardly like the idea of forty of their militants getting charged with riotous assembly, especially not after members of their security squad were charged with drug trafficking."

"Maybe. I just don't know. I'll go and see what I can find out at the gendarmerie," Bruno said, grabbing his cap and heading for the stairs.

"And I'd better go and see if there's anything we can do for Rashida at the café, and we'd better call Momu. He may not know about this yet," said the mayor.

"If Karim's convicted of violent assault he's likely to lose his tobacco license, and that means the end of his café and probably bankruptcy," Bruno said. "If those bastards insist on a deal where we have to drop all charges against them, we may not have a lot of choice but to agree."

18

Bruno always savored a long stroll along the Rue de Paris, the main shopping street of St. Denis. Built in the days when a street had to be wide enough for a horse and cart to turn in, not a single building was less than two centuries old, and only the church stood more than three stories tall. Despite the modern shop fronts on the ground floor, women still leaned from the balconies of the apartments above as their grandmothers and great-grandmothers always had, summoning their kids from playing in the alleys, calling to one another across the street and hanging their washing out to dry on the wrought-iron railings. There was something slow and timeless in the ways of his town and in the familiarity of the street and its people that he found calming, despite the bustle of errands and commerce and the constant metallic ballet of cars trying to squeeze themselves into the narrowest of parking places.

But today, the Rue de Paris slowed him down even more because everybody wanted to talk about the riot. He had to shake the hands of all the old men filling out their horse-racing bets at the Café de la Renaissance, though he refused their offers of a *petit blanc.* The women standing in line at the butcher's shop all wanted to kiss him and tell him they were proud of him. More women wanted to do the same at the pâtisserie, and Monique insisted on giving him one of his favorite *tartes au citron* as a token of her renewed esteem. He walked on, shaking hands at the barber's shop and again at Fabien's Rendezvous des Chasseurs, where Bruno bought his shotgun cartridges.

Fabien wanted his opinion on a new lure he was inventing to tempt the fish in that fiendish corner of the river where only the most perfectly cast fly could evade the trees and boulders. Jean-Pierre was tinkering with a bike in front of his shop and raised an oily hand in salute. Not to be outdone, Bachelot the shoemaker darted from his shop, nails still gripped between his lips and carrying a small hammer, to shake Bruno's hand warmly. Didier came out from the Maison de la Presse to make sure Bruno had seen the newspapers and to assure him that at least three small boys had bought scrapbooks to record the sudden fame of their local policeman, and he was joined by the ladies in the flower shop and Colette from the dry cleaner. By the time Bruno had reached the open ground in front of the gendarmerie and greeted the two rugby forwards who were making a success of their Bar des Amateurs, refusing their offer of a beer, he felt restored by the familiar rhythm of the town and its people.

Francine was at the desk in the gendarmerie, and she had been stationed in St. Denis long enough to understand Karim's importance to the town as its star rugby player, which had to be the reason for Bruno's visit. After he kissed her cheeks in greeting, she jerked a thumb toward the closed door of Duroc's office and rolled her eyes to signal her own view of Karim's arrest. She beckoned him closer and spoke very quietly.

"He's in there with Karim and a magistrate from Périgueux who just turned up this morning with a couple of videotapes," she whispered. "He's the one behind this arrest, Bruno. Duroc is just obeying orders."

"Did you recognize the guy from Périgueux?"

She shook her head. "He's new to me, but a very fancy dresser. And he came in a car with a driver, parked over there by the vet's office. He made the driver carry in the video machine."

"*Merde,*" said Bruno. It must be Tavernier, already armed with the TV film of Karim's part in the brawl. He thanked Francine and strolled out to the trees that shaded the old house containing the office for Dougal's Delightful Dordogne. There he pulled out his cell phone and called the mayor to warn him that Tavernier was now the problem.

"I'm with Rashida at the café and she's in hysterics," the mayor said. Bruno could hear Rashida in the background. "I called Momu's house to get Karim's mother over here," he went on, "but then she called Momu at school and he's heading for the gendarmerie. You'd better make sure he does nothing foolish, Bruno, and I'll have to tackle Tavernier. The moment you have Momu calmed down, get hold of Tavernier and say that I want to see him urgently, as an old friend of his father."

"Do you have a plan?" Bruno asked.

"Not yet, but I'll think of something. Is there a lawyer in there with Karim?"

"I don't think so. Can you call Brosseil? He's on the board of the rugby club."

"Brosseil is just a notary," the mayor said. "Karim will need a real lawyer."

"We can get a real lawyer later. We just want Brosseil to go in there, tell Karim to say absolutely nothing, and insist that anything he *has* said so far be struck from the record since he was denied legal representation."

"You know that's not French law, Bruno."

"Yes, but it is European law, and Tavernier won't want to run afoul of that. Brosseil has to keep on saying so. That will buy us time and keep Karim quiet. And do you have the deposition yet from the minister or those two generals on what they saw in the square?"

"From the generals, yes. They faxed it. Nothing yet from the minister," said the mayor.

"Tavernier won't know that. If he thought that his prosecution of Karim called into question the deposition of a minister, not to mention two senior figures in the defense ministry, he might have second thoughts."

"Good thinking, Bruno. We'll try it. But first you had better stop Momu."

Bruno poked his head in around the door and told Francine to block Momu at all costs and to call him as soon as Momu appeared. Then he stationed himself at the end of the Rue de Paris, one of the two routes that Momu could be taking, just in time to see Momu pedaling furiously toward him.

"Hold it, Momu," he said with his hand up. "Let me and the mayor take care of this."

"Out of my way, Bruno," he shouted angrily, steering around him and thrusting out a powerful arm to push him away. Bruno hung on to his arm and the bike began to topple. Momu was stuck, his feet on the ground, his bike between his legs and his arm still in Bruno's firm grip.

"Get off, Bruno," he yelled. "The rugby boys are on their way, along with half the school. We can't have them rounding people up like this. It's a damn *rafle* and we've had enough."

"Rafle" was the term the Algerians had used for the mass roundups staged by the French police during the Algerian war, and before that to refer to Gestapo raids against French civilians.

"It's not a *rafle*, Momu," Bruno said, trying to match his intensity.

"The Nazis kill my father and leave him like a piece of butchered meat and now you take my son into your dungeons. Out of my way, Bruno! I've had it with French justice."

"It's not a *rafle*, Momu," Bruno repeated, trying to catch the man's eyes with his own. He let go of Momu's arm and gripped his handlebars instead. "It's Karim answering some questions and the mayor and I are on your side. The town's on your side. We have a lawyer coming and we're going to do this right. If you go charging in there you'll make things worse for Karim and do yourself no good. Believe me, Momu."

"Believe you?" Momu scoffed. Then he braced himself and seemed to calm but his face turned cold. "I might believe you, Bruno, but I've had it with that uniform you wear and this damned system it stands for. It was French police who killed hundreds of us in those *rafles* back during the war. Police like you rounded up Algerians and bound them hand and foot and threw them in the River Seine. Never again, Bruno. Never again. Now get out of my way."

A crowd was gathering, led by Gilbert and René from the Bar des Amateurs.

"Have you heard?" Momu shouted. "The gendarmes arrested Karim. He's in there. I have to get to him."

"What's this, Bruno?" asked Gilbert. "Is this right?"

"Calm down, everybody," Bruno said. "It's true. The gendarmes came and picked him up and there's a magistrate now questioning him about the brawl in the square with those Front National guys. The mayor and I are trying to get things fixed. We have a lawyer coming and we're standing by Karim, just as we expect you all to do. We can't have people charging into the gendarmerie—it will just make things worse."

"What's Karim supposed to have done?" René wanted to know.

"Nothing, nothing," said Momu. "He's done nothing. He was defending himself against those Nazi bastards, defending you."

"We don't know yet," said Bruno, keeping firm hold of Momu's handlebars. "It looks as if they are considering a charge of assault because Karim threw that garbage can."

"Bruno, Bruno," shouted a new voice, and Brosseil came up trotting, trying to tighten the knot of his tie. "The mayor just called me, said I'd find you here."

Whatever the mayor had told the notary, Bruno had an angry Momu and a gathering crowd to deal with and a scene that threatened to turn ugly. He had to keep the town on his side and that meant explaining what he planned to do. Keeping one hand on the bike he raised his voice as he addressed Brosseil.

"We want you to go in and insist on seeing Karim as his legal representative, and tell him to say nothing and sign nothing. No statements. And then you say you demand anything he has said should be struck from the record because it was said while Karim was denied a lawyer. Then you tell them you will be filing a formal complaint in the European Court of Justice for denial of legal representation, and suing Captain Duroc personally."

"Can I do that?" Brosseil asked. He was usually a self-important man but he suddenly looked deflated.

"It's European law, and it holds good in France," Bruno said, suddenly grateful for those tendentious pamphlets in European law that regularly arrived on his desk. "They might try to deny it, but just bluster and shout and threaten, and above all stop Karim from saying anything and we'll get a criminal lawyer here as soon as we can. Just refuse to take no for an answer."

Brosseil, whose main work was to draw up wills and notarize sales of property, squared his shoulders like a soldier and marched off to the gendarmerie. This might just be his finest hour.

"You have to trust me, Momu," Bruno said, turning back toward the swelling crowd. "I have to go in there now and try to help sort things out and I can't have an angry mob shouting outside or forcing their way in." He slowly let go of Momu's handlebars and handed him his own phone. "Call the mayor. It's on speed dial, so just hit number one and then press the green button and you'll reach him. The mayor and

I have a plan. Talk with him. Calm down and calm these people down. René, Gilbert—I'm relying on you to help keep things under control here." With that, Bruno followed Brosseil.

The door to Duroc's office was wide open and the shouts of angry men mingled with the soundtrack of the riot from a video playing on the TV. Duroc was standing beside his desk roaring at Brosseil to get out, but the usually meek notary was standing his ground and yelling back with dire threats about the European Court. Tavernier was sitting calmly behind Duroc's desk, watching the confrontation with an air of amusement. Karim sat, hunched and baffled, before the desk. Bruno sized up the situation, then moved to the TV and switched it off. Brosseil and Duroc stopped shouting in surprise.

"Gentlemen, please," he said. "I have an urgent message for the magistrate. A confidential matter." He turned to Duroc, shook him warmly by the hand and began steering him out of the door. "*Mon Capitaine,* please, just a brief moment. Thanks so much." Bruno kept murmuring smooth platitudes while his other hand grabbed Brosseil's coat and tugged him along until he had them both in the hallway. He extricated himself, told Karim to join his lawyer in the hall and closed the door. He leaned his back against it and scrutinized Tavernier, whose expression was sardonic.

"So what about this message for me?" Tavernier said mockingly.

"An old friend and classmate of your father, Senator Mangin, requests the pleasure of your company," said Bruno.

"Ah yes, the mayor of St. Denis, making up for the disappointments of his political career in Paris by running the affairs of this turbulent little town. My father tells amusing stories of his old classmate. Apparently he was out of his depth even then. Please convey my sincere respects to the mayor, but tell him I am detained on judicial business."

"I think the mayor's business is more urgent, monsieur," Bruno said.

"I don't agree. Please send the others back in when you leave, except for that ridiculous little notary—you can take him with you."

"I can do that, but I thought you'd be interested in the depositions from the generals and the minister who witnessed the events. I think the mayor wishes to discuss them with you before any further judicial decisions are made."

"Very clever," said Tavernier after a long silence. "Are the depositions very flattering about the role of our Arab?"

"I wouldn't know. I haven't seen them. I only know the mayor wants to discuss them with you, in the interest of furnishing all possible assistance to the judicial authorities."

"Like sending that pompous little notary in here spouting about the European Court of Justice."

"I don't know what you're talking about," said Bruno. "I do know that no responsible policeman would stand in the way of allowing someone the benefit of legal advice if they're being questioned. I'm sure you and Captain Duroc would agree."

"A country policeman who follows the judgments of the European Court of Justice," Tavernier said. "How very impressive."

"And the European Court of Human Rights," Bruno said.

"The law everywhere is evenhanded, *Monsieur le Chef de Police*. The outside agitators involved in the riot are facing prosecution, and so are the local townspeople who reacted with undue force. And we are still seeking to establish who was responsible for starting the violence."

"Then, monsieur, I am sure you will want to waste no time in consulting the depositions of such eminent witnesses as the generals and the minister, as the mayor invites you to do."

A silence ensued as Tavernier kept his eyes fixed on Bruno's, and Bruno could only guess at the calculations of personal and political ambition that were taking place behind the young man's calm features. He kept his own face similarly immobile.

"You may inform the mayor that I shall be in his office within thirty minutes," Tavernier said finally, and turned his gaze away.

"One last thing. The mayor and I kindly request that you release into our protection the young man you were questioning," Bruno said. "We guarantee that he will be available to you at any time for further questioning, along with a suitable legal representative."

"Very well," said Tavernier. "You may take your violent Arab along for the moment. I think we have all the evidence we need anyway." He gestured toward the video.

"He was born here, so the law says he's a French citizen. He's as French as you or me, but I'll remember you said that." Bruno turned and walked out. He collected Karim and Brosseil on the way and made to leave. Duroc started to protest but Bruno looked at him and pointed back to the closed door of Duroc's office. "Check with the boy wonder in there," he said.

As they emerged from the gendarmerie, a cheer came up from the crowd that had gathered at the corner of the Rue de Paris as Momu trotted forward joyfully to embrace Karim. Half the town seemed to be present, including the two old enemies of the Resistance, Bachelot and Jean-Pierre, both of them beaming. Bruno thanked Brosseil, who was jaunty with pride at his own part in the proceedings and too excited even to think about whether he might send someone a bill for his services. Bruno knew Brosseil's forgetfulness would not last long. He slapped Karim on the back, and Momu came up apologetically to shake his hand.

"Was that true what you said about the *rafles,* throwing people in the Seine?" Bruno asked.

"Yes. Over two hundred of us. Nineteen sixty-one. They even made a TV program about it."

Bruno shook his head, and not in disbelief. "I'm very sorry," he said.

"It was the war," said Momu. "And at times like this I get worried that it isn't over." He looked across to where Karim was being led into the Bar des Amateurs for a celebratory beer. "I'd better make sure he just has the one and gets back to comfort Rashida. Thank you sincerely, Bruno. I apologize for my actions and my words."

"I understand how hard a time this is for you with your father and now this. Give my respects to Rashida," Bruno said, and walked off alone up the Rue de Paris to brief the mayor.

19

As Bruno fed his chickens, he pondered what to wear for dinner that evening. He had decided on a pair of chinos, a casual shirt and a sports jacket. A tie would be too much. He took a bottle of his unlabeled Lalande de Pomerol from the cellar and put it on the seat of his car beside the bunch of flowers he had bought, so that he would not forget. He showered, shaved and dressed, fed Gigi, and then drove off wondering what Pamela and her friend were going to feed him. He had heard much of English cooking, none of it reassuring, although Pamela was clearly a civilized woman with the excellent taste to live in Périgord. But still, he was nervous, and not only for his stomach. The invitation to "a real English dinner" had come by hand-delivered note to his office, and was addressed "To our defender." The women in the Mairie loved it.

It had been a tiresome day, with half the newspapers and TV stations in France wanting to interview "the lone cop of St. Denis," as *France-Soir* had called him. He turned them all down, except for his favorite, Radio Périgord. The interviewer, however, seemed disappointed when he said that the lone cop was being overwhelmed and it was the presence of Inspector Isabelle Perrault that had made the difference. Isabelle had then called him to complain that *Paris Match* wanted to photograph her in her karate uniform and the damn female media expert at police headquarters was insisting she submit. But she accepted his invitation to dinner the following evening, only, she said, because she wanted to get a good look at his black eye and bruises.

It was still fully light outside as Bruno parked at Pamela's, yet there were lights blazing throughout the house, an old oil lamp glowing softly on the table in the courtyard, and some gentle jazz playing. An English voice called out "He's here," and Pamela appeared, looking formal in a long dress and her hair piled high. She was carrying a tray with a bottle of what looked like Veuve Clicquot and three glasses.

"Our hero," she said, putting the tray on the table and kissing him soundly on both cheeks as he offered his flowers and wine. Standing so close she realized how many stitches his wound had required.

"That's one of the best black eyes I've ever seen, Bruno," she said. "I'm not surprised, after seeing that club he hit you with." She turned as Christine appeared. "Just look at Bruno's stitches."

Christine came up, kissed him on both cheeks and hugged him tightly, bathing him in her perfume. "Thank you, Bruno. Truly, thank you for saving us the other day."

"We heard you on the radio this afternoon," Christine said. "And we bought all the newspapers."

He wanted to shift the discussion. "I'm just sorry that St. Denis now has this reputation for fighting and racial troubles," he said. "Some of the tourist businesses have had cancellations already. I hope it won't hurt your rentals this summer, Pamela. I was told there was something in the English newspapers."

"And on the BBC," said Christine.

"I should be fine," Pamela said, handing him the Champagne to open. "I don't use St. Denis in the address of this place, only the postal code. I just give the name of the house, then the name St. Thomas et Brillamont, the hamlet that we are part of, and then Vallée de la Vézère. It sounds so much more French to the English ear."

"I didn't know the house had a name," he said, gently tapping the hollow at the base of the bottle to prevent the foam from overflowing.

"It didn't before I christened it—Les Peupliers, for the poplars," she said. "There were certainly enough on the property to justify that."

"I think you would call that *le marketing*," Christine said, making him smile as he began pouring the wine. She was wearing a long dark skirt and blouse, and her hair had been freshly curled. They had dressed up for him and he began to regret not wearing a tie.

"I'm really curious to know what you cooked—a real *English* dinner," said Bruno.

"Christine helped me with the menu."

"But that's really all I did," said Christine. "My contribution was to spend the day on the computer on your behalf, researching your Arab soccer team."

"I tried the sports editor of *la Marseillaise* today," said

Bruno. "He was very helpful when it dawned on him that I was the same St. Denis cop whose picture was in his newspaper, but there was nothing in their files. He even looked through the back issues of those months in 1940, but he said they didn't seem to cover amateur leagues. He said he would ask some of the retired journalists about it."

"Well, I have something," Christine said. "I decided to check the thesis database. You know there are all these new graduate studies in areas like sports and immigration history? Well, they all have to write theses, and I found two that could be useful. One of them is titled "Sport and Integration: Immigrant Football Leagues in France, 1919–1940," and the other is called "Remaking Society in a New Land: Algerian Social Organizations in France." I couldn't get the texts from the Internet, but I did get the name of the authors, and I tracked down the first one. He teaches sports history at the University of Montpellier, and he thinks he knows about your team. There was an amateur league in Marseilles called Les Maghrébins, and the team that won the championship in 1940 was called Oran, after the town in Algeria where most of the players came from. And here is his telephone number. He sounded very nice on the phone."

"This is amazing," Bruno said. "You got all that from your computer?"

"Yes, and he e-mailed me a copy of his thesis and I have it all printed out and ready for you."

"This is very kind," said Bruno.

Pamela intervened. "Enough of crime and violence. We're about ready to eat, so tell us what you expect of English cooking," said Pamela.

"Roast beef that is overcooked," said Bruno. "Mustard that

is too hot, sausages made of bread, fish covered in soggy thick batter and vegetables that have been cooked so long they turn to mush. Oh yes, and some strange spiced sauce from a brown bottle to drown all the tastes. That's what we had when we all went over to Twickenham for the rugby international. We all liked the big egg-and-bacon breakfasts, but I have to say the rest of the food was terrible."

"Well, Pamela's cooking will change your mind," said Christine. "What did you think of the Champagne?"

"Excellent."

"It's from England." Pamela turned the bottle so he could see the label. "It has beaten French Champagnes in blind tastings. The Queen serves it. Christine brought me a bottle and it seemed a good time to serve it. I should confess that the winemaker is a Frenchman from the Champagne district."

"I'm still impressed."

Bruno was beginning to relax. It was the first time he had dined in an English home and also the first time he had dined alone with two handsome women. Dining alone with either one would have been easier, on the familiar territory of flirtation and discovery. The evening had already more than justified itself, thanks to the news of Christine's research.

The women led him indoors, and Bruno looked around with interest to see what the English would do with a French farmhouse. He was in a large, long room with a high ceiling that went all the way to the roof, and a small balustraded gallery on the upper floor. There was a vast old fireplace at the end of the room, two sets of French windows, an entire wall filled with books, and half a dozen wide and evidently comfortable armchairs, some of leather and some covered in chintz.

"I like this room very much," he said. "But I can't imagine it was like this when you arrived here."

"No," said Pamela. "I had to repair the roof and some of the beams, so I decided to do away with half the upper floor and make this high ceiling. Come through to the dining room."

This was a smaller, more intimate room, painted a color somewhere between gold and orange, with a large oval table of dark and ancient-looking wood and eight chairs. Three places were set at one end, with glasses for both red and white wine. On one wall was a carefully spaced array of old prints. The flowers he had brought had been placed in a large pottery vase on the table. As in the living room, the floor was laid with terra-cotta tiles, scattered with rugs of rich reds and golds that glowed in the soft light of some lamps and the two candelabras on the table. On the long wall hung a large oil portrait of a woman with auburn hair and startlingly white shoulders, wearing an evening dress from an earlier era. She looked very like Pamela.

"My grandmother," Pamela said. "She was from Scotland, which helps explain the one part of the meal where I cheated, just a little. I'll explain later, but do sit down and we'll begin."

She went to the kitchen and returned with a large white tureen of steaming soup. "Leek and potato soup," she announced. "With my own bread, and a glass of another English wine, a Riesling from a place called Tenterden."

The bread was thick and brown, with a solid, chewy texture that Bruno found unfamiliar but decided that he liked, and it went well with the filling soup. The wine tasted like something from Alsace, so he declared himself impressed again.

"Now comes the bit where I cheated," said Pamela. "The fish course is smoked salmon from Scotland, so it isn't quite English, but Christine and I agreed that it still counts. The butter and the lemons are French, and the black pepper comes from heaven knows where."

"This is very good *saumon fumé*," Bruno said. "It's paler than the kind we usually have here. Very delicate. Delicious!" He raised his glass to the women.

Pamela cleared away the fish, then brought in a large tray that held warmed plates, a carafe of red wine, two covered vegetable dishes and a steaming hot pie with golden pastry.

"Here you are, Bruno. The great classic of English cuisine: steak-and-kidney pie. The young peas and the carrots are from the garden, and the red wine is from Camel Valley in Cornwall. They used to say you could never make good red wine in an English climate, but this proves them wrong. And now, prepare for the most heavenly cooking smell I know. Come on, lean forward, and get ready for when I cut the pie."

Bruno dutifully obeyed, and as Pamela lifted the first slice of pastry he took a deep breath, savoring the rich and meaty aroma. "*Magnifique*," he said, peering into the pie. "Why so dark?"

"Black stout," said Pamela. "I would normally use Guinness, but that's Irish, so I used an English version. And beefsteak and kidneys, some onions and a little garlic." She piled Bruno's plate high, then Christine served the peas and carrots. Pamela poured the wine and sat back to observe his reaction.

He took a small cube of meat from the rich sauce and then tried a piece of kidney. Excellent. The pastry was light and crumbly and infused with the taste of the meat. The young peas in their pods were cooked to perfection and the carrots were equally right. It was wonderful food, solid and traditional, like something a French grandmother might have prepared. He sniffed the wine, enjoying the fruity bouquet, and twirled the glass in the candlelight, watching the crown where the wine fell away from the sides of the glass as it leveled. He took a sip. It was heavier than he had expected, unlike a red Gamay from the Loire, which was his only experience of red wine grown that far to the north. It had a pleasantly solid aftertaste—a good wine, reminding him slightly of a Burgundy, and with the body to balance the meat on his plate. He laid down his knife and fork, took up his glass, sipped again and then looked at the two women.

"I take back everything I've said about English food. So long as you prepare it, Pamela, I'll eat any English food you put before me. And this pie, you must tell me how to make it. It's not a kind of dish we know in French cuisine."

"Yes!" exclaimed Christine, and to his surprise, the Englishwomen raised their right hands, palms forward, and slapped them together in celebration. A curious English custom, he presumed, smiling at them and addressing himself once more to his Cornwall wine.

The salad, the ingredients again from Pamela's garden, was excellent and fresh, although crisp lettuce mixed with *roquette* did not seem particularly English to Bruno. But the cheese, a fat cylinder of Stilton brought from England by Christine, was rich and splendid. Finally, Pamela served ice cream she had made with her own strawberries, and Bruno confessed himself full, and wholly converted to English food.

"So why do you keep this a secret?" he asked. "Why do

you serve such bad food most of the time in England, and why is its reputation so terrible?"

"You explain your theory, Christine, while I get the finale," said Pamela.

"I think it's that Britain was the first country to experience both the agricultural and the industrial revolutions of the eighteenth century, and they very nearly destroyed the peasantry. Small farming was replaced by sheep farming because the sheep needed less care, just as better plows and farming techniques needed less labor and more investment. So small farmers and farm laborers were pushed off the land, while the new factories needed workers. Britain became an urban, industrial country very fast, and the mass urban markets needed foods that could be easily transported and stored and quickly prepared because so many women were working in the mills and factories. Then the new farmlands of North America and Argentina were opened, and with its doctrine of free trade Britain found its own farmers beaten on price and became a massive importer of cheap foreign food. It came in the form of tinned meat and mass-produced breads. And this happened just as the old traditions of peasant cooking that were handed down through the generations were disappearing, because families dispersed into the new industrial housing."

"Some would say that similar forces are at work now in France," Bruno said. He turned to Pamela, who brought to the table a small tray with a large dark bottle, a jug of water and three small glasses.

"I agree with all that Christine says about the history," Pamela said. "But World War II and rationing, which continued for nearly ten years after the war, made everything worse. After depending so long on cheap imported food, Britain was nearly starved by the German submarine campaign. People were limited to one egg a week, and hardly any meat or bacon or imported fruits. Even the tradition of better cooking in restaurants nearly died because there was a very low limit on how much they could charge for a meal. It took a generation to recover and to get people traveling again and enjoying foreign food, and to have the money to go to restaurants and buy cookbooks."

She lifted the dark bottle off the tray. "And now I want you to try this as your digestif instead of Cognac. It's a Scotch malt whisky, which is to ordinary whisky what a great château wine is to *vin ordinaire*. This one is called Lagavulin, and it comes from the island where my grandmother was born; it has a taste of peat and the sea."

"You sip it like Cognac?"

"My father brought me up to sniff it first, a really long sniff, then to take the tiniest sip and roll it around your mouth until it evaporates, and then take a deep breath through your mouth so you feel the flavor all down your throat. Then you take a proper sip."

"It feels warm all the way down," said Bruno, after taking his deep breath. "That's very good," he said, after a long sip. "The smoky taste is very unusual, but very satisfying, especially after a wonderful meal and great conversation. Thank you both."

He raised his glass to them, trying to decide which of the two he found the more attractive.

"So let me sum up," he said, "by asking whether I've really

had English cuisine this evening?" Pamela looked puzzled. "I've had Scotch malt whisky and Scotch salmon, wine from Cornwall, French beef and French kidney, French salad and vegetables and strawberries, and French-style Champagne that was made in England. The only wholly English part of this meal was the cheese. And it was all wonderfully cooked by an Englishwoman who lives in the Périgord."

He raised his glass to them both as they smiled at him. "And now I have the challenge of deciding what I can serve that will be half as good when you come to dine with me."

20

With the taste of the whisky still lingering pleasantly in his mouth, Bruno cruised to a halt at the end of Pamela's driveway. He took out his mobile phone and checked the time. Just after ten-thirty. Not too late. He called his friend Jean-Luc. A woman's voice answered.

"Francine, it's Bruno. Are they out tonight?"

"Hi, Bruno. You'd better take care. Captain Duroc has the boys out just about every night these days. The bastard wants to break the record for drunk-driving arrests. Hold on, I'll get Jean-Luc."

"Out drinking again, Bruno?" said his friend, his voice a little blurred with wine. "You ought to set a better example. Yes, Duroc sent some of us out again. He had me and Vorin on the Périgueux road last night, and he took the road junction that goes off to Les Eyzies—with Françoise. I think he likes her but she can't stand him. Neither can any of us. He's got us on alternate night shifts and we're all getting fed up with him. I tell you what. Young Jacques is out on patrol tonight. I'll call him and see where he's stationed and call you back."

Bruno waited and let his thoughts linger on the two women with whom he'd spent the evening. Christine was conventionally pretty, a dark-eyed brunette of the kind he always liked, and her liveliness and quick intelligence made her seem somehow familiar. Aside from her accent, she could almost be French. But Pamela was different, handsome rather than pretty, and with that wide and graceful stride of hers and her upright posture and strong nose, she could only be English. There was something rather fine about her, though, he reflected. She was serene and self-confident, a woman out of the ordinary, and a very good cook. He was already thinking what he should cook for them. They had probably had more than enough Périgord cuisine, and he had, too, of late, so he could forget the *tourain* soup, the foie gras and the various ways with duck. But he still had some truffles stored in oil. A risotto with truffles and mushrooms would be interesting.

His phone rang, jolting him out of his reverie. "Bruno, it's Jean-Luc. I rang Jacques and he's on the bridge. He said Duroc has gone out to the junction at Les Eyzies again. Apparently he found good pickings there. Where are you? Up near the cave? Well, you could come back by the bridge and give a wave to Jacques as you pass, he knows your car. Or you could go around by the water tower and have a clear run home."

"Thanks, Jean-Luc. I owe you a beer."

He took the long way home, past the water tower. If only Duroc knew! The man had a lot to learn about rural France. And other things, too, like Françoise, a plumpish blonde from Alsace with a sweet face and generous hips, who was said to have a small tattoo on her rump. The other gendarmes speculated that it might be a spider or a cross, a heart or a boyfriend's name. Bruno's bet was a cockerel, the symbol of France. Nobody had yet claimed the prize. Bruno hoped it would not be Duroc who succeeded, although perhaps an affair was just what Duroc needed. But the man went so carefully by the book that he would never break the strict gendarmerie rule against romantic attachments with junior ranks. Or would he? If the others suspected he was stricken with Françoise, he was getting into risky territory already. Bruno filed the thought away as his car climbed the hill to his cottage. Turning the corner, he saw faithful Gigi sitting guard at his door.

He took the printout of the thesis with him to bed, turning first to the back for the chapter headings, and frowning slightly as he saw there was no index. This could take longer than he thought, but there was an entire chapter on Marseilles and the Maghreb League, which from its name was presumably composed of teams and players from North Africa. He lay back and began to read, or at least he tried to. The first two pages were devoted entirely to what previous scholars had written about North African life in Marseilles and about the theory of sports integration. When he had read one paragraph three times, he thought he understood it to say that integration took place when teams of different ethnic groups played one another. Why didn't the man say so more clearly?

He battled on. The Maghreb League had been founded in 1937, the year after Léon Blum's Popular Front government came to power with its commitment to social welfare, paid holidays and the forty-hour week. Blum had been Jewish and a socialist, Bruno knew, and his government depended on communist votes.

The Maghreb League was one of several sporting organizations that had been started by a group of social workers employed by Blum's Ministry of Youth and Sport. There was also a Catholic Youth League, a Young Socialists League, a Ligue des Syndicats for the labor unions and even an Italian League because southeast France from Nice to the Italian border had been part of the Italian duchy of Savoy until 1860. Then the Emperor Louis Napoleon had taken the land as his reward for going to war against Austria in support of a unified Italy. But the Young Catholics, Young Socialists and young trade-union members did not want to play against the North Africans, Bruno read. Only the Italians agreed to play them and this was encouraged by the Ministry of Sport as a way to integrate both minorities. Bruno was happy things had changed. The French national soccer team that won the World Cup in 1998 was captained by Zinedine Zidane, a Frenchman from North Africa. Even the young sportsmen of St. Denis had grown out of this nonsense and played happily with blacks, browns and even young English boys.

The Maghrebians were enthusiastic players but not very skillful, and invariably lost to the teams of young Italians. So, in the interests of getting better games, the Italians offered to help the North Africans with some coaching. Very decent of them, thought Bruno. And the main coach for the Italian League was a player for the Marseilles team called Giulio Villanova.

Bruno sat up in bed. Villanova was the name of the man that Momu had remembered. This was Momu's father's team!

Bruno read on avidly. In those days of amateur teams before soccer players could dream of commanding the fantastic salaries they earned these days, Villanova was happy to coach the Maghreb League in return for a modest wage from the sports ministry.

Under Villanova's coaching, the Maghreb teams became better and better, and some of them began to win matches. The best team of all was the Oraniens, who won their league championship in March 1940, just before the German invasion that led to France's defeat in June and the end of organized sports for the young North Africans. The chapter went on to analyze the possibility that, had the war not intervened, the success of the Oraniens and the Maghreb League might have secured them the chance to play the Catholic and socialist youth and thus begin the process of assimilation.

But Villanova, the social workers and the players over the age of eighteen had already been conscripted into the Army. The young Arabs that were left began to play among themselves informally and the Maghreb League collapsed. Bruno thumbed quickly through the rest of the thesis, looking for photos or lists of the players' names or more references to the Oraniens or Villanova, but there was nothing. Still, he had the phone number of the author, and that was a lead to be followed up in the morning. Well fed, happy with finding the name of Hamid's team and deeply satisfied at having evaded Duroc's trap for motorists, Bruno turned out his lamp.

Bruno called the author of the thesis as soon as he got to his office in the morning. The young teacher of social history at

Montpellier University was delighted that his thesis turned out to have been useful to someone other than himself and his teaching career, and declared himself eager to help. Bruno explained that he was involved in a murder investigation following the death of an elderly North African named Hamid al-Bakr, who had kept on his wall a photograph of a soccer team dated 1940. The police were very interested to learn more about this, he said. The victim's son believed that his father had played on that team and had been coached by Villanova, and since the victim had been holding the ball when the photo was taken, he was either the captain or the star of the team. Was there any more information?

"Well, I think I have a list of team names somewhere," said the teacher. "I wanted to check whether any of the players became famous after the war, but none of them seemed to make it into the professional teams in France. They may have done so in North Africa, but I had no funds to do my research over there."

"Can you find the team list for the Oraniens, the champions in 1940? And might you have any team photos?" Bruno asked. "Or anything more on Villanova—that seems the only name we have."

"I'll have to check, but it won't be until I get home this evening. My research notes are stored there and I have to teach all day. I do have some photos, but I'm not sure if they'd be relevant. I'll check. And Villanova seems to have dropped out of sporting life during the war. He doesn't reappear on any team lists that I came across, nor at the sports ministry when it reopened in 1945. I'll call you back this evening, if that's okay."

Bruno gave him his home and fax numbers, told him to leave a message and hung up, hopeful but cautious. He looked forward to sharing the news with Isabelle. The inquiry had made little real progress that Bruno knew of. The tire tracks had matched, but only confirmed what they already knew, that both young Gelletreau and Jacqueline had been in the clearing in the woods overlooking Hamid's house. A second forensic sweep of the clearing had failed to produce any new evidence that could break their story. There was still Jacqueline's lie about being in St. Denis on the day of the killing. She claimed that she had simply come to pick up Richard to take him back to her house, but that rang false. Playing truant from his lycée, Richard would have stayed at her home in Lalinde. He had firmly denied being in St. Denis at all that day. Even when confronted with Richard's testimony, Jacqueline stuck to her story. J-J and Isabelle assumed that her visit to St. Denis probably had something to do with the drugs, making a pickup or a delivery, and that she was more frightened of the drug dealers than she was of the police.

Bruno knew that most of the Ecstasy pills in Europe were said to come from Holland. Why hadn't he thought of that sooner? He picked up the phone and called Franc Duhamel at the big campground on the river bend below the town.

"*Bonjour,* Franc, it's Bruno and I have a question for you. Didn't you mention in the mayor's office the other day that you had some Dutch guys who stayed at your place for the motocross rally? How long did they stay?"

"They were here the whole week. They came down late Friday night, stayed the week and went back the next Sunday. There were about thirty of them, a couple of those big camping vans, a couple of cars and the rest on motorbikes. Then we also had some of the teams that were competing, so I was nearly full that weekend. It was just what I needed."

"Franc, I know you have that wooden pole across the entrance and a night watchman, but do you run security during the day? Do you take note of car registration numbers and all that?"

"Sure. The insurance requires it. Every vehicle that comes in gets recorded in the book."

"Even visitors, even local cars from around here?"

"Everybody. Visitors, delivery trucks, even you."

"Do me a favor. Look up the visitors' book for May tenth, and see if you have a listing for a local car with a twenty-four registration." He gave Franc the number of Jacqueline's car, and waited, listening to the rustling of pages.

"Hello, Bruno? Yes, I found it. The car came in at twelve and left at three-thirty. It looks like whoever it was they came for a good lunch."

"Any idea who was driving the car, or whom they visited?"

"No, just the number."

"Do you have the names of the Dutchmen who were staying with you?"

"Yes. Names, addresses, car and bike registrations, and some credit cards. Mostly they paid cash, but some paid with cards." Franc spoke hesitantly, and Bruno smiled to himself at Franc's new dilemma, whether he would now have to declare to the tax man even the cash income he had taken from the Dutchmen.

"Don't worry, Franc. This is about the Dutchmen and their visitor, nothing to do with you or taxes. Can you get the paperwork together with the names and addresses and all the information you have on them and I'll be down in twenty minutes to make copies."

"Can you tell me what this is about, Bruno? It's not involved with the murder of that Arab, is it?"

"It's just a hunch, Franc, but we're investigating the way some drugs have been getting into the area, that's all. Twenty minutes."

With Franc's paperwork in hand, Bruno thought he had better tie up another loose end and drove on through the town to Lespinasse's garage on the main road to Bergerac. It was a Total filling station, with gas slightly more expensive than at the supermarket but well placed for the tourist trade, and it was where Jacqueline had filled her tank. Lespinasse's sister ran the pumps, while he, his son and a cousin tinkered happily with engines and gearboxes and bodywork in the vast hangar of their garage. It was a big local family; another cousin ran the town's *tabac*.

As always, he found Lespinasse under a car, chewing on a matchstick and singing to himself. He called out and the plump, jovial man wheeled himself out on the small board on which he lay and rolled off to greet Bruno, presenting his forearm to be shaken rather than cover Bruno's palm with oil.

"We saw your picture in the newspaper," said Lespinasse. "Saw you on TV, too. You're a celebrity. Everybody says you did a great job with those bastards."

"Thanks. I'm here on police business, Jean-Louis, about a

credit card of one of your customers. I need to look at your fuel sales records for May tenth."

"The tenth? That would have been Kati's day off, so the boy would have been running the pumps." He looked back into the garage and whistled, and young Edouard came out, waving cheerfully. He was the image of his father but for a full set of teeth. The boy was eighteen now but he had known Bruno ever since he'd first learned to play rugby, so he came and kissed Bruno on both cheeks.

"You still write down the registration numbers on the credit-card slips?" Bruno asked.

"Always, except for the locals that we know," said Edouard.

Bruno gave him the number of Jacqueline's car, and Edouard leafed through the file to the right day.

"Here we are," he said. "Thirty-two euros and sixty centimes at eleven-forty in the morning. Carte Bleu. I remember her, she was a real looker. Blond. When she came back she was with a bunch of guys, though."

"She came back?"

"Yes, after lunch, in one of those big camper vans with a bunch of Hollanders. I filled them up. Here it is, eighty euros exactly at two-forty in the afternoon, paid with a Visa card and here's the registration number." Bruno checked his own list. It was one of the numbers from the campground.

"And there were a couple of them on motorbikes at the same time and I filled them, too," Edouard went on. "They must have paid cash. I remember asking myself what a girl like that was doing with a bunch of tough-looking guys. I saw her in the back of the van with them when the guy who paid opened the back door to get his wallet. I don't think we saw them again, and I'd have remembered if we'd seen her."

"If you hadn't given up playing tennis you might have met her at the tournament last year. She came and played at the club."

"Well, it was either tennis or rugby, but maybe I made the wrong choice," said Edouard.

21

Bruno left the garage feeling he was making progress and went directly to see Isabelle in her temporary office above the tourist board. At her desk he laid down three thin files and said, "New evidence."

Isabelle, in dark trousers and a white shirt of masculine cut, was sitting pensively with a pencil in her hand and wearing earphones. She looked startled to see him at first, and then pleased. She took off the earphones and switched off a small machine, then rose and kissed him in greeting.

"Sorry," she said. "I was listening to the tape of the last round of interrogation. J-J e-mailed it to me. You said there was new evidence?"

"I've identified the missing photo," he said. "It's of a team called les Oraniens, who won the Maghreb League trophy in Marseilles in 1940. They were coached by a professional player named Giulio Villanova. By this evening we should have a full list of who was on that team, thanks to a sports historian who wrote a thesis on it. Here are my notes and his phone number." He pushed out one of the files he had brought.

"I've traced Jacqueline's movements on the day in question." He put his finger on the next file, which contained the list of Dutch names and credit-card numbers and a photocopy of the campground's visitors' book with Jacqueline's registration number. It also contained the numbers of the vehicles that had left the campground while Jacqueline's car was there.

"We can also put Jacqueline in the company of the visiting Dutch guys for almost all of the time during which we think the murder was committed. This third file has photocopies of the credit card they used to buy diesel, and the name of an eyewitness who saw her with them, and who earlier saw her fill up her own car."

Isabelle poured him some of her own coffee before returning to her desk and looking through the files Bruno had brought. "So why would she not explain to us that she was simply visiting some Dutch boys at the campground?" she asked.

"That's what I asked myself, too. You know you thought it might be drug-related, and she was frightened of her suppliers if talked? Well, the Dutch produce most of the Ecstasy pills. The Dutch guys at the campground came down in cars, camping vans and bikes, mainly for the motocross rally, but they stayed on. That's not a bad cover for distributing drugs. I have a list of names here, some of them with credit-card numbers, and I thought you might want to see if any of them are known to your Dutch colleagues or to any of those Europol cooperation agencies."

"I'm impressed, Bruno. I'll brief J-J and send off a report to Tavernier. We'll need J-J's signature to send the request to the Dutch police. I presume the Dutchmen have all left St. Denis, so they're out of our reach?" He nodded, still standing before her desk. "You realize this could give the girl an alibi for the period when the murder was committed?"

"Of course," he said. "It looks as if she left her car at the campground and then went out in one of the Dutch vans. Look at the page of the visitors' book, and the times of various vehicles coming and going while her car was there. You might want to ask the Dutch police to check whether any of those guys had connections with the extreme Right."

"You sure you want to remain in the Police Municipale, Bruno? We could use someone like you."

"Every time I see J-J he tells me how much he envies my life here."

"Seriously, Bruno. Why not transfer to the Police Nationale? You're wasted here."

"I'm happy here, Isabelle," he said. "I'm busy, I think I'm useful and I'm certainly not wasted. It's a way of life that pleases me and I've seen enough violence and drama in my time. I like J-J, but I don't envy him his life."

"You don't want more out of life?"

"Not now. Maybe not ever. I have enough money to live as I please. I have friends and I get satisfaction from my work. I love living here." Bruno knew from the look on Isabelle's face that he was not saying what she wanted to hear. "You're able and ambitious and you want to follow your talents as far as they will take you. You like challenges. That's your nature and I admire it," he said.

"But we're different people with different priorities and our lives will take different trajectories," said Isabelle. "That is what you're saying. Am I right?"

"Trajectories? Now there's a word. Our careers will probably take different trajectories because you have that kind of drive." He got the feeling he had suddenly been drawn into another kind of conversation altogether, where the language was strange and the meanings had shifted.

"Drive for what?" she said. He noticed her fingers were clenched around her pencil.

"To get to the center of things, to fulfill your talents."

"You mean I want power?" She was looking almost fierce.

"Isabelle, Isabelle. Why are we having this confrontation? You're putting words into my mouth and I like you too much for this." Her fingers seemed to relax on the pencil. "What I'm saying is that you're a dynamo, Isabelle. You want to change things. I'm the kind of person who likes to keep them the same. But I've been through enough to know that people like you are needed, probably more than people like me. But we have our uses, too."

They looked at each other.

"You promised to take me to dinner, remember?" she said.

"Of course I remember. What would you prefer? A bistro, pizza, not very good Chinese food, more Périgord cooking? Your choice."

"I loved your cooking. Why don't we do that again?"

"You're still free this evening?" She nodded, and smiled. "I'll pick you up at seven. Here, or at your hotel?"

"The hotel. I'd like to bathe and change."

"Okay. Don't dress up."

He had to rush. There were the final details to clear with the company that had the contract for the three firework displays of St. Denis—the June 18 event that launched the season, Bastille Day and the town's own feast day at the end of August. The company had wanted sixty thousand euros for the three events, but with a little trimming of the display and a lot of negotiation he managed to reduce the cost to forty-eight thousand, just short of his fifty-thousand-euro budget. That meant more money for the sports-club fund. Then he had to call all the local businessmen to persuade them to take out their usual ads in the tournament brochure for the tennis club, and each had to grumble about the bad season and cancellations. But finally it was done. A tourist had lost a purse and he had to take a statement. He had to brief the mayor on the latest developments in the murder case, fend off two interview requests and check over the mayor's deposition describing the riot. He just had time to get to the tennis club at four o'clock and change for his *minimes* class of five-year-olds.

By now the kids could hold a racket, and were starting to put together the hand-eye coordination that allowed most of them to hit the ball most of the time. He lined them up at the far end of the court, and with the big wire basket of balls beside him at the net, he tossed a gentle bounce to each of the kids, who ran forward in turn to try to hit the ball back toward him. If they were lucky enough to send the ball his way, he would tap it back gently with his racket and the child was entitled to another hit. Two was usually all they could manage, but in every class there would be one or two kids who were naturals, who struck the ball surely. These were the ones he would keep his eye on. But for the young mothers, who stood watching in the shade of the plane trees, each child was a future champion, to be cheered on before hitting the ball and applauded after it. After a while, he signaled that it was time for them to start preparing the milk and cookies that ended each session of the *minimes*.

The kids went around ten times. They all counted carefully, and knew that after three rounds there would be no more balls in the wire basket and they could scamper around the court to pick them all up and replace them. Sometimes he thought that that was the part they most enjoyed.

He thought he saw one of the mothers still watching, but when he turned to look he noticed that it was Christine. He left the children running after the balls and then strolled across to the fence to greet her.

"That was a wonderful dinner last night," he began, wondering what had brought her here. She looked dressed for a walk, in strong shoes, loose slacks and a polo shirt.

"That was Pamela's cooking, not mine," she said. "It's strange after seeing you fight the way you did in the square, and here you are like every kid's favorite uncle. You have a remarkable range of skills. I didn't know that tennis lessons were part of your duties."

"It isn't exactly a duty, more a tradition. I enjoy it. Besides which, it means I get to know every kid in the town long before they start getting to be teenagers and ripe for trouble, so that counts as crime prevention. Speaking of crime, I wanted to call you this evening. That thesis you found for me was very useful. It was exactly what I needed to track down the missing photo."

"Good, I'm pleased. Listen, I was just passing by and saw the courts and thought I'd take a look. I didn't know you'd be here. But since you are, is there anything specific you'd like me to look up in Bordeaux before I leave for England? I'm going there for a couple of days on Thursday, to that Centre Jean Moulin I told you about, you remember? Resistance research."

He nodded. "Let me think about it and get back to you tomorrow. I don't really know what I'm looking for. More information on Hamid, I suppose, and which group he was with before he joined the Army near Toulon in 1944. If I get the rest of the names of his team, maybe we could see if any of them crop up. And then there's this Giulio Villanova."

"I think I know what to look for. I read the thesis. You'd better go to your children. You're very good with them; you'd make quite a father." She blew him a kiss and sauntered off slowly toward the road that led to the cave, now and then bending to pick a wildflower. He watched her for a moment, enjoying the swing of her hips. She turned and saw him, and waved. She had used the phrase "your children" and Bruno did not think it was accidental from a woman with no children herself. He waved back and went into the clubhouse to be greeted by the usual bedlam of a score of five-year-olds and as many mothers. The latter eyed him gleefully, giggling like a pack of schoolgirls as they rolled their eyes and asked about his new lady friend.

22

In the low light of the hotel lobby, Isabelle looked striking and almost mannish. Her hair, still wet from her shower, was slicked back from her brow, and she was dressed entirely in black: flat black shoes, black slacks and blouse, and a black leather jacket slung over one shoulder, all set off by a bold crimson suede belt at her waist.

"You look lovely," he said, kissing her cheeks. She had on the merest hint of eye makeup, lipstick to match her sash, and no perfume but the fresh scent of her shampoo. He led her to his van, which he had cleaned out specially, at least the front seat. As he showed her in, Gigi put his head over from the back and licked Isabelle's ear. Bruno set off over the bridge.

"This isn't the way to your place," she said.

"We're going to a place you probably don't know, but you should. Relax, it's a pretty drive." He had thought carefully about this dinner and toyed with the idea of taking her home, but decided on balance against it. They had been together frequently enough and clearly liked one another, so there was going to be sexual tension in their evening anyway. It would be all the more loaded if they were just a few steps away from his bedroom. Isabelle, he judged, was a woman who would decide for herself whether and when and where to take a lover, and yet it would feel odd to him and probably to her if he did not make an advance on his own turf.

He drove up the long hill past the water tower and out onto a plateau that gave the best views along the sweeping bends of the river. At a road so small it looked like a path, he turned off. They climbed another low hill, and came to the foot of a high and almost vertical cliff, where he parked on a small patch of ancient gravel, opened her door for her and then released Gigi. He took a small picnic bag from the back and she heard the tinkling of glasses.

"I want you to meet a friend of mine," he said. He led her up a track, around a corner and there, nestling into the base of the cliff, was a small house. It had a door and two windows, and its roof was the great rock itself. A small stream flowed from the base of the house through a gutter to tumble down the hill with a soft sound. In front of the house was a narrow terrace, with an old metal table and three chairs, and beyond it was a small vegetable garden. A black-and-white mongrel dog was tied to a hook screwed into the doorframe, and growled when it first saw Gigi. But Bruno's dog knew his manners and approached slowly and humbly, his tail wagging as if asking permission, and the two dogs sniffed each other courteously.

"They're old friends," Bruno said. "We go hunting together."

The door opened and a small elderly man poked his head

into the open. "Ah, Bruno," he said, as if they had last met a few minutes ago. "Welcome, welcome, and who is your friend?"

"Isabelle, this is Maurice Duchêne, owner and keeper of the Sorcerer's Cave, who was born in this cliff house and has lived here all his life. Maurice, meet Inspector Isabelle Perrault of the Police Nationale, a colleague but also a good friend."

"I'm honored to receive you, my dear mademoiselle," said Duchêne. He was terribly bent with age, and as he came forward to shake her hand he had to cock his head sideways to peer up at her, but Bruno noticed that his glance was almost roguish.

"You are a real beauty, my dear. And my magnificent Gigi, prince among hunting dogs. This is a pleasure, such a pleasure."

"Come, sit and have a drink with us, Maurice, and then with your permission I'd like to show Isabelle the cave. And could you bring us some of your water? Isabelle is from Paris and she will never have tasted anything like it."

"Gladly, gladly. Sit down and I'll be with you in a minute." He turned and hobbled back into the house. Isabelle sat, and Bruno took a dark wine bottle with no label and three small wineglasses from his bag, and poured. Isabelle turned to look at the view, a vast sweep of the valley with trees marking the river's meandering course and more cliffs on its far side.

"Here we are, here we are, the finest water of mother nature and father Périgord," said Duchêne, coming out with a tray bearing a jug of water and three tumblers that were opaque with age. "Straight from the rock, straight into my kitchen and bathroom, always running water. It never runs dry. And Bruno has brought my favorite aperitif. He makes it himself, you know, every year on Saint Catherine's Day. This must be last year's vintage."

"No, Maurice, in your honor, and for Isabelle, I have brought the '99 that you like. Let's drink a toast to friendship, but first, Isabelle, I should tell you that this is *vin de noix,* made from our local green walnuts, Bergerac wine and eau-de-vie from my own peaches. You won't find this in Paris."

"Delicious," she said after tasting it. "And what a magnificent view you have, Monsieur Duchêne. But isn't it cold up here in winter?"

"Cold? Never. The water never freezes and the rocks keep me dry. I have plenty of wood and my stove is all I need, even on the coldest nights when there's snow on the ground. Now you must try my famous water, my dear. If there were much more of it, I'd call it a source and bottle it and become richer than Monsieur Perrier."

She took a sip. It was cool, so lightly *pétillant* that she could barely taste the bubbles, and without any of the chalky taste of some mountain waters. She took some more, swirling it around her mouth.

"It tastes like freshness itself," she said, and Duchêne rocked back and forth with glee.

"May I show her the cave, Maurice?" Bruno asked. "I brought two flashlights. And the *vin de noix* is for you, along with some pâté I made this spring." He took a large glass jar with a rubber seal from his bag and placed it on the table, and Duchêne handed Bruno an ancient key and poured himself another glass from Bruno's bottle.

They walked on past the vegetable garden, along an

increasingly narrow winding track, where only a flimsy rope fence protected them from the drop, and then around a steep buttress in the cliff. They came to a patch of brilliant green turf that led to an ancient iron-bound door in the rock. Bruno opened it with the key, gave Isabelle a flashlight and told her to watch her footing. He took her arm to guide her in, and they stood for a moment to let their eyes get accustomed to the darkness. Gigi stayed at the entrance, backing away from the cave's black interior and growling softly. Bruno was very conscious of Isabelle's closeness as he steered her forward, his feet carefully feeling their way over the rough rock.

"They call this the Cave of the Sorcerer, but hardly anyone knows about it and even fewer come to see it," he said. "Maurice prefers it that way, so he doesn't put up any signs and won't let the tourist board advertise it. But it has something very rare among the cave paintings of this district."

He stopped and turned her with a gentle touch to her arm. It gave her a small start. Then she leaned slightly toward him as if she expected to be kissed, but he shone his flashlight high and told her to look carefully. As she followed the movement of the beam of light she saw that he was illuminating the outlines of a creature, crouching and heavy and somehow touched with power and menace.

"Is it a bear?" she asked, but the light was moving on. Next to it was another image; Bruno was playing the light up and down along a strange curve that seemed at first to be part of the rock. He let her take in the dark painted shape.

"It's a mammoth!" she said, marveling. "I see the tusks, and that's a trunk, and those massive legs."

"Twenty thousand years old," said Bruno softly, and

directed the beam farther along to a small creature on all fours, its face turned toward them.

"Its face is so human," Isabelle said. "Is it a monkey, an ape?"

"No tail," said Bruno, moving the torch to the rump. "This is just about unique, the only identified humanoid face in all the Périgord cave art that is known. Look: the eyes, the curve of the jaw and shape of the head, and the gap that seems to be an open mouth."

"It's wonderful, but it looks almost evil."

"That's why Maurice calls it the Sorcerer." He paused, and she shone her own flashlight around the cave, up to the jagged, sloping roof and back to the mammoth. "There's one more thing I want to show you, something I find very moving," he said, and steered her around a pillar of rock and into a smaller cave, his flashlight darting back and forth at waist height before he found what he was looking for. Then the beam focused on a tiny hand, the print of a child's palm and fingers, so clear and precise that it could have been made the day before.

"Oh, Bruno," she said, clutching at his hand and squeezing it. "A child's handprint. That's so touching, it's marvelous."

"Can't you just see the little one at play?" he said. "While his parents are painting mammoths and sorcerers, the child puts a hand in the paint and then makes a mark that lasts forever."

"Twenty thousand years," she whispered, then impulsively reached up and touched his cheek and kissed him. She let her mouth linger on his as the light from their flashlights darted aimlessly around the cave. Bruno responded, tasting the wine on her lips, until she moved her hand up to stroke his cheek. She drew back, her eyes glinting in the light and smiling questioningly, as if asking herself whether he had brought other women to this cave, and whether it had worked the same magic on them.

They bade farewell to Maurice and his dog, and the sun was still an hour or more from sinking as they returned to the van, hand in hand.

"Now what?" she asked.

"Now for your picnic," he said. He drove up the narrow, winding road. They came out on a wide plateau formed by the cliff that harbored the cave. He drove on toward a small hillock topped with a ruined building, but the distance was deceptive. The hillock was far larger than it seemed at first sight, and the ruined building was tall and imposing.

"It's a ruined castle," Isabelle said with delight.

"Welcome to the castle of Brillamont, seat of the seigneurs of St. Denis, built eight hundred years ago. It was twice taken by the English and twice recaptured and sacked, and ruined over four hundred years ago by fellow Frenchmen in the religious wars. But it's the best place I know for a picnic. You have a look around with Gigi while I organize things. Just don't climb the walls or the staircase—it's not safe."

Bruno watched as Gigi bounded ahead, occasionally glancing back to see what took this human so long, and Isabelle climbed the hill past the crumbled castle walls to a large sloping expanse of turf dominated by a central tower.

Three of its walls still stood, but the whole of the interior was open to her view. A stone staircase that looked solid enough climbed up the interior of all three walls. Bruno glanced up from the fire he was making as she paced the exterior walls and looked out over the plateau, where the view was even grander than it had been from the cave, with the river Vézère flowing into the Dordogne as it came from an adjoining valley.

Swifts and swallows were darting above Isabelle as she rejoined Bruno. He had built a small fire inside a nest of stones and laid across it a metal grill he had brought with him. Two freshly gutted fish were steaming gently above the coals. He had spread a large rug and some cushions on the ground, and two Champagne glasses stood on a large tray. He'd put a fresh baguette with a hefty wedge of Cantal cheese and a block of pâté on a wooden board. As she knelt on a cushion, he reached into a cooler and pulled out a half bottle of Champagne.

"Now there's a responsible policeman. Only drinking a half bottle because he has to drive," she said, sinking to her knees on the rug. "This looks even better than I could possibly have dreamed when I asked for a picnic, Bruno. Where did you get the fish?"

"From my friend the Baron. He caught those trout less than half an hour before I met you at the hotel."

"What would you have done if he hadn't caught anything?"

"Some sausages from the pig we killed in February are in the cooler."

"Can we have one of those as well?" she asked, clapping

her hands. "Just so I can try them? I don't think I have ever had a homemade sausage before."

"Certainly, anything for the lovely lady of Brillamont," he said, handing her a glass of Champagne, and then digging out a long skein of sausage which he laid carefully over the coals.

"That's much too much. I just want a little taste."

"Yes, but Gigi has to eat, too." He raised his glass. "I drink a toast to my rescuer, with my deepest appreciation. You saved me from a real beating in the square."

"My toast is to you and your wonderful imagination. I can't think of a better evening or a better picnic, and there's no one I'd rather enjoy it with." She leaned forward and kissed him briefly, letting her tongue dart out between his lips, then sat back, smiling almost shyly.

"I'm glad," he said, and poured the rest of the Champagne into their glasses. "Drink up, before the sun goes down and it gets too dark to see what we're eating."

"Knowing you, Bruno, you'll have thought of that, and some elderly retainers will march out from the castle ruins holding flaming torches."

"I think I'd prefer privacy," he said, and handed her a tin plate from his picnic box. He moved across to the fire to turn the fish and sausage, and looked back briefly. "Help yourself to the pâté and break me off some bread, please." He turned back to his cooler, and came out with two fresh glasses and a bottle of rosé. "This is why we only had the half bottle of Champagne."

The fish were just right, the blackened skin falling away from the flesh and the backbone pulling easily free. She saw thin slivers of garlic that he had placed inside the belly of the trout, and he handed her half a lemon to squeeze onto the pink-white flesh, and a small side plate with potato salad studded with tiny lardons of bacon.

"I couldn't make a feast like this in a full kitchen, and you produce it in the middle of nowhere," she said.

"I think they probably had very grand banquets up here in the castle in the old days. That sausage looks about ready, and we still have another hour of twilight after the sun goes down."

"I wonder what the cave people ate," she mused, picking up a piece of sausage with her fingers. "This is delicious but I'm getting full." She put her plate down, and when Gigi came up to sniff it, the dog looked inquiringly at Bruno. He put the plate down in front of his dog and stroked its head, giving Gigi permission to eat.

"They ate reindeer. There were even glaciers up in Paris in those days. It was the Ice Age, and reindeer were plentiful. The archaeologists found some of their rubbish heaps and it was almost all reindeer bones, and some fish. They didn't live inside the caves—they saved them for painting. Apparently they lived in huts made of skin, probably like the American Indians in their tepees."

He tossed the fish bones into the fire and put their plates and the cutlery into a plastic bag. This went into his cooler after he'd brought out a small basket of strawberries and placed it beside the cheese.

"This is it, the last course. But no picnic is complete without strawberries." Then he put some more sticks onto the fire, which blazed up as they lay on their sides on the rug, the strawberries between them, and the sun just about to touch the horizon.

"It's a lovely sunset," Isabelle said. "I want to watch it go down." She pushed the strawberries aside and turned to lie close to him, her back against his chest and her buttocks nestled into him. He pulled her ever so gently toward him. On the far side of the fire, Gigi was discreetly asleep. Bruno put his arm around her waist and she snuggled into him more tightly. As the sun finally sank she took his hand and slipped it inside her blouse and onto her breast.

23

When Bruno woke up at home, he reached across for Isabelle. He was surprised she wasn't there. Then, with his eyes still closed, he smiled broadly at the memory of the previous evening by the fire before, reluctantly, they had dressed and Bruno had driven Isabelle back to her hotel, stopping the car every few hundred yards to kiss again as if they could never taste each other enough.

He sprang from his bed and into his familiar exercises, his mind fresh and alert and alive with energy as he ducked into the shower, turned on the radio and dressed to go outside and enjoy the new day. He fed himself, his dog and his chickens and stood awhile gazing at the familiar view of his land and the hills that rolled away toward the river, enjoying his happy mood and the freshness of the morning air. He looked over his garden, suddenly noting that it must have rained in the night while he slept. At least the rain had held off for them, he thought, and he felt himself smiling once more.

He felt ready for anything, and turned back to the house to get his cap and briefcase, and noticed the red light of a message flashing on his phone. Thinking only of Isabelle, he must have missed it when he got back last night. It was the young professor at Montpellier, telling him that the list of players for the Oraniens team had been faxed to him at the Mairie.

After deleting the message, he was heading for the door when his phone rang and he leaped toward it, a lover's intuition persuading him that it was Isabelle.

"I just woke up," Isabelle said. "And it's so unfair that you're not here. I miss you already."

"And I miss you," he said, and they exchanged the delightful nothings of lovers, content just to hear the other's voice in the electronic intimacy of a telephone wire. In the background of her room, another phone rang.

"That'll be J-J on my cell for the morning report. I think I'll have to go to Bergerac for the drug case."

"Can we meet this evening?" he asked.

"I can't wait, *chéri*. I should be back later this afternoon. I'll call when I'm on my way."

Once in his office, where the fax from Montpellier awaited him, Bruno read through the list of names—and assumed there had to be some error. How else to explain why the final list of the Oraniens championship team contained no Hamid al-Bakr, when the young man had pride of place in the official photograph? He called the professor in Montpellier again, and double-checked the spelling of every name. Still no Hamid. He looked at the name that was listed as the team captain: Hocine Boudiaf. Beside the word "Hocine," Bruno had written in brackets "Hussein," which the Montpellier lecturer said was an alternative spelling and which looked more familiar. He had not been able to come up with a team photograph, but he had faxed Bruno another photo that included Boudiaf. That might help solve the puzzle. He checked his watch. Momu would not yet have left for school. He called him at home.

"Bruno, I want to apologize again, to apologize for my words and actions and to thank you," Momu began.

"Forget it, Momu, it's all right. Listen, I have a question. It comes from trying to track down your father's missing photograph. Have you ever heard the name Boudiaf, Hussein Boudiaf? Could he have been a friend of your father?"

"The Boudiaf family were cousins, back in Algeria," Momu replied. "They were the only family my father stayed in touch with, but not closely. I think there might have been some letters in the stuff I went through at his house, just family news, deaths, weddings and children being born. I suppose I should write and tell them of Hamid's death and of Karim's child, but I haven't kept in touch. My father felt he could never go back to Algeria after the war."

"Did you know any of his friends from his youth, soccer friends or teammates? Do you remember any names?"

"Not really, but try me."

Bruno read down the list of the Oraniens team. He put a small cross beside two of the names that Momu said sounded vaguely familiar. After he hung up he called Isabelle again.

"I knew it was you," she said, laughing happily. "I am just out of the shower and thinking of you."

"I wish I were there with you, but I have a business question. That helpful man you spoke to in the military archives.

If you have his number, would he speak to me? I have the list of the Oraniens team and the mystery is that Hamid's name is not on it. I want to see if we can trace any of the other team members. One or two might still be alive."

She gave him the number. "If you don't get very far, I can try him. I think he was an old man who liked talking to a young woman."

"Who could blame him, Isabelle? I'll call your cell if I need help. Until tonight."

The photo that had been faxed with the list was grainy and not too clear. It had come from an unidentified newspaper and showed three men in soccer gear. In the center was Villanova with his arms around two young North Africans. One of them was identified as Hussein Boudiaf and the other as Massili Barakine, which was one of the names that Momu had half remembered. Bruno felt he was getting somewhere. He dialed the military archives number that Isabelle had given him, and a quavering voice answered.

"This is Chief of Police Courrèges from St. Denis in Dordogne, monsieur. I need your help with regard to an inquiry in which you've already been very helpful to my colleague Inspector Isabelle Perrault."

"Are you the policeman I saw on TV, young man, in that riot?"

"Yes, that probably was me."

"*Chapeau,* monsieur. You have the admiration of sous-officer Arnaud Marignan, of the seventy-second of the line. What can I do for you?"

Bruno explained the situation, gave the names and reminded Marignan of the connection with the Commandos d'Afrique who had landed near Toulon in 1944. Did the archives have a photograph of the young Hamid al-Bakr?

"We should have an identity photo on the copy of his pay book, if not for the Commandos d'Afrique then certainly after his transfer. Give me your phone number and I'll call back, and a fax so I can send a copy of the pay-book photo. I'm afraid we can't send the original. And please convey my regards to your charming colleague."

Bruno smiled at the effect Isabelle seemed to have on the telephone. He was anxious to get the fax but he had another task in mind, and began thinking what other lines to pursue. He took a piece of notepaper from his desk and wrote a brief letter of thanks for his English dinner. Then he called Pamela, exchanged amiable courtesies and asked for Christine. He gave her the new names to be researched in Bordeaux and made sure they had one another's cell-phone numbers. The second he hung up the phone rang again. It was J-J.

"Bruno, I want to thank you for that good work on Jacqueline's movements," he said. "It turns out that those Dutchmen she was with are well known up there. Drugs, porn, stolen cars, you name it, they're into it. From what I see of their convictions, in France we'd have locked them up and thrown away the key, but you know how the Dutch are on prisons. To get to the point, we showed Jacqueline the evidence you collected and she cracked last night. We have a full confession on the drugs, but she's still saying nothing on the murder."

"That's great, as far as it goes, J-J. What about Richard? Was he involved in the drugs?"

"She says not, so I don't think we can still hold him. We can't shake his story, and now that she's come clean on the drugs I'm inclined to believe her on the killing. If it were up to me, Richard would be out today, but that decision is up to Tavernier. By the way, what did you guys do to him yesterday? He came back steaming and spent hours on the phone to Paris."

"I think our mayor gave him a talking-to, as an old friend of his father's. You know Tavernier got the gendarmes to arrest Karim, the grandson who found Hamid's body. Arrested for assault, after Karim charged into those Front National jerks in the riot."

"Tavernier must be out of his mind. Half of France saw the riot and they all think the men of St. Denis are heroes."

"Not Tavernier. Anyway, the mayor made him see sense. We got Karim out."

"Tavernier's a menace. Still, I'm glad you worked it out. Anything else?" said J-J.

"We seem to be making some progress on that photo of the soccer team. I'll keep you posted."

"It's a bit of a subplot, Bruno, but keep at it. We're still looking for a killer, and we don't have any other leads."

As he hung up, Bruno heard Mireille's voice in the corridor greeting Momu. He should have been at school at this hour. He waved and Momu came over to shake his hand.

"I can't stop," he said. "I just came up in the morning break to sign these papers closing down my father's social security account."

"Give me ten seconds, Momu. I have a picture to show you." He got the fax from his desk, with little expectation that Momu might recognize anyone in it, but since he happened to be here . . .

"Where did you get this?" Momu asked. "That's my father

as a young man, or his identical twin." He pulled out his reading glasses to read the caption. "Hussein Boudiaf, Massili Barakine and Giulio Villanova. The Boudiafs are our cousins, so I suppose it's a family likeness, but that's an extraordinary resemblance. And Barakine? I recall that name from somewhere. Villanova is the coach my father talked about. But that Boudiaf—I'd almost swear it was my father as a young man."

Consumed though he was by the murder investigation, Bruno had to keep abreast of routine matters, too. He sighed as he opened his mail and read three anonymous denunciations of neighbors. It was the least pleasant aspect of the citizens of St. Denis, and of every other commune in France, that they were so ready to settle scores new and old by denouncing one another to the authorities. Usually the letters went to the tax office, but Bruno got his share. The first was a regular letter from an elderly lady who liked to report half the young women of the town for "immorality." He knew the old woman well, a former housekeeper for Father Sentout who was probably torn between religious mania and acute sexual jealousy. The second letter was a complaint that a neighbor was putting a new window into an old barn without planning permission, and in such a way that it would overlook other houses in the village.

The third letter was more serious. It concerned Léon, an alcoholic who had been fired from the amusement park for placing Marie Antoinette on the guillotine in such a way that it cut her in half rather than just decapitating her, much to the horror of the watching tourists. They were even more appalled when he fell drunkenly on top of her. Now Léon was reported to be working *noir* for one of the English families that had bought an old ruin and had been persuaded that Léon could restore it for them. The anonymous letter claimed he had demanded payment in cash to evade taxes.

He sighed. He wasn't sure whether to warn Léon that somebody was probably reporting him to the tax office, or to warn the English family that they were wasting their money. Still, Léon had a family to support, so Bruno had better get him onto the right side of the tax authorities. He checked the address where he was supposedly working, out in the tiny hamlet of St. Félix, where he had also had a report of cheeses being stolen from a farmer's barn.

He looked again at the letter about the offending window. That was St. Félix as well; *mon Dieu,* he thought, a crime wave in a hamlet of twenty-four people. He sighed, grabbed his hat, phone and notebook, plus a leaflet on the legal employment of part-time workers, and went off to spend the rest of the day in the routine work of a country policeman. Halfway down the stairs he remembered that he would need his camera to photograph the window. Fully burdened, he went out to his van, thinking glumly that Isabelle would not be very impressed if she knew how he usually spent his days.

Three hours later he was back. The English family spoke almost no French, and his English was limited, but he impressed upon them the importance of paying Léon legally. He would leave it to them to discover the man's limitations. The owner of the allegedly offending window had not been at home, but Bruno took his photographs and made his notes for a routine report to the planning office. The affair of the stolen cheeses had taken most of his time, because the old farmer insisted that somebody was destroying his livelihood. Bruno had to explain repeatedly that since the cheeses were homemade in the farmhouse, which fell well short of the standards required by the European Union, they could not be legally sold, and thus they had to be listed as cheeses for domestic consumption in his formal complaint of a crime. Then he had to explain it all over again to the farmer's wife. She finally understood when he pointed out that the insurance company would seize the chance to refuse to pay for the theft of illegal cheeses.

The phone was ringing as he got back to his office. He lunged and caught it just in time. It was the *sous-officier* from the military archives.

"This name Boudiaf," the caller said. "The name you gave me was Hussein, and we have no trace. But we do have a Mohammed Boudiaf in the Commandos d'Afrique. He was a corporal, enlisted in the city of Constantine in 1941, joining the Tirailleurs. He then volunteered for the Commando unit in '43, and on the recommendation of his commanding officer he was accepted. He took part in the Liberation, and was killed in action at Besançon in October 1944. No spouse or children listed, but a pension was paid to his widowed mother in Oran until her death, in 1953. That's all we have, I'm afraid. Does that help?"

"Yes, thank you," said Bruno automatically. "Does the file list any siblings or other relatives?"

"No, only the mother. But I think we can assume that Corporal Mohammed Boudiaf was a relative of your Hussein Boudiaf. I know it's Hamid al-Bakr you are interested in, but there is a coincidence here. Al-Bakr joins the unit in August '44 in an irregular way, a unit where his acceptance would have been made a lot easier if he knew Corporal Mohammed. Is there a possibility of a name change here? It's just speculation, but in cases like this we often find that the new recruit had some good reason to want to change his name when he enlisted. They do it all the time in the Legion, of course, but it's not uncommon in other branches of the service. If your al-Bakr was originally called Boudiaf and wanted to change his name, there would be no easier way to do that than to join a unit where his brother or his cousin was already well installed."

"Thank you, that's a great help. If we need copies of this for the judicial proceedings, may I contact you again?"

"Of course. I looked up your own file and read the citation for that Croix de Guerre you won in Sarajevo. I'm honored to give you any help I can. Now, did you receive my fax of the pay-book photo?" Bruno checked the fax machine. It was there, the first two pages of an Army pay book, featuring a passport-size photo of a young man known to the French Army as Hamid al-Bakr. Beneath it were two thumbprints, an Army stamp and on the previous page the details of name, address, date and place of birth. The address was listed as Rue des Poissonniers, in the Vieux Port of Marseilles, and the date of birth was given as 14 July 1923.

"Yes, it's here. Thank you."

"Good. Feel free to call on me anytime, Sergeant Courrèges. Good-bye."

Bruno focused on the notepad in front of him and the two photos. Hamid al-Bakr of the French Army was the spitting image of Hussein Boudiaf, the soccer player. Could they be the same person? Momu's reaction had been real. If Hamid had changed his name, the question was why. What was he so intent on covering up that he hid his real name from his own son? And could this secret of the past explain Hamid's murder, more than sixty years after the young soccer player decided to join the Army and change his name?

He could talk this through with Isabelle that evening, he thought, smiling at the prospect, then admitting to himself that there probably wouldn't be a lot of time spent talking about crime and theories—or talking about anything. He remembered the way she had kissed him in the cave, just a millisecond before he was going to kiss her. . . . The phone broke into his reverie.

"Bruno? It's Christine, calling from Bordeaux. I'm at the Moulin archive and I think you had better get down here yourself. There's nothing about Hamid al-Bakr that I could find, but we have certainly tracked your Villanova and that new name you gave me, Hussein Boudiaf. It's dynamite, Bruno."

"What do you mean, dynamite?"

"Have you ever heard of a military unit called the Force Mobile?"

"No."

"Look, Bruno, you're not going to believe it unless you come and see this stuff for yourself. Your men Villanova and Boudiaf were war criminals."

"War criminals? How do you mean?"

"It's too complicated to explain on the phone. There's so much background. Go to Pamela's house. Ask her to let you see two of my books that she'll find on the desk in my room. The books you need are *Histoire de la Résistance en Périgord* by Guy Penaud, and *1944 en Dordogne* by Jacques Lagrange. Look up Force Mobile in the indexes and read all you can about it. I'll call Pamela and get her to put them out for you, but you have to read the bits about the Force Mobile and call me back. I— Dammit, my phone's running down. I'll recharge it and wait for your call. And my hotel in Bordeaux is the Hôtel d'Angleterre in case there's a problem. Believe me, you have to get here as soon as you can."

24

In Pamela's large living room, where the walls were glowing gold in the sunlight and her grandmother's portrait stared serenely down at him, Bruno plunged back nearly sixty years into the horror of war and occupation in this valley of the Vézère.

The Force Mobile, he read in the books Christine had identified, was a special unit formed by the Milice, the much-feared police of the Vichy regime that administered France under the German occupation after 1940. Under German orders, transmitted and endorsed by French officials of the Vichy government, the Milice rounded up Jews for the death camps. As the tide of war turned against Germany after 1942, the Resistance grew, and its ranks were swollen by tens of thousands of young Frenchmen fleeing to the hills to escape the STO, the Service du Travail Obligatoire, which rounded them up for forced labor in the factories of Germany. They hid out in the countryside, where they were recruited by the Resistance and took the name Maquis, from the word for the impenetrable brush of the hills of Corsica.

To them came the parachute drops of arms and radio operators, medical supplies, spies and military instructors from Britain. Some came from the Free French led by de Gaulle, some from Britain's Special Operations Executive, or SOE, and others from British Intelligence, MI6. The British wanted the Maquis to disrupt the German occupation, or, in the words of Winston Churchill's order establishing the SOE, "to set Europe ablaze." But as the invasion neared, the prime British objective was to disrupt military communications in France, and to force German troops away from defending the beaches against an Allied invasion, driving them into operations against the Maquis deep inside France. The Gaullists wanted to arm the Maquis and build the Resistance into a force that could claim to have liberated France, thus saving the country's honor after the humiliation of defeat and occupation. They also wanted to mold the Resistance into a political movement that would be able to govern France after the war and prevent a seizure of power by their rivals, the Communist Party. On occasion, Gaullists and communists fought it out with guns, usually in disputes over parachute drops.

The Milice and their German masters crafted a new strategy to crush the Resistance in key areas. Specialist German troops, anti-partisan units, were shipped in from the Russian front and from Yugoslavia, where they had become experienced at battling similar guerrilla forces. But the real key to the new strategy was to starve out the Resistance by terrorizing the farmers and rural people on whom the Maquis depended for their food. Rural families whose sons had disappeared were raided, beaten and sometimes killed, and the women raped. Crops and livestock were confiscated, farms and barns were burned. This reign of terror in the countryside was carried out by a unit specially recruited for the task, the Force Mobile. In the Périgord, it was based in Périgueux.

Sitting in Pamela's peaceful home, Bruno read on, rapt and appalled. He knew that the Occupation had been rough, that many in the Resistance had been killed and that the Vichy regime had become engaged in a civil war of Frenchmen killing Frenchmen. He knew about atrocities like the one at Oradour-sur-Glane, a village to the north where German troops, in reprisal for the death of a German officer, had locked hundreds of women and children in the church and set it on fire, machine-gunning any who tried to escape the flames. He knew of the small memorials dotted around his region: a plaque to a handful of young Frenchmen who died defending a bridge to delay German troop movements; a small obelisk with the names of those shot *pour la Patrie*. But he had never known about the Force Mobile, or the wave of deliberate brutality inflicted on this countryside he thought he knew so well.

The Force Mobile in Périgord was commanded by a former professional soccer player from Marseilles named Villanova, Bruno read. The name leaped out at him. Villanova, it seemed, brought a new refinement to the rural terror. He believed that the French peasants would be even more effectively intimidated if the reprisals and rapes and farm burnings were carried out by North Africans, specially recruited for the job with promises of extra pay and rations, and all the women and loot they could take from the farms they raided. Villanova found his recruits in the immigrant slums of Marseilles and Toulon, Bruno read, where unemployment and poverty had provoked desperation, and where he had many acquaintances on the local soccer teams, including young Arab immigrants.

Bruno shivered as he realized where this was leading. It looked likely that Hamid al-Bakr, war hero of France, had also been Hussein Boudiaf, war criminal and terrorizer of Frenchmen. Christine was absolutely right. He would have to go to Bordeaux in the morning, and gather the evidence about Villanova, Boudiaf and other members of the Force Mobile. This theory was indeed dynamite. The evidence for it would have to be complete and unassailable. The names of the victims of the Force Mobile would also have to be found. They would have every reason to want vengeance against any of Villanova's North African troops still living. They would certainly have the motive to kill an old Arab whom they recognized from those dark days of the war.

He couldn't help thinking of Momu. What would it do to him, to Karim and Rashida, if they were to learn that their beloved father and grandfather had been a war criminal, a terrorist in the employ of Vichy, acting under Nazi orders? What kind of shock would it be to learn that the man you respected as a war hero, as a brave immigrant who had established his family as French citizens with education and prospects and family pride, had in reality been a villain who had spent most of his life living a lie? How could the family stay in St. Denis with that knowledge hanging over them? How would the rest of the little North African community in St. Denis react to this revelation? And how would everyone else react?

Bruno could scarcely bring himself to think about the reaction of the French public, or to imagine how the Front National vote would swell. He bent forward in his chair, his head in his hands. He had to make some plans, talk to the mayor, brief J-J and Isabelle, and arrange to go to Bordeaux in the morning. How on earth could he prepare his town for a bombshell such as this?

"Are you all right, Bruno?" Pamela had come into the room. "Christine said you would have some pretty grim news and would probably need a stiff drink, but you look quite devastated. You're as white as a sheet."

"Not right now, but thanks."

"Christine said she thought what you were going to read related to Hamid's murder. It's funny how the past never quite goes away."

"You're right. The past doesn't die. It even keeps the power to kill. Look, I have what I need now. I'll take these books and leave you in peace. I have to get back to my office."

As he drove away he looked with new eyes at this placid countryside that had known such events, and known them within living memory. He thought of smoke in the sky from burning farms, blood on the ground from slaughtered fathers; he imagined French policemen giving the orders that deployed military convoys on the country roads—convoys packed with Arab mercenaries in black uniforms, with license to rape, loot and pillage. He thought of half-starved young Frenchmen, hiding in the hills with only a handful of weapons, helplessly watching the reprisals unleashed against their families and their homes.

And, Bruno wondered, whatever can we do with the Frenchmen who took their long-delayed revenge against one of their tormentors? At least now he knew why a swastika had been carved into Hamid's chest. It signified not the politics of the killers, but the real identity of the corpse.

. . .

Once back in St. Denis, Bruno drove immediately to the mayor's house by the river on the outskirts of town and explained why he now believed Hamid, their dead Arab war hero, had been in the Force Mobile. Shocked but convinced, the mayor agreed that the chain of evidence had to be made solid. They sat down and, from memory, composed a partial list of all the families they knew in St. Denis or the surrounding region who had been part of the Resistance. They could flesh out the list the next day from the records of the Compagnons de la Libération in Paris.

"So the police are now going to start investigating half the families of St. Denis to see which of them might have known that Hamid had been in the Force Mobile. My God, Bruno."

"They will question the old ones first, those who might have recognized Hamid. It could take weeks, a lot of detectives, and the media and the politicians will get involved. We could have a national scandal on our hands. There can be no winners in this, nothing but a political nightmare when the Right-wingers make hay about French families being burned out and terrorized by Arabs in German pay. It's awful. But I've got to go and brief the investigation team."

"You haven't told them yet?" the mayor looked off into the distance. "So we have some time to think how much to tell them."

"No time at all, sir," Bruno said sharply. Whatever thoughts might be stirring in the mayor's mind, he wanted to squash them. "They know I'm working on this, and Isabelle has already been looking into Hamid's mysterious war record. They are on the trail, and I have to go."

Bruno left the mayor sitting hunched and looking slightly shrunken in the overdecorated sitting room that was his wife's great pride. Bruno walked out to his van to call Isabelle. They met in his office at the Mairie where he laid out the evidence for her. Together they rang J-J and agreed to meet in Bordeaux the next morning. He phoned Christine at her hotel, got from her the phone number of the curator of the Jean Moulin archives, and arranged for the next morning's visit. He decided it was not his job to alert Tavernier. J-J could do that.

More depressed than he had ever felt, except for those last days in Bosnia, Bruno could not think of food. But Isabelle insisted that they go to the nearest pizzeria, where he ate mechanically and drank too much wine. She drove him home and put him to bed. She fed the chickens, gave Gigi dinner in his kennel, and then went back inside, undressed and climbed into bed beside him. He awoke in the early hours and headed for the shower, where she joined him under the steaming water and they made urgent love amid the soapsuds. They returned to bed. There, he turned more gently to her, and they were still engrossed in each other's bodies when the cockerel crowed to signal the dawn, which made them both laugh and Bruno knew that he was better. They showered again, and Bruno watered his garden and fed Gigi, then made coffee while Isabelle went back to her hotel to dress. She returned with a bag of fresh croissants from Fauquet's and they took her car to Périgueux. Bruno kept his hand resting lightly on her thigh for the entire journey.

"You're a very remarkable woman," he told her as they reached the new motorway at Niversac. "Twice now you've rescued me."

"You're worth it," she said, taking his hand, putting it between her thighs and squeezing it.

"I'm not looking forward to when we have to make an arrest."

"The law's the law, Bruno. Whatever Hamid was or whatever he did, he was unlawfully murdered."

"I know," he said. "But if it had been your family, your farm, your mother, you would have killed him yourself. That's justice."

"It may be justice, but it's not the law," she said. "You were in Bosnia, so you know what that leads to better than I do."

"Was that what Bosnia was about?" he asked. "I suppose it was, in a way. People making their own rules, taking their own revenge. No authority but the gun."

And sometimes justice was inflicted even without guns, he thought, and the memory came back of the day they had found the battered old motel that the Serbs had used as a brothel. He and his troops had disarmed three Serbian soldiers, left one man guarding them and gone on to clear the perimeter. When they came back, the Serbs were dead, their heads crushed into pulp. The Bosnian women they had used were standing over the bodies, some fierce and some sobbing, stones still bloody in their hands. One of them was Katarina. The trooper they had left to guard the prisoners just shrugged and said, "I thought they were entitled."

In his report, Bruno had written that the Serbian troops were already dead when they arrived at the motel. The lie had come easily. It seemed like justice then. It still did.

. . .

Bruno and Isabelle met J-J and a liaison officer from the Bordeaux police on the steps of the Centre Jean Moulin at nine a.m. Christine was already inside with the elderly French historian who ran the archives. The center was named after one of the most famous of France's Resistance leaders, who had sought to unify communists, Gaullists and patriots into a common command, and had been betrayed to the Gestapo. It stood in the city center, an elegant neoclassical building of white stone. Best known to the public as a museum of the Resistance, it contained showcases of domestic objects from the Occupation: wooden shoes, wedding dresses made of flour sacks, ration cards and other realities of daily life in wartime. Also on show were bicycle-driven dynamos that produced electricity for clandestine radios, and cars with giant bags on the roof that contained carbon gas made from charcoal, to use in the absence of gasoline. There were displays of the different contents of the weapons containers, Sten guns and bazookas, grenades and sticky bombs, dropped by British aircraft for use by the Resistance. Underground newspapers were laid out to read. And playing in the background was a quiet but continuous soundtrack of the songs they sang, from the love songs of Charles Aznavour to the defiant heroics of the Resistance anthem, "Le Chant des Partisans."

But as Bruno discovered, the real heart of the Centre Jean Moulin was to be found on its upper floors, which contained the written and oral archives and the research staff who worked there, focusing on this tortured period of French history.

Christine and J-J sifted through the fragmentary records

of the Force Mobile. They established that Hussein Boudiaf and Massili Barakine had been recruited to a special unit of the Milice in Marseilles in December 1942. After two months of basic training, they were assigned to the Force Mobile, a unit of 120 men commanded by Captain Villanova, which specialized in what were described as "counterterrorist operations" in the Marseilles region. In November 1943, after the British and Americans had invaded Italy and knocked Mussolini out of the war, the Germans had spread their occupation into the previous "autonomous" zone run by the Vichy government, and the Force Mobile came under Gestapo rule. The outfit was expanded, and Villanova's unit was assigned to Périgueux in February 1944, charged with taking "punitive measures against terrorist supporters."

They found pay slips with Boudiaf's name, movement orders for Villanova's unit, payroll listings that included Boudiaf and Barakine, and requisitions for special equipment that included explosives and extra fuel to destroy "terrorist support bases." The curator, cross-checking with the records of the Force Mobile's pay office, found a record of Boudiaf's promotion to squad leader in May, after one of Villanova's trucks was destroyed in a Resistance ambush. The promotion listing included a new Milice pay book and identity card, complete with photograph, that had never been collected by Boudiaf. The Milice records stopped in June 1944, with the Allied invasion of Normandy and the collapse of the Vichy regime.

Bruno and Isabelle went through the Force Mobile mission reports, the punitive sweeps, staged from the Périgueux base, north into the Limousin region, west to the wine country of St. Emilion and Pomerol, east toward Brive and south into the valleys of the Vézère and the Dordogne. The Force reached the region around St. Denis in late March 1944, raiding farms where the sons had failed to appear for forced labor service. They hit again in early May, based on intelligence from interrogations of Resistance prisoners after a Wehrmacht anti-partisan force, the Bohmer division, had surprised and destroyed a Maquis base in the hills above Sarlat. Bruno noted the names of the interrogated prisoners, who had all been shot; the names of the families listed as having sons who failed to appear for the Service du Travail Obligatoire, and the names of the towns and hamlets where the Force Mobile had been deployed. St. Denis was not among them, but the surrounding hamlets of St. Félix, Bastignac, Melissou, Ponsac, St. Chamassy and Tillier had all been raided.

Bruno, J-J and Isabelle spread out the photographs on the curator's desk and compared them. There was no doubt that Hussein Boudiaf the soccer player was also Hussein Boudiaf the newly promoted squad leader of the Force Mobile. And if he was not also Hamid al-Bakr then he was his double. But all bureaucracies tend to operate in the same way, Bruno thought. He looked at the French Army pay book, which contained two thumbprints of al-Bakr. The Milice pay book had been designed in precisely the same format and contained two thumbprints of Boudiaf. They were identical. The dates and place of birth were also identical, 14 July 1923, in Oran. Only the addresses were different. Boudiaf's address was given as the police barracks in Périgueux, al-Bakr's as Rue des Poissonniers, Marseilles.

"So that's our murder victim," said J-J. "*Cochon.*"

"Wait a moment," said the curator, making his way to a large bookshelf where he removed a fat volume. He began leafing through the index, and then looked up with satisfaction. "Yes, I thought I remembered that. Rue des Poissonniers was part of the Vieux Port of Marseilles that was destroyed in the bombing before the invasion, which makes it a useful address for someone who wanted to hide his true identity."

They went back to the Force Mobile mission reports, signed by Villanova. The raids around St. Denis on 8 May 1944 had included Squad Leader Boudiaf's unit. They claimed to have destroyed fourteen "terrorist supply bases," which meant farms. May 8, thought Bruno, the day that France celebrated her part in the victory that came exactly a year after the Force Mobile raided the outlying hamlets of the commune of St. Denis. He would never think of the annual May parade at the town war memorial in quite the same way again.

Suddenly, a memory of this year's parade came to him in a series of distinct but clear images, almost like the frames of a film in slow motion. It had been just two days before Hamid's murder, and Bruno conjured up the image of Hamid in the crowd with his family, proudly watching Karim carry the flag to the war memorial. Hamid, who had been a recluse, never seen in the town, never going to the shops or sitting in the café to gossip or playing *pétanque* with the other old men. Hamid, who had mixed only with his own family and kept himself carefully out of sight. And then Bruno remembered Jean-Pierre from the bicycle shop and Bachelot the shoemaker, the two Resistance veterans who never spoke but who carried the flags side by side at each May 8 parade. He saw the two rivals of so many years staring intently at one another in unspoken communication. He saw the Englishman's grandson playing "The Last Post," remembered the tears it brought to his eyes. He had assumed that Jean-Pierre and Bachelot had connected through the music and the memory. But that was not what had triggered their sudden transformation.

Bruno played each scene back carefully in his mind, then he went to the interrogation reports that came from the prisoners taken by the Bohmer division. He examined the list of captured men who were to be shot. The third name was Philippe Bachelot, age nineteen, of St. Félix. Jean-Pierre's family name was Courrailler, but he found no Courrailler in the list of prisoners. There was still a branch of the Courrailler family, though, in Ponsac, where they kept a farm, and a daughter who bred Labradors. He knew the farm. Bruno excused himself and walked down the stairs, through the museum and into the open air of the square. There he took out his phone to call the mayor.

"It's him all right, sir," Bruno said. "Photograph and thumbprint. Hamid al-Bakr was also Hussein Boudiaf of the Force Mobile, a squad leader who did a lot of damage in our commune in May 1944. There's no question about it, the evidence is solid. But it gets worse. One of the farms that was hit was that of Bachelot's family, after his elder brother had been interrogated. Another was in Ponsac, and I think it was the Courrailler farm, but could you get someone to check the compensation records in the Mairie archives? I remember that the families all got some kind of compensation after the war."

"That's right," said the mayor. "There was a lawsuit in the Courailler family about who got what after the Germans paid a lot of money in war damages. And of course half the family still doesn't speak to the other half because of the lawsuit. I'll get hold of the full list and call you back. Is this leading where I think it is, to Bachelot and Jean-Pierre?"

"It's too soon to say. I'm outside, but when I go back into the archives I assume we'll just collate all the evidence, make copies and get them certified by the curator. And of course we'll collect the names of families who were victimized by the Force Mobile. We could end up with a long list of possible suspects and it could take some time. A lot of potential witnesses have died and memories aren't what they were."

"I understand, Bruno. Will you be back in time for tomorrow's parade?"

The next day was June 18, the anniversary of the Resistance, of de Gaulle's message from London in 1940 for France to fight on. Bachelot and Jean-Pierre would carry the flags, just like always.

"I'll be there. And everything is in order for the fireworks display tomorrow night."

"Let's hope those are the only fireworks we get," said the mayor. With a heaviness in his step but a sense of justice in his heart, Bruno went back into the building.

25

Bruno drove back with J-J to police headquarters in Péri-gueux, Isabelle following behind with thick files of photo-copies in the back of her car. He would have driven with Isabelle but J-J held open the passenger door of his big Renault and said, "Get in."

J-J waited until they were out of Bordeaux and on the autoroute before saying, "If you screw me around on this, Bruno, I'll never forgive you. I think you already know who killed the bastard, and you are pretty sure that nobody else will ever find out. You and your local knowledge. Am I right?"

"I may have some suspicions, but I have no evidence. And I don't see anybody confessing. Some of these old Resistance types went through a Gestapo interrogation without talking. They won't confess to you. If this case goes public and we charge someone, can you imagine the lawyers who'll be stand-ing in line to represent them for free, out of patriotism? It will be an honor to stand up and defend these old heroes. Any ambitious and clever young lawyer can build a career on a case like this. If this ever comes to trial, a guy like Tavernier would fight tooth and nail for the privilege of representing them."

J-J grunted a kind of agreement and they drove on in silence.

"Dammit, Bruno," J-J finally said. "Is that what you want? An unsolved murder? Dark suspicions of racial killing? It will poison St. Denis for years to come."

"J-J, this is not going to be decided by you or me. This is going to be decided in Paris. They're not going to want a trial of some old Resistance heroes who executed an Arab war criminal sixty years after he burned their farms, raped their mothers and killed their brothers. The Minister of the Interior, the Minister of Justice, the Minister of Defense and the prime minister will all have to troop into the Elysée Palace and explain to the president of the republic how the TV news and the headlines for the next few weeks are going to be about gangs of armed Arabs collaborating with the Nazis to terrorize patriotic French families. Arabs who evaded justice by hiding out undiscovered in the French Army, war criminals awarded the Croix de Guerre. Can you imagine how that will play out in the opinion polls, on the streets, in the next election? Tell me, what would the Front National do with that?"

"As you said, Bruno, those are not our decisions. We do our work, collect the evidence. It's up to the law, not us."

"J-J, you know as well as I do it's up to Tavernier, and he'll do nothing without considering every possible political angle and checking with every minister he can reach. When we explain all this to him, he will understand instantly that this case is political dynamite. He'll probably take one look at all this and decide to take a prolonged leave of absence for reasons of health. Either that or resign from the bench to become their defense lawyer."

"I'm not as sure about things as you are," said J-J.

"I don't know. Right now I just want to go with you into Tavernier's conference room and lay out the evidence, and then I want to drive to St. Denis with Richard Gelletreau and bring him back to his parents with no charges against him. You have your drug conviction with the girl, and you'll get points for cooperation with the Dutch police when Jacqueline's evidence convicts those guys. You have Jacqueline's Front National pals on narcotics charges. You and Isabelle come out smelling of roses no matter what happens."

"That will be a nice farewell present for her," J-J said. "You know she's being transferred back to Paris? The order came in last night and I haven't even told her yet."

"That's great," Bruno said automatically, not allowing himself to display any emotion. "The mayor predicted that she would be assigned to the minister's staff."

"She'll probably end up as my boss in a year or two," said J-J.

Tavernier knew all about the promotion. He strode into the conference room with a cheerful smile and a comradely handshake. "Let me be the first to congratulate you, Inspector Perrault," he said. J-J handed her the transfer order and Bruno watched her smile radiantly until she looked in his direction. He made himself smile back.

"Now, I hear you have made a breakthrough in the case," Tavernier said. "New evidence from Bordeaux, they tell me. Explain."

Bruno laid out the photocopies of the pay books from Vichy and from the French Army. Then he added the fax photo of Hussein Boudiaf with Massili Barakine and Villanova, and the Force Mobile action report that cited Boudiaf's role in the raids around St. Denis.

"Our murder victim was a hired killer for the Vichy Milice, who changed his name and his identity to hide out in the French Army," Bruno said. "That is why his executioner carved the swastika onto his chest."

Tavernier looked at J-J, then at Isabelle and finally at Bruno. He had a half smile on his face as if he were expecting someone to tell him it was all a joke.

"Obviously, the higher-ups are going to have to consider some of the wider national implications of this," Isabelle said coolly. "As far as I know, the fact that North Africans were specially deployed by the Vichy regime to inflict brutal retaliations on the French population during the Occupation has not become widely known. It's now likely to become very well known indeed."

Tavernier looked at the papers Bruno had put out before him.

"Notice the thumbprints on the pay books," said Isabelle. "They match. And when the forensics team searched the home of the deceased, they naturally took all the victim's fingerprints. Here they are." She shoved another sheaf of papers across to Tavernier. "It's the same man."

"Do you have any recommendation for me, any proposal on how you plan to proceed?" Tavernier asked.

"We have a list of the known Resistance families in the region, including those who were targets of the Force Mobile," said Isabelle. "Any of them would have a motive to murder their old tormentor. The obvious next step would be to question them all, about forty families, altogether. That is just in the commune of St. Denis. We may have to spread our net wider."

"Why on earth did the old fool ever come back to St. Denis and run the risk of being recognized?" Tavernier asked, almost to himself.

"It was the only family he had," Bruno said. "He was about to become a great-grandfather. He was old and tired and lonely. He took a chance."

"And you think he was murdered by someone who recognized him from the old days?"

"Yes," said Bruno. "I do. I think he was executed by someone who felt he had a right to vengeance. And of course, that's how I would make the case if I were his lawyer."

"I see," said Tavernier. "Let me review all of this overnight." He looked up at them, a determined smile on his face. "You three have obviously had a very long day. I congratulate you on first-class detective work. Now why don't you take some time off while I consult with Paris and we decide how best to proceed. So, no questioning of the old Resistance heroes for the moment. I'll call when I have a decision."

He stood up, gathered the papers and was about to leave the room.

"Just one thing before you go, Monsieur Tavernier," said Bruno. "Would you be good enough to sign the release order for Richard Gelletreau, the teenage boy? He's obviously no longer a suspect."

"We have nothing on him for the drug charges," said J-J.

"Bruno is right. The girl has given us all the testimony we need to nail the Dutchmen. It's a good result."

"Right," said Tavernier, "a good result." Bruno looked across to see Isabelle smiling at him. Tavernier took some notepaper and his seal of office from his elegant black leather attaché case. He scrawled the release order with a flourish, and then stamped it with the seal. "Take him home, Bruno."

Bruno awoke with Isabelle still sleeping beside him, her hair tousled from the night and one arm flung out above the covers and resting on his chest. Gently, he crept out and tiptoed to the kitchen to make coffee, to feed Gigi and his chickens. June 18 would be a busy day for him. He knew that if he turned on the radio, some announcer on France-Inter would play de Gaulle's full speech. He also knew that there was no copy of the original broadcast of 1940, and de Gaulle had recorded it all over again after the Liberation: *"Français et Françaises, la France a perdu une bataille. Mais la France n'a pas perdu la guerre!"*

While the water boiled, he walked out to his garden, Gigi by his side. As he turned he saw Isabelle in the doorway, looking particularly fetching in the blue uniform shirt he had worn the previous day.

"Police Municipale—it suits you." When he was standing just in front of her he said, "I'm going to miss you." It was the first time he had raised the subject.

She stretched out her arm and put her hand on his. "Not until September," she said quietly. "I have to be here for the drug case, and with all the bureaucracy of the Dutch liaison I'll probably be here until the middle of July. Then I have my vacation and my reassignment leave. That's the rest of August. You'll probably be tired of me by then."

He shook his head, suspecting that whatever he said would be wrong, and leaned across and kissed her instead. She smiled, took his hand and led him back into the kitchen.

"I saw you'd put the photograph of you and the blond girl away," she said. "You didn't have to do that for me, not if she was important to you. Particularly not if she was important."

"Her name was Katarina and she was important." He looked directly into Isabelle's eyes as he spoke. "But that was a long time ago, a different Bruno, and it was in the middle of a war. The rules all seemed to be different then."

"What happened to her?" she asked. "You don't need to answer. It's just curiosity."

"She died. The night that I was wounded, she was in a Bosnian village beside our base that got attacked and burned out. The Serbian paramilitaries did it to set a trap for us. When we went to help with the fire they hit us with mortars and snipers. She was among the dead. My captain went looking for her after the battle and told me when I got out of the hospital. He knew that she meant a lot to me."

"At least you knew some happiness with her."

"Yes," he said. "We knew some happiness."

Isabelle rose and came around to his side of the kitchen table. She opened the shirt she was wearing and put his head against her breast and stroked her hands through his hair.

"I know some happiness now, with you," she murmured, and bent to kiss him.

. . .

When Bruno reached the Mairie later that morning, he immediately reported to the mayor.

"The case is suspended until Tavernier gets his orders from Paris," Bruno told him. "My guess is they're not going to pursue it."

"Good," said the mayor. "I've wrestled with this. Murder is murder, after all. But what good would it do to put two Resistance members on trial for killing a Nazi collaborator?"

"Have you spoken to them?"

"I can't bring myself to do it. I'm not proud of that."

"I'm tempted to tell them I know what they did," Bruno said. "Maybe then they would take the decision out of our hands."

"I don't know what to say, Bruno, having lived through all of it. They are old men, and Father Sentout would tell you that they will soon face a far more certain justice than our own."

"Two unhappy old men," said Bruno. "They fought on the same side and lived and worked opposite one another for sixty years and refused to exchange a single word because of an old political feud, and they all but poisoned their marriages by constantly suspecting their wives of deceiving them. Think of it that way and the good Lord has already given them a lifetime of punishment."

"Perhaps. But there's something else: What do we do about Momu and his family?"

"I saw them yesterday when I got back, and told Momu and Karim that we had new evidence that convinced us that Richard and the girl could not possibly have been responsible for Hamid's murder. I had to explain why Richard had been freed to come home. They asked what the police would do now and I said that in the absence of any other evidence, the police would have to start work on the theory that the swastika was a distraction carved onto the corpse to mislead us. So one of the next lines of inquiry would have to be Islamic extremists who saw the old man as a traitor."

"It must have been hard for you to tell such a blatant lie."

"It would have been worse to tell them the truth about Hamid."

"What did they say?"

"Momu kept silent at first. Karim said the old man had a good long life and died proud of his family and knowing that he had a great-grandson on the way. He seemed fatalistic about it. Then Momu said that having taught the boy, he'd never been able to believe that Richard was involved in the murder. He was glad Richard was free and he supposed that now we'd never find the killer and he'd just have to live with that failure of justice. He was used to that in France, he said, which made me feel even lower. He seemed to realize that I was feeling terrible about it and it was as if he then set out to comfort me. He said he'd been thinking a lot about the *rafle* of 1961 that he told me about, and how much things had changed since then. He was touched by the way so many neighbors came out to be sure that Karim was released by the gendarmes, he said. When I left, he came after me and said that as a mathematician he always knew that there were some problems beyond human solution, but none beyond human kindness."

"I was in Paris at the time of the *rafle*," said the mayor. "But do you know who was then the prefect of police in Paris, the man responsible? It was the same man who had been prefect of police of Bordeaux under the Vichy regime in the war; a man who rounded up hundreds of Jews and had Force Mobile troops under his orders. Then the same man went on to be prefect of police in Algeria during that dirty war. Maurice Papon. I met him once, when I was working for Chirac. The perfect public servant, who always followed orders and administered them with great efficiency whatever they were. Every regime finds such men useful. It's our dark history, Bruno, Vichy to Algeria, and now it all comes home to St. Denis again, just as it did in 1944."

The mayor's voice was calm and measured, but tears formed in his eyes as he spoke.

"This isn't right, Bruno. We both know that."

"I don't know what's right, but I know I can live with it, at least for now. And I want it to be over," said Bruno.

"Should we go back to Momu, do you think? Tell him the truth in private and in confidence?"

"I'm content to let it lie. They'll accept it in time, get on with their lives. Think what they will go through if all this becomes public. As it is, Momu goes on teaching the children how to count, Rashida will still make the best coffee in town and Karim continues to win our rugby games."

"And the younger generation uses Resistance tricks with potatoes to immobilize the cars of our town's enemies." The mayor smiled. "They are our people now, three generations of them. One of the things that troubled me most was that Momu and the whole family would feel they had to leave St. Denis if all this became public."

"They don't even know that the old man was not who he claimed to be," said Bruno. "Maybe it's better that it stays that way."

The mayor donned his sash of office and Bruno polished the brim of his cap as they walked down the stairs together to the square, where the town band had already begun to gather for the parade and Captain Duroc had his gendarmes lined up to escort the march to the war memorial. Bruno called Xavier, the deputy mayor, and the two of them posted the ROUTE BARRÉE signs by the bridge and brought up the flags from the basement of the Mairie. Montsouris and his wife took the red flag, and Marie-Louise took the flag of St. Denis. Bruno smiled and hugged her extra hard. The Force Mobile, he remembered, had destroyed her family's farm after she was sent to Ravensbrück. There was no sign of Bachelot and Jean-Pierre.

A crowd was beginning to gather, and he went across to the outside tables of Fauquet's café, where Pamela was sharing a table with Dougal, wineglasses in front of them. "We're celebrating Waterloo day," said Pamela. He kissed her in greeting and shook Dougal warmly by the hand. Bruno's eyes were searching everywhere. Then he turned and saw Isabelle striding jauntily toward him. They were meeting in public, so he contented himself with a fond smile and a barely perceptible shrug as he kissed her formally on both cheeks. She squeezed his arm and let her hand linger to show she understood. With a burst of cheery greetings, Monsieur Jackson and his family arrived, his grandson with his bugle brightly polished. Pamela introduced them to Isabelle, who dutifully admired Jackson's British flag.

It was less than five minutes to twelve when Momu arrived with Karim and his family. Bruno kissed Rashida, who looked ready to give birth there and then, and hugged Karim as he handed him the flag with the stars and stripes, and the mayor came across to greet them. Bruno checked his watch. Bachelot and Jean-Pierre in years past would have been there by now. The siren was about to sound, and the mayor looked at him anxiously.

And then Jean-Pierre and Bachelot emerged, walking slowly, almost painfully, up opposite sides of the pavement from the Rue de Paris into the square. They made their separate ways to the Mairie to collect their flags. The two men were very old, Bruno thought, but neither one would stoop to use the assistance of a walking cane while the other walked unaided. What power of rage and vengeance had it required, he marveled, to endow these enfeebled ancients with the strength to kill with all the passion and fury of youth?

He stared at them curiously as he handed them the flags, the Tricolor for Jean-Pierre and the cross of Lorraine for Bachelot the Gaullist. The two men looked at him suspiciously. He looked back, his eyes shifting between them. They know, or do they? The two men of the Resistance shared the briefest of glances.

"After all that you've been through together, and I include the secret you have shared for the past month, do you not think in the little time remaining to you that you two old Resistance fighters might exchange a word?" he asked them quietly.

The old men stood in grim silence, each one with his hand on a flag, each with a small Tricolor in his lapel, each with his memory of a day in May more than sixty years ago when the Force Mobile had come to St. Denis, and a day in May more recently when the story had come full circle and another life had been taken.

"What's that supposed to mean?" snapped Bachelot.

"What did you do with the old man's medal—the one he earned fighting for France? Not for what he did in the Force Mobile," Bruno asked.

Bachelot turned and looked at his old enemy, Jean-Pierre. A look passed between them that Bruno remembered from the schoolroom, two small boys stoutly refusing to admit that there was any connection between the broken window and the slingshots in their hands; a look composed of defiance and deceit that masqueraded as innocence. So much contained within a single glance, Bruno thought, so much in the initial look they had exchanged when they first saw the old Arab at the victory parade. That had been the first direct look between the two veterans in decades, a communication that had led to an understanding and then to a resolve and then to a killing. Bruno wondered where they had agreed to meet, how that initial conversation had gone, how the agreement had been reached to murder. Doubtless they would have called it an execution, a righteous act, a moment of justice too long denied.

"If you've got something to say, Bruno, then say it," said Jean-Pierre. "Our consciences are clear." Bachelot nodded grimly.

"Vengeance is mine, sayeth the Lord," Bruno said.

This time they did not need to look at one another. They stared back at Bruno, their backs straight, their heads high, their pride visible.

"*Vive la France,*" said the two old men in unison, and marched off with their flags to lead the parade as the town band struck up "The Marseillaise."

Acknowledgments

The author wishes to thank Gabrielle Merchez and Michael Mills for luring him to the Périgord, and Rene Millot for making the place so comfortable, and Julia and Kate and Fanny Walker and our dogs Bothwell and Benson for filling it with life. This is a work of fiction, and all the characters are invented, but I am indebted to the incomparable Pierrot for inspiration and for his cooking, to the Baron for his wisdom and his wines, to Raymond for his stories and his bottomless bottle of Armagnac, and to Hannes and Tine for their friendship, tennis and memorable meals. The tennis club taught me how to roast wild boar, everybody taught me how to make *vin de noix* and those who taught me how to ensure that nothing of a pig was wasted had better remain nameless in view of the European Union regulations. The inhabitants of the valley of the river Vézère in the Périgord call it a tiny corner of paradise, and I am honored to share it. Jane and Caroline Wood and Jonathan Segal between them whipped the book into shape, and I am deeply grateful.

An excerpt from

The Dark Vineyard

By Martin Walker

Available in paperback from Vintage Books

1

The distant howl of the siren atop the *mairie* broke the stillness of the French summer night. It was an hour before dawn but Bruno Courrèges was already awake, his thoughts churning with memories and regrets about the woman who had until recently shared his bed. For a brief moment he froze, stilled by the eerie sound that carried such a weight of history and alarm. This same siren had summoned his neighbors in the small town of Saint-Denis to war and invasion, to liberation and peace, and it marked the hour of noon each day. Its swooping whine also served to call the town's volunteer firemen to their duty. Such an emergency invariably required his presence as the sole municipal policeman of Saint-Denis. The brusque summons shook him from his melancholy thoughts, and he thrust aside the tangled sheets.

As Bruno dressed and swigged from a carton of milk by way of breakfast, his cell phone rang. It was Albert, one of the two professionals who led the town's team of *pompiers,* and he, his truck and his night patrol were already en route.

"There's a big fire up on the old road to Saint-Chamassy," Albert began, an urgency in his voice. "It's at the top of the hill, just before the turn to Saint-Cyprien. A barn and a big field. This time of year it could spread for miles if the wind gets up."

"I'll join you there," Bruno said, tucking the phone between his shoulder and his ear as he tried to fasten his shirt buttons. He squeezed his eyes shut to draw on the map of the sprawling commune of Saint-Denis that he kept in his head. It was composed of the roads he patrolled, the isolated homes and hamlets he visited, the farms he knew, with their flocks of geese and ducks and pigs and goats that made this the gastronomic heartland of France. His familiarity with the ground over which he hunted, and searched for mushrooms after it rained, meant that he knew his district like a woman knows her own face.

"There's no report of any casualties," said Albert. "But you'd better alert the hospital as soon as you've told the mayor. I'm calling Les Ezyies and Saint-Cyprien for support. Can you stop at the station and make sure they send up the spare water tankers when the rest of the guys get in? Drive one of the tankers yourself if you have to. We'll need all the water we can find. I'll see you at the scene."

"What about evacuation? There are four or five farms up there."

"I don't know yet, but the mayor had better start phoning people to put them on alert. Get a warning out on Radio Périgord."

Bruno prayed that his elderly and sometimes temperamental van would start right away. He quickly fed his dog, left his chickens to fend for themselves and ran to the vehicle. It started at once, and he drove one-handed down the lane from his cottage toward town, thumbing the auto dial on his phone to alert first the mayor and then the chief doctor, each of whom already had been awoken by the siren. Lights were on inside people's homes, and the town was stirring as Bruno drove at high speed to the gendarmerie to tell old Jules on the night desk to call the radio station in Périgueux and to dispatch men to seal off the road near the fire. As Bruno hurried back out to his van, Captain Duroc rushed into the main building from the small barracks next door, still pulling on his uniform jacket. Bruno left Jules to explain the situation. At the fire station, Ahmed and Fabien were struggling with the towing rig for the tankers as the other volunteers were arriving, sufficient to man the trucks and tenders. Bruno drove on as fast as his van could manage, his blue light flashing and the town siren still howling into the night behind him.

By the time he reached the open road by the railway line to Sarlat, he could see the broad glow in the hills above. Bruno shivered with apprehension. Fire frightened him. He had always treated it with a wary respect, which had become something close to fear since he'd hauled some wounded French soldiers from a burning armored car during the Balkan Wars. His left arm still carried the scars. In his bedside drawer was the Croix de Guerre the government had awarded him for his efforts, after a lengthy debate among bureaucrats as to whether the Bosnian peacekeeping mission was actually a war.

Bruno wondered if there was anything in the jumble in the back of his van that might serve as protective gear. There would be gloves and a cap in his hunting jacket, his hunting boots and some swimming goggles and a bottle of water in his sports bag. Maybe there was an old tennis shirt he could soak and use as a face mask. He pushed the accelerator harder as the van labored up the hill. He knew this area well but tried in vain to remember where there might be a barn this high up on the plateau, where the land was too poor for farming. It was mainly woods and thin pasture, some tumbledown shepherds' *bories* of old stone, plus the tall microwave tower.

As Bruno rounded the last bend before the plateau, the whole night sky ahead seemed to pulse and glow red above the trees. He remembered the dry summer, the river so low that the tourist canoes had to search out the deeper channels. Now he could smell the burning. He slowed down. At least some of the pulsing red was the flashing light of Albert's fire truck. Bruno parked off the road. He put on his boots, gloves and hunting cap, looked at his swimming goggles and stuffed them into a pocket, poured water on the tennis shirt he had found and ran up the road to the truck, where two *pompiers* stood bracing the spouting hose, silhouetted against the flames.

"Not a barn, just a big wooden shed. We couldn't save it," shouted Albert over the crackling of the flames and the roaring noise of the truck. He reached into the back of the vehicle and pulled out a heavy yellow fireman's jacket and handed it to Bruno, nodding his approval of the stout boots on Bruno's feet.

"It could have been a lot worse. We were here in time to stop it from spreading to the woods."

More pulsing lights began to grow on the road as Ahmed approached with the second fire truck and the big water tanker, and then there were flashes of blue as the gendarmes arrived in their big van. Albert was calling the neighboring fire chiefs to say their help would not be needed.

"No sign of any people?" Bruno asked. Albert shook his head and ran off to direct the second truck. "How did you hear about the fire?" Bruno called after him.

"Anonymous call from the phone booth in Coux," Albert shouted back.

Bruno made a mental note of that as he tried to get his bearings. He remembered this road being thickly wooded on both sides, but where he stood there was a break in the trees, and a new-looking dirt track curved into the wide stretch of field and pasture that was burning low but steadily. What little breeze he felt on his cheeks was coming toward him and toward the woods, where the *pompiers* were soaking the brush to deny the flames any fresh fuel. The biggest fire was the ruin of what had been the shed, standing amid the charred crop. Bruno's foot caught on something. He looked down and saw a small metal flag, like the one farmers used to identify which seeds they had sown in which rows. He plucked it from the ground and, in the light from the truck headlights, read the words AGRICOLAE SÉCH G71. That meant nothing to him, but he stuffed the flag into his pocket. Shouts came from behind, and he turned to see more yellow-clad *pompiers* struggling up with a second hose, which bucked in their hands as it filled and a much more powerful jet of water lanced onto the edge of the woods.

"Smell anything funny?" Albert asked, suddenly looming beside him. "Come on, this way."

He led Bruno across the still smoldering ground and around the side of the shed until they were upwind, where it was quieter. Inside the shed, a metal table supporting some charred machinery was still hot enough to spit as water dripped from what was left of the roof beams. Two smoking roof timbers thrust into the sky, perched on top of what looked like an old filing cabinet. Bruno caught a stink of burned plastic and rubber, and something else.

"Gasoline?" he asked.

"That's what I think. We'll send some trace evidence off to the lab in Bordeaux, but I'll bet this was deliberate. If you go over to the far side of the field, you'll smell it again. Somebody was thorough—he got the crops, the shed, everything. This is going to be a job for you a lot more than for me."

"If it's arson, it's the Police Nationale," said Bruno. It would be a good idea to seal off the phone booth in Coux to check fingerprints, Bruno thought.

"If it's arson against crops," said Albert, "it's local. Some farmers' feud or somebody's been playing games with another man's wife. And that means the Police Nationale won't have the first idea where to start."

Bruno nodded, peering at something in the shed that struck him as odd. "Albert, have you ever seen a filing cabinet and office stuff like that in a farmer's shed in the middle of a field?"

"No. Looks like it could be a computer, though there's no electricity up here. Maybe it's an old typewriter."

Bruno turned away and was walking across to the point where the charred crops stopped when an explosion came with a flat crunch. Light flared, and a rush of heat stunned him as he turned and saw Albert topple to his knees amid the debris of the shed, which was bright with new flames.

His forearm up to protect his eyes against the searing heat, Bruno ran instinctively toward Albert and grabbed him by the collar. Fighting down fear as he plunged into the flames that seemed hungry to engulf him, Bruno hauled Albert back. The fire chief's legs dragged limply through the flaring wood of the shed, and his trousers were on fire. Once the two men were clear of danger, Bruno spread-eagled himself over Albert's legs to douse the flames with the fireproof material of his jacket. And then the other firemen were there, spraying them both with foam from handheld extinguishers.

Ahmed hauled Bruno up and shone a flashlight into his face, shouting, "You okay?" while others tended to Albert. Bruno nodded, shook himself and rose a little jerkily to his feet, brushing away the thick foam that covered him.

"A bit scorched, but nothing serious thanks to that jacket Albert gave me," he said. "What the hell was that explosion?"

"An aerosol; maybe a can of paint or kerosene. Some bastards leave an almost empty fuel container at the scene and close the cap. The vapor can make it go off like a bomb once it's hot enough," Ahmed said with a shrug. "Albert never should have gotten that close. We'd have carried on hosing it but we had to put water on the edge of the fire, stop it from reaching the woods."

"My fault," said Bruno. "I was asking him about the equipment inside the shed."

Albert had been lifted to his feet and was shaking his head to clear it, flecks of the foam flying off from his helmet and jacket. Bruno asked him how he was.

"I'll live to make a fool of myself another day. Some damn thing hit me on the ear," said Albert. He put his hand up to the side of his head and it came away bright with blood. One of the firemen gave him a bottle of water; he drank deeply, then rinsed his mouth, spat and looked across at Bruno and nodded once. "Thanks," he said quietly, handing him the water. Albert's hand was trembling. So, Bruno noticed, was his own.

"How are the legs?" Bruno asked. His voice was hoarse, and his throat hurt. The thought of the gasoline and of the fire being set deliberately brought a surge of anger and a sudden sharp memory of the airfield at Sarajevo, the crunch of mortars and the screams of the men inside the armored car. Bruno had often wondered if he'd ever be able to go back into a fire. Now he knew, but he shuddered and took a deep breath to control himself.

"Not bad. I wear flameproof undertrousers, just like the race car drivers," Albert said, his voice raised. He spoke quickly as the adrenaline rushed through his system. "I'm okay, just a bit dizzy from whatever hit me."

More shouting erupted from behind them, and another fireman came running up.

"Hey, Chief, there's a water main. The gendarmes just ran into a standpipe."

Albert looked at Bruno and rolled his eyes. "Probably the first time our Captain Duroc ever found anything, and even then he had to run into it."

They headed back to the road, where a jet of water was fountaining high from a broken standpipe and Fabien was doing something violent with a heavy wrench in the light of the only headlight on the gendarmes' van that wasn't broken. Captain Duroc could be heard shouting angrily at his men. Fabien gave a final twist of his wrench and the water stopped.

"We can use this now," he said. "There's not much pressure, but enough to damp down the embers."

"Where's that pipe going? Why isn't it on my maps?" Albert demanded angrily, mopping at his bloodied ear with a handkerchief.

"Looks like it goes from the water tower to the microwave station. That's Ministry of Defense, so they have a guard post," said Fabien. "And this standpipe is here because they have another pipe going off to that shed and the field. Looks to me like there's some fancy irrigation system installed."

"Irrigation? Up here?" said Albert. "Somebody's got more money than sense."

"Funny that the one field that has its own piped water supply is the one that gets torched," said Bruno. "You ever heard of this Agricolae?" He reached into his pocket and pulled out the small metal flag he had plucked from the ground.

"No. Could be some experimental seed, I suppose, but I never heard of anything like that up here."

They went back to the truck, where the elderly mayor, Gérard Mangin, stood patiently by the road. Behind him was a row of parked cars belonging to locals who had come to watch the excitement. The mayor stepped forward, smiled a greeting and shook hands with Albert and Bruno. A camera flashed. Philippe Delaron was recording the scene for the local paper.

"Not much to report," said Albert. "The danger's over, and there's no sign of anyone hurt. Not even me, thanks to Bruno. There's a burned-out shed, a field of crops destroyed and one broken standpipe. I have my suspicions about what started this, but we'll have to wait for the lab report."

"You mean the fire was set deliberately?"

"It looks that way, *Monsieur le Maire*. And I think that explosion you saw was of a gasoline can going up. Whatever it was, it could have killed somebody. Could have killed me, if Bruno hadn't pulled me out."

"I hadn't realized this was so serious," the mayor said.

"Now I'd better go and see about getting my guys back to the station. And, Bruno, I'll take that fire coat back. Those things cost a small fortune."

"Whatever they cost, they're worth every centime," said Bruno, shedding the coat. He turned back to the mayor. "There's more to this than meets the eye. That field had its own water supply, and the shed contained what looked like office equipment. Not what you expect to find in a bare upland field in the middle of nowhere. I'll have to inform the landowner, probably have to make a report for the insurance and so on."

"Have you told the gendarmes about this?"

"Not yet. Captain Duroc is a bit preoccupied with the damage to his van. It appears they ran into a standpipe."

"Yes, I saw that." In the strengthening light of dawn, Bruno watched a smile twitch at the mayor's lips. "Well, it seems clear there's been a crime here."

"Right, and that means the Police Nationale, not the gendarmes. They might even want to send a forensics team."

Bruno walked on to the row of parked cars and the small knot of locals to tell them there was no danger, that the show was over, and to ask them to move their cars so the fire trucks could turn around and leave. Big Stéphane the dairy farmer, a friend of Bruno's from the hunting club, was there with his pretty young daughter Dominique. Their farm was just down the hill, probably one of the first that would have been hit if the fire had spread, and this was normally the hour when they would start the milking. Bruno shrugged off their questions and persuaded most of the onlookers back into their cars. Then he walked over to Captain Duroc to arrange for a gendarme to seal off the phone booth in Coux. It was just past 6 a.m. Fauquet's café would be open, and Bruno needed a proper breakfast.

Bruno walked toward two familiar cars, an elderly Citroën DS from the 1960s and an even older Citroën *deux chevaux,* a design with a canvas hood that traced back to the 1930s. His friend the baron, a retired industrialist whose trim figure belied his age, leaned against his big car. Beside him stood Pamela, the owner of the *deux chevaux* and of a local guesthouse, who was known to most of Saint-Denis as the Mad Englishwoman. Bruno had introduced them over a game of tennis, and Pamela and a visiting friend had thoroughly trounced them.

"The baron woke me with a phone call. I hadn't heard the siren," Pamela said. A handsome woman whose features were too strong to be described simply as pretty, she was wearing an Hermès head scarf and a battered version of the English waxed cotton jacket that had become highly fashionable in France. Whether she was standing, walking or on horseback, Bruno could recognize her at a distance from her posture alone, the straight back and the proud neck, the bold stride of a woman wholly at ease with herself.

"Where's your horse?" Bruno asked, leaning forward to kiss her on both cheeks. She shrank back, laughing.

"Sorry, Bruno. Normally I love this French obsession with kissing, but you look terrible and smell worse. Of burned wool and I suppose that awful foam all over your trousers. And I think you've lost your eyebrows. It's hard to see under all the black smears over your face."

"I'm fine," he said, touching his fingers to his eyebrows. They felt like the bristles on his chin.

"I didn't bring the horse," she said, "because I thought the fire might frighten her. I only came up to see if we'd have to evacuate."

"What's that building that was on fire?" asked the baron. "I thought I knew every inch of these hills but I never knew it was there."

"Nor I," said Bruno. "There's a break in the trees, and then a track that curves away toward the field so you can't see it from the road. I want some breakfast. See you back at Fauquet's?"

"Good idea," said the baron. "It's far too late to go back to sleep. Pamela, please be our guest, so long as you promise to prefer our company to your English crossword puzzle."

"But of course, Baron. You're more entertaining than any crossword puzzle. But I think Bruno needs to wash and change first." She studied him. "You'd better throw those trousers away. I hope the town pays for a new uniform."

A TASTE FOR VENGEANCE
A Mystery of the French Countryside

When a British tourist fails to turn up for a luxuriou cook-ing vacation in the idyllic village in the south of France that Bruno calls home, the chief of police is quickly on the case. Monika Felder is nowhere to be found, and her husband, a retired British general, is unreachable. Not long after Bruno discovers that Monika was traveling with a myste-rious Irishman with a background in intelligence, the two turn up dead. Was she running away? How much does her husband really know?

Mystery

ALSO AVAILABLE
America Reborn

BRUNO, CHIEF OF POLICE SERIES
The Dark Vineyard
Black Diamond
The Crowded Grave
Bruno and the Carol Singers (eBook Only)
The Devil's Cave
The Resistance Man
A Market Tale (eBook Only)
The Children Return
The Patriarch
Fatal Pursuit
The Templars' Last Secret
The Chocolate War (eBook Only)
A Birthday Lunch (eBook Only)
The Shooting at Chateau Rock

VINTAGE BOOKS
Available wherever books are sold.
www.vintagebooks.com